Praise for Jackson's Pond, Texas

Teddy Jones has vividly painted the thirsty wide fields and searing sun of West Texas and the lives of families who've farmed this land for generations. In this large and generous book, we see the complicated inter-generational knots and feel the deep, implacable longings of individuals who pull against long-established social conventions. Like the setting's wide horizon, *Jackson's Pond, Texas* is steady at its center and suggestive of life's infinite possibilities beyond its edges. Its clear, honest language is suffused with compassion, humor, and grit; at its heart is the tenacity and resilience of people whose lives have not been easy, and the intricate, profound, and complicated love which binds mother to daughter, brother to sister, grandmother to grandson, lover to lover.
—Eleanor Morse, author of *White Dog Fell from the Sky*

Teddy Jones writes a gorgeous story of a Texas ranching family and a fading small town that carries their name. The matriarch who emerges to lead them all through hard times is Willa Jackson, a spirited, independent, complex and brilliant woman--beautifully drawn, memorable, and resonant with our times. Teddy Jones' story and voice on the page will stay with you for years.
—Philip F. Deaver, author of *Silent Retreats*, Winner of the Flannery O'Connor Award for Short Fiction

"One day you realize that there is much less water than there was in the past and that certain types of plants and animals are not so plentiful as they once were. The bottom is even thicker with muck. ...The result is that the pond becomes smaller, until finally its opposing shores meet and there is no longer any open water. The pond has ceased to exist; it is now only a wet spot in a meadow, and soon, that too fills in and dries."
William Amos in *The Life of the Pond*

Dedication

This story is for my husband, Jim Bob Jones,
the best man I know.

Acknowledgments

Thanks beyond measure to Robin Lippincott and to Philip F. Deaver, mentors who guided the development of this novel. Eleanor Morse, teacher extraordinaire, deserves thanks also for guidance that helped make me a better writer. Many colleagues and faculty at Spalding, too numerous to list individually, have influenced and supported me, and now travel with me. I thank you all. Also due gratitude are colleagues from the Taos Summer Writers' Conference for the past five summers and mentors at that conference, Robert Boswell and John Dufresne. I also am ever grateful to my two continuing cyber-critique partners, Martha Burns and Candace Simar.

Jackson's Pond, Texas

By

Teddy Jones

Cold Front

Willa had predicted a brief upset, something like a line of clouds developing far out on the horizon, producing nothing but thunder. But as soon as she told her daughter her plans for the Christmas holiday, she saw a real norther begin to roll in. On the High Plains of Texas, a norther reminds folks that a day, like a life, can change from pleasant to ominous before they realize it. Sudden stillness precedes a wind shift that pushes clouds of dust up into the northern sky; the temperature drops; and after the dust rolls over everything, hail batters anyone caught out in it. A snowstorm may follow. Willa Jackson had weathered plenty of abrupt changes and had provoked a few in her time. Another storm wouldn't bother her.

She'd gone into town specifically to stop by her daughter's house. In her book, telephone conversations were poor substitutes for face-to face discussions of touchy subjects.

"You caught me working. Finishing some things from the office," Melanie said. Her job as Assistant Superintendent at the Consolidated School District in Calverton consumed a great deal of her time. By her own design, little was left for anything resembling a life.

"I won't keep you long. I wanted to let you know about my plans for Christmas, so that you won't be surprised," Willa said. She followed Melanie into her office. Watching from behind, she admired Melanie's perfect posture and the beige sweater and wool slacks she'd selected for this Saturday—less stern than the navy blue business suits she armored herself in for work.

Her daughter sat behind her desk. Willa took the only available chair, a straight-backed model that faced the desk. She thought it must have come from a school equipment catalog. Willa began. "I'm going on a cruise. There's one that departs December nineteenth and returns on the twenty-eighth." She didn't mention the ticket in her purse–the one bearing a December twenty-eighth departure date.

Melanie sat very still in her executive model chair. She had arranged this office in her house exactly like the one at school. Willa felt like a parent called in for a conference about an unruly student—surely to blame for the bad behavior, required to explain. Staring directly at her mother, Melanie uttered not a sound. Willa waited. Her daughter was a very bright woman, but Willa often wondered if Melanie was so dazzled by her own light that she underestimated others.

She wondered if Melanie hadn't heard what she'd said, but only for a second; she'd seen this before. Melanie had cultivated the use of long silences, something she learned in a counseling class. At first, as a counselor, she used silence as a therapeutic technique. Since she'd become an administrator, she used the long silences to intimidate. Willa waited, imagining the smell of a dust cloud gathering in the room.

Melanie continued her silence at least another full minute, a twitch at the corner of her left eye her only observable movement. The temperature seemed to drop. Then she spat out a hail of icy syllables. "You're doing what? What is *wrong* with you? You have to be here. Families are supposed to be together at Christmas. Sometimes I wonder about you, Mother." She heaved a gust of a sigh and shook her head. A wrinkle between her eyes matched the two vertical lines bracketing her mouth. Etched there by reacting to the many things she disapproved of, those lines spoiled an otherwise pretty face. She'd been "Miss Jackson's Pond 1973" and the Sweetheart of Ray's fraternity chapter at Tech in 1975. In the years since she and Ray divorced, everything about her seemed to have tightened—eyes narrowed, jaw clenched, shoulders squared, chin up.

Before Melanie could cloud the atmosphere further, Willa said in a steady voice, "To answer the questions you asked, first, what I said was, 'I'm going on a cruise.' And to the second, nothing's wrong with me. I feel great. It's time I did something different. So I've decided I will take a cruise, maybe the first of many. Would you like to see the brochure?" She held back on responding to the declaration about families being together at Christmas. Melanie often stated opinions that assumed the tone of facts. Willa didn't take the cruise brochure from her purse just yet.

"I can't imagine how you can be so selfish. The whole family will be upset by this whim of yours. Taking a cruise."

Willa sat straighter in her chair and leaned forward just the tiniest bit. Willa had skills of her own, not learned in courses but in countless meetings of committees and boards she had served on, here in town, in the county, and across the state. One thing she had learned was to take whatever time was necessary to resolve a dispute. Another was to listen very carefully. Melanie might be good with silences, but Willa could not be matched in listening. A person would always tell you, intentionally or not, what was important to her. All you had to do was wait, and listen. She had plenty of time. Today was only December fourth.

"I should think that in your position you would honor your obligations, not trot off on some expensive tour. There are functions to attend, gifts to buy, Christmas trees to decorate, cookies to make, guests to entertain. For God's sake Mother, it's the holidays. I can't do it all," Melanie said. "No, you just can't do this to me." She opened a drawer and took out a tissue, began dabbing at her eyes, sniffed loudly twice.

Willa did not respond to the display. As much as she loved her daughter, Willa disliked some of her tactics. She reached for her purse.

"No, no," Melanie said, waving her tissue, "I don't want to look at any brochure. There's nothing you could show me that can make going on a cruise the right thing for you to do."

Willa held up the notepad she'd gotten from her purse. "Let's make a list. We can see how the things you're concerned about can be handled so my absence won't cause problems." Neither tears nor hailstones had ever worried her much. "Let's see, you mentioned gifts to buy." She wrote on the pad. "I have mine wrapped already so if there's some shopping you'd like me to do to help you, I can drive to Lubbock any day next week."

Melanie blinked her dry eyes, discarded the tissue. "No, I prefer to do my own shopping. Thank you for the offer." She straightened in her chair, matching Willa's posture.

Willa nodded and wrote a few more words. She said, "Functions to attend. I haven't received any invitations. So, my calendar is clear. Apparently, the local citizens who still live here are not the type to entertain, or if they are, I'm not on their guest lists. And the Chamber of Commerce is so busy trying to decide whether to disband they haven't planned any holiday reception this year."

The 2003 reception had been a fiasco. All that food wasted. The disagreements about trying to get a Dollar Store located in Jackson's Pond had ended the Economic Development Board and would probably be the end of the Chamber.

Melanie's mouth tightened. She consulted her desk calendar. Reading upside down, Willa could see her daughter's every hour documented in tiny precise handwriting. Staff meetings; grocery shopping; continuing education; play time with the grandkids; choir practice; cook and freeze next week's meals—each day filled. No wonder she couldn't do it all.

"I have several school functions in Calverton, but no, I haven't gotten any invitations for anything here in town. People probably expect *us* to host something." She raised her right eyebrow a fraction and said, "Grandmother always did."

Willa resisted the urge to respond. Melanie amazed her. One day she could be so genuinely caring and kind and the next she would use any means she could to provoke her. Instead of rising to the bait, she thought about Delia Jackson's final party, in 1974, the year before she died. It had been quite the big event—a band, lots of out of town guests, five Christmas trees in the house, excellent food, and Melanie and her college friends dancing till early morning. Thinking of Jackson's Pond's better days saddened Willa for a moment. There had been a motel, a grocery store, places to eat, two dry goods stores, and a drugstore. No empty storefronts. Jackson's Pond had once been a real town. She doodled a Christmas tree on her notepad. She looked up and saw Melanie studying her as if she were a specimen.

"Oh, cookies. I have fifteen dozen baked and in the freezer, three different kinds. I did that one weekend last month when the weather was gloomy. So, that's one less thing for you to do," Willa said.

"Mother, nothing would make up for your not being here for Christmas. Your great-grandchildren should have the kind of family Christmas children are supposed to have. You can't possibly think it's right to deprive them of that." After a second, she snapped her calendar closed and added, "My grandmother would never have done such a thing."

Willa could see that Melanie was not ready to compromise and certainly not willing to concede. No surprise. Willa understood. Sometimes being stubborn is the only thing that keeps a person going. She smiled at her daughter, thinking she actually admired that tenacity. She said, "It's good to know that I'm important to you and Claire and the children. I won't keep you from your work any longer. Let's both think about this overnight and talk about it tomorrow. Come out to the house after church. I'll have lunch ready." Willa dropped the pad into her purse and stood, not giving Melanie time to respond. Next time she came to visit, she'd bring a heavier sweater.

There had always been dogs on the ranch, strays that found a home and plenty of food there. Frank had hated to see any animal go hungry, and Willa enjoyed the puppies that inevitably appeared soon after a female arrived. She hated that people would take their animals out on a dirt road and dump them if they were unwanted or pregnant. Those dogs came to mind as she drove the eleven miles from town back to the house. A couple of the female strays had been favorites of hers. After the old dog that had been the prime female died, Willa watched as those two had vied to become the new alpha. Like two prizefighters, they circled and avoided one another—an older, experienced, heavyweight and a quick-punching agile middleweight—as if each was convinced she had an advantage that she preferred not to press, neither one wanting to land a fatal blow.

Snarling and barking had brought Willa running from the kitchen to the back door one afternoon. Not about to stop what she knew would only erupt again later, she watched from the porch, the only spectator. And in no time, it was finished. For all the noise and bared teeth, no blood was shed. The only injuries were invisible ones, nips inflicted on ears, bruising bites to haunches, blows to status. Both dogs stalked away, each refusing to look at the other, each with the hair on the ridge of her back standing erect. The morning after the dog fight, one of the dogs was gone. They never saw her again. Frank said that she was an independent kind of dog that wasn't willing not to be number one, so she left. Willa told him she admired that. He said it was too bad one or the other couldn't just learn to wait; her time would come.

She let herself in the back door. Even though the kitchen had a familiar smell, she'd never thought of this house as her home. It was the Jackson home place, this big house with all the family areas downstairs and the huge room that covered the entire fifteen hundred square feet of the second floor. That room had been the site of Frank's mother's parties. A dumbwaiter connected the kitchen downstairs with a serving area in the upstairs room; a bandstand occupied half of the north wall; satin draperies, a coatroom, powder room with a chaise longue, soft lighting from Tiffany sconces, and four French doors opening onto a terrace made guests feel elegant. As long as Mrs. Jackson lived, the "Jackson Ballroom" was alive with parties, and the room and its hostess always merited a mention in any discussion of the town.

Willa and Frank had moved in not long after Mr. Jackson died in 1958. Frank's mother convinced him that she couldn't manage alone, even though she continued directing every household function as long as she lived. Delia Jackson's devotion to Melanie, who was three at the time, convinced Willa that her own resistance to her mother-in-law's continuing to run the house was selfish.

Willa dedicated herself to helping Frank with the ranch and farm activities. At the time, she had been sure that hard work was the only thing that might save her sanity—mending fence, working cattle, planting wheat—outdoor, physical work—and being with Frank. She and Frank worked as partners. Unlike his mother, he was naturally at ease with sharing decisions and cooperating in hard work. With a hired hand and occasional custom harvesters to help them, he and Willa made the family's living from the 3000 acres of Jackson land.

For seventeen years, until Delia Jackson died in 1975, she and Willa coexisted without open warfare. "I know that living all those years with Mother wasn't easy for you," Frank had said during his long weeks in the hospital. "You should do whatever you want to when I'm gone. You deserve it."

She cried and held his hand. All she wanted was for him to be well and to live the rest of their lives together. But he didn't live. He never got to leave the hospital. That was in 1989, and she still missed him every day, particularly in the evening, here in this big house.

The slight chill didn't penetrate the knit leg warmers Willa wore over her tights. Soon her barre exercises would make her welcome the ballroom's coolness. Melanie had never asked if her mother still danced. As a child she resisted Willa's encouragement to join her in her three-times-weekly ballet practice. She'd preferred tea parties with her dolls and her grandmother. And now, as an adult, she still understood nothing about choreography.

After Frank died, and she became the lone occupant of the large house, Willa had metal doors installed behind the ballroom's French doors, added locks to those and all the windows, put a deadbolt on the door at the top of the stairs, closed the heating and cooling vents to the upper floor, and had a false wall built to hide the dumbwaiter on both the upper and lower floors.

Although she hadn't been asked, Melanie had approved. "A sensible reduction in energy use and the resulting heating and cooling bills. A very good idea, Mother," she'd said. Her voice had reminded Willa of Delia Jackson's. Willa heard that same tone again not long ago when Melanie told her she should begin making plans to move to a smaller house. "Mother, the ranch house is too much for a woman of your age to maintain." Willa heard Delia's voice and she heard the warning in it.

Willa asked her father for ballet lessons as a child. "I'm sorry honey, you know I'd do it if I could," he'd said. "But a tenant farmer's share don't stretch far these days. Maybe later." She'd felt bad for even asking. Raising her alone after her mother died when she was five, he did all he could to make her childhood better than his own. Saving for her college education, his own dream for her, was the only extra he could manage.

"I hope you'll never stop dancing," Frank had said. He whispered the words to her just before their wedding ceremony. He told her he was proud of the fact that the girl he'd waited for four years had honored her father's dream by graduating from the University of Texas before she would marry. And prouder still that she'd studied ballet along with the art classes that were her major, even though he would be her only audience.

The last strains of the Peer Gynt Suite ended as she opened the double sets of doors to stand on the terrace. A breeze cooled her as she faced north and watched the hypnotic revolutions of the wind turbines' fins. Amazing. The portion of the project's turbines that were on Jackson land towered above the grass pastures and the Angus cattle that grazed there. Like a flock of gentle, watchful birds, the towers lent an additional sense of peace to the landscape she loved. J. D. called the wind turbines their new cash crop. For her, those generators represented hopes soon to be realized. This cruise would be her first step.

Off to the east, she could see the small house where she had grown up and where she and Frank lived as newlyweds—Melanie's daughter, Claire, and her husband, J. D.'s, place now. A mile south from there the pond that had given the town its name lured a small circling flock of geese. As the years passed and the pond aged and shrank, fewer geese settled there each year. In the pink twilight she could see the low mesquites that were creeping up from the edge of the Caprock moving steadily to surround Jackson's Pond.

Willa opened the front door before Melanie could knock. She gave Melanie a hug that seemed to take her by surprise. Before her daughter slipped off her coat, Willa saw in her face a glimpse of the sweet young bride who had been so in love with Ray. "It's been a while since you've been out here. You know you never need an invitation. How was church?" she asked.

"Oh, all right, I suppose. Standard Methodist service. I'm concerned, though, about the choir. We're down to ten members. With so few voices, it's easy to hear every missed note. I admit my own voice was not what it should be today. But poor Mary Lee is far worse. Someone's going to have to encourage her to turn in her robe. She seems to forget both words and melody more every week." Melanie scanned the living room as they passed through it. Willa thought she might be taking an inventory. Melanie stopped and turned to face her mother. "How old is she anyway? About your age?"

"No, she's seventy-two. I'm two years older."

"Well," Melanie said, leaving the word to stand alone.

Willa didn't respond for a few seconds, thinking that Melanie had been in administration too long. Relying on her position for authority had apparently caused her to lose all subtlety. She said, "Mary Lee. Memory problems seem to run in her family. Both her mother and her younger sister were burdened with forgetting—spent hours making lists. You and I are fortunate that our genes don't carry that." She smiled, as if her genes were the source of immense pleasure. "We'll eat here in the dining room. A little party. We're using your Grandmother Jackson's china and crystal in your honor. I know how you love these pieces. I might as well tell you now, I've packed all the rest of it and you can take it with you today. Think of it as a late inheritance, or an early one."

"Oh, my goodness. Are you sure?" Melanie looked

genuinely surprised, or maybe puzzled was more accurate. She traced her index finger around the gilt edge of her bread plate. "You're right. I do love this china." She raised her goblet toward her mother in a silent toast, smiling a tentative, complicated smile. "Thank you, so much. But what will you use if I take these?"

Willa said, "Oh, I have some colorful new pottery I bought on the Internet. Chris definitely did me a huge favor when he gave me his old computer."

At the mention of her son's name, Melanie's expression changed from pleasant to carefully neutral. Willa considered grabbing her and shaking her until her tight French twist came undone. She behaved as if Chris was Ray's son, not hers, too. Willa suspected, although her tight-lipped daughter had never told her, that battles over her attitude toward Chris were part of the reason for their divorce.

Sure, Chris had done his share of adolescent experimenting with alcohol and drugs and fighting. He had even been delivered home by the deputy sheriff late one night after he'd lost a brawl with two football players. They'd started the trouble by calling him a "clarinet-playing band-pussy." But he had never been arrested and he had graduated from high school on schedule.

Melanie had complained to her that Chris was defiant and borderline delinquent. He spent as much time as possible away from home; almost every weekend he stayed with Willa on the ranch. His grandmother didn't see defiance or delinquency in him. She saw sensitivity and talent. If Melanie would have listened, she could have told her that he saw life from an artist's perspective; his was not a world of rules. The facts—that he'd graduated from UT and that now, at twenty-eight, he supported himself as a news photographer and had two successful exhibitions of his paintings to his credit—convinced Willa that her view was correct.

Willa reminded herself that her plan didn't involve a discussion of Chris, not today, anyway. She breathed deeply and showed Melanie a serene-appearing smile. "I'll bring in our lunch. I made something light, a chicken salad plate, because we're having dessert. Bread pudding, your favorite."

After a few bites of her chicken salad, Melanie said, "Mother you invited me here so we could finish our discussion. After you thought about it overnight, do you see why you really must cancel your trip?"

"I did think about what you said. Honoring my obligations. I wondered exactly what you had in mind when you chose the word obligations."

Melanie balanced her fork precisely diagonally on her plate. "Obligations might have been a poor choice of words. Expectations is probably a better one. I think that the town has expectations of you that you should consider."

"The town? Half of the handful of people who still live in town don't know me at all. The others are acquaintances and a few I'd call friends." She chuckled; it sounded a little like a snort. "No, I think we can safely eliminate any expectations from the town as a reason for me to stay here."

"Well, the town *is* named for the family," Melanie said. She raised her wadded napkin from her lap, frowned at it.

"Your grandmother Jackson often said that. But the fact is that the town is named for the pond, not for the Jackson family. If a Jackson must be here for Santa's arrival or the birthday of Jesus, you should be the one with that job. I'm only a Jackson by marriage." Willa took a long time completing the last bite of her roll and the final asparagus spear on her plate. "Melanie, exactly what Christmas arrangements have you made that I spoiled by making my own plans?"

"I assumed that it would be like it always has—gifts on Christmas Eve and on Christmas, dinner around noon, both at my house." As she spoke, she tore her roll into four almost equal segments and placed them apart on her plate–north, south, east, and west. She pushed everything toward the center of the plate and then looked up and met her mother's eyes. "You'd help me cook. The children will have Christmas morning Santa gifts at home with their parents. Christmas Eve and Christmas dinner will be the family, the five of us."

That confirmed that Chris would not be included. Whether he had not been invited or had declined an invitation was not clear. "I see. Does that fit with Claire and J. D. 's plans? What about his parents? Or have you made plans for everyone?" Willa asked. The words sounded calm when she said them, just as she intended.

Melanie's face now wore the mask of the Assistant Superintendent. "J. D. and Claire and Amy and Jay Frank will go to J. D. 's parents' after Christmas dinner. It's all arranged."

After a pause that Willa knew she was expected to respond to, Melanie resumed eating. Willa looked in her direction, beyond her and out the window. A thin line of clouds paralleled the horizon to the north. "How did you like the chicken salad? I tried a new recipe."

Melanie exhaled; almost a sigh. "It's quite good."

"So, I'm the only one who hadn't been consulted yet about the schedule?"

Melanie's fork paused halfway to her mouth. She looked at it as if it had arrived there by surprise. "I see what you're pointing out. Yes, I made assumptions. And I didn't stop to consider that you might have other plans. That was an oversight. It never occurred to me that you wouldn't want to be included."

Willa thought she saw a trace of sadness in her daughter's eyes. She mentally scored a point in Melanie's favor. "Do you agree it's reasonable for me to make my own plans?"

"I suppose it is, if you want to disregard the feelings of your only daughter, granddaughter and great-grandchildren."

Willa erased the point.

Melanie's voice rose, "And besides our feelings, there are other considerations. Concerns about your going on a cruise at all, regardless of when."

"What concerns?" Willa pushed her plate back and gave Melanie her full attention.

"Your age, for one, and safety, and preparations one must make for traveling out of the country. A woman of your age can be taken advantage of. And someone as attractive as you would definitely be a target. Is there any security on this cruise? Where will you be stopping? Do you know anyone who has ever gone on one of these?" She paused briefly and started again, "And what about—"

Holding up a hand, stopping the word-flood, Willa responded with the itinerary–Galveston, Cancun, Belize—the cruise line's thirty-year history of satisfied customers, and the details of security aboard.

Melanie shook her head and rolled her eyes. "And what about preparations? Isn't a passport necessary? And immunizations? What if you got sick or had an accident?"

"No immunizations are required. I've had a passport for years. There's a medical clinic on the ship, which I might point out we don't have in Jackson's Pond. It's not as if I will be going unaccompanied on a trek in the jungle. It's a cruise with a thousand other passengers, not the Lewis and Clark expedition. Besides social activities, there are art lectures. That's one of the main reasons I chose this company." With a hint of a smile she added, "That and the dance hosts."

"Dance hosts?" Melanie's eyebrows arched. "Is that a euphemism for gigolos?"

Willa laughed. "More chicken salad?" Melanie stared at her.

"Here's an idea, Melanie. Clear your calendar; we'll have Christmas early, and then you come with me on the cruise. We'll have fun. Maybe you'd like the dance hosts. They're screened and employed by the cruise line. I haven't had a partner in years. Would you prefer that I find one in a dance hall in Lubbock?"

"God no. I'd prefer you act your age."

"I am acting my age. I'm a healthy seventy-four year old woman interested in life. I know not to get into vehicles with strangers or to trust siding salesmen or traveling roofers. And I'm going on a cruise to have fun and to learn, to meet new people."

"What's wrong with people you know? Besides, I think it's just too risky."

"Risky? Having fun in general or going on this cruise in particular? Nothing worth doing is entirely without risk. Come on, go with me. What do you say?

Melanie shook her head. "No, I have too much work to do. I have obligations." The frown lines were back.

Willa returned from the kitchen with a tray holding two dessert bowls and two small pitchers, one filled with heavy cream and the other with lemon sauce. "Just the way you like it, Melanie. Pecans inside, lemon sauce and cream for the top."

Melanie stared at her pudding, hesitating before taking a bite, just one. And then another. She stopped eating for a second and added more lemon sauce. She tested the new mixture and nodded. She held her spoon as if it might try to escape.

"Mother, if you're dead set on going on a cruise, couldn't you do it some other time?"

"Maybe I could, but this one has the art lectures."

"Surely you're not thinking of teaching art again. It's been years."

Willa shrugged. "I might. Some of my paintings have sold."

They both continued eating in silence.

Willa added cream to the last of her pudding. "That was good, if I do say so myself—and the cook should never boast." She ate the final bite, then nodded and pushed her chair back from the table. "I'll look into other schedules. Does that seem reasonable?"

"Yes, Mother, it does. I'm sorry to have to be hard on you, but years from now you'll be glad you were here for the children's Christmas." Melanie patted Willa's hand and leaned back in her chair for the first time since she'd arrived. Then she polished off her dessert.

"You're probably right; Amy *was* a delight last year," Willa said. "Tell you what, I'll get a big tree for your living room. You and I can decorate it one night next week. I'll bring all the ornaments from the attic. We can make cocoa and eat some of those cookies I baked." She had gathered the ornaments the same day she packed the china, the same day she bought the ticket.

Willa waited until ten-thirty the next morning to phone Melanie. "Sorry to call you at work, especially on a Monday, but I wanted to let you know there is another cruise—same destinations, with the art lectures. Leaves on the twenty-eighth. I'll be here for Christmas."

She listened to the rhythm of Melanie's approving sounds. The words were what she might have predicted—"just the way a real, true family Christmas should be; you won't regret any aspect of your decision; Amy and Jay Frank will remember this when they're older." She smiled at her reflection in the hall mirror and bobbed her head in time to her daughter's voice on the phone.

When Melanie paused, Willa said, "I won't keep you. I know you have work to do." Yes, I'll bring the tree on Saturday. It's on my calendar, the eleventh. Sure, that's a great idea, a slumber party; just us girls."

Her smile disappeared as she hung up. She shivered; she could have sworn she'd seen Delia Jackson's reflection in that mirror.

FLOYD COUNTY TRIBUNE
Thursday, December 2, 2004
Wind Project At Full Power

Texas Wind Coalition announced this week that its project near Jackson's Pond reached full generating power as the final turbine came on line. The project's operational phase culminates nearly five years of negotiation, leasing, and construction activities.

County Judge Don Thompson said, "The increased property tax revenues related to the project will significantly benefit the county. Our fire protection and EMS are important priorities for new spending, along with road maintenance. Another possibility is funding the library to provide service for Jackson's Pond where the city had to close their library due to lack of funds."

Jackson's Pond Mayor Mark Bradley said, "It's a boon for the county. But, I am sorry that none of the turbines are on Jackson's Pond city land. The town has lost significant tax revenue over the past fifteen years and as a result many city services have had to be cut."

Public Notice

Floyd County Consolidated Independent School District Meeting
December 6, 2004 7 p.m.
District Offices 1206 Morgan Street
Agenda
1. Invocation
2. Superintendent's Report
3. Athletic Director's Report
4. Action Items
a. Budget draft approval
b. School calendar for 2005-06 school year
c. Approval of contractor for new Athletic Fieldhouse
d. Schedule for demolition of Jackson's Pond Junior High School Building

5. Executive Session—Discussion of personnel matters

News and Notes From Floyd County Communities

by Andrea Wigley

Jackson's Pond

The Jackson's Pond Chamber of Commerce and Agriculture announced this week that the annual town square Christmas tree lighting and visit from Santa and Pancho Clos is cancelled due to budget constraints.

Centrifugal Force

Melanie opened her mouth, an answer beginning to form. Lucille Jones sat, coffee cup raised, head cocked, waiting. Lucille reminded her of a magpie, all bright eyes and beak-like nose, plucking around for something to turn into fodder for gossip. Melanie said, "I'm sorry, Lucille, I wasn't listening. I was thinking about arrangements for the staff Christmas Tea." Melanie had come very close to breaking one of her own rules—don't discuss personal matters with co-workers. Better to admit she wasn't listening than to join in the discussion. Her position demanded she be professional at all times, all business. What had she been thinking? Her Christmas plans and her mother's cruise were inappropriate topics. But when Lucille complained about her own mother "driving her nuts at holiday time," Melanie had come dangerously close to crossing the line.

"What about the tea? I thought there was a committee taking care of that," Lucille said.

"Yes, there is, but I'm the administrative liaison to the committee. I need to see if any special support is needed." As Melanie spoke, she took a small tortoise shell compact from her purse. She checked her lipstick, smoothed a few stray hairs back into the clip at the nape of her neck and snapped the compact closed. "I'll see you Monday, Lucille."

Several brisk steps toward her office, she remembered. She executed a quick turn back toward the lounge, speaking before she reached the door, "Did you file a personal leave form for me, a half day for today?" Before Lucille could answer,

Melanie stood in the doorway. "I have some appointments in Lubbock this morning and then on school business at the Education Service Center there beginning at two p.m." She concentrated on operating her PDA, handling its stylus like a dagger. She looked up to see Lucille's tiny, sharp eyes on her. Melanie said, "Also, if you haven't already done so, please complete a travel form—round trip to Lubbock for the afternoon meeting. I'll be back in the office early Monday. I've left several items in your in-basket." With that she buttoned her coat and marched back down the hall. She didn't glance back. She'd done that last week and caught a clear view of Lucille mocking her brisk exit.

Not ready. Those words hung in Melanie's mind. Her first appointment was with a new counselor. The drive to Lubbock would give her time to plan her approach. She ignored the bank of dark clouds far out to the north and the temperature, already several degrees lower than forty-five minutes earlier when she had arrived at the office. She wouldn't allow herself to think about the possibility of a snowstorm and the havoc it would wreak in her schedule. Christmas preparation in Jackson's Pond and end of term work in the office loomed larger than any weather threats. And to top it all off, her mother had to be dealt with. She'd already had to talk her out of going on a cruise and missing Christmas in Jackson's Pond with the family. As a result of that encounter, she'd obligated herself to spending Saturday evening with her decorating the Christmas tree. She could have used that time.

A cruise! If anyone deserved to go on a cruise, Melanie was her own favorite candidate. But of course, that was out of the question. Too much to do. She needed twenty-six hours a day. She banished a brief image as soon as it appeared—of herself among a crowd of happy people in a ship's ballroom. As she started the car and adjusted the heater and the mirrors, she smiled and waved briefly across the lot at Mr. Owens who was just arriving. He nodded, head down against the wind. She raised an eyebrow as she noted the time—8:14 a.m. A charitable thought, that the Superintendent might have been late because he attended a breakfast meeting of the Lions Club, disappeared as she felt the first dull pain behind her left eye.

Just what she needed now, one of her headaches. Her smile froze on her face, and she felt gravity flattening out her features, the sensation she'd first felt when she was ten, when she rode the Tilt-a-Whirl at the Tri-County Fair. She was simultaneously being flung apart and held together by a force over which she had no control. These days she created her own busy whirl. When one of her headaches developed, she feared that some pieces, tiny bits of her, might fly loose and never be retrieved.

She checked both directions before pulling slowly onto the highway. *Where was that Imitrex?* She felt in the bottom of her purse, keeping both eyes on the road, aware of a constellation of tiny black spots in her upper left field of vision. No time for her migraine today. She had to be ready. That new counselor. Melanie's first order of business was to decide if the woman was trustworthy before she would tell her anything. She stopped on the side of the road, took several deep breaths. The Imitrex she'd finally grabbed from the bottom of her purse burned in her nose as she sprayed in a dose. Eight slow deep breaths later, she drove again, toward Lubbock.

Nothing in her life was as frustrating as her headaches. At the most critical moments, when she needed most to be capable and calm, one would attack—that's how it felt, like an attack—and the pain would turn her into a weak, pitiful husk of a woman. She even could see that husk sometimes—a lone stalk of wheat, sere and seedless—in among the black spots that diminished her vision.

Why, the question she always asked when one of these started, why couldn't she control these headaches? Stress was the main trigger; she knew that. She had never had one until she and Ray began having problems. The divorce should have taken care of all that. The last counselor implied that her job might be a source of stress. He couldn't have been more wrong. Her job was where she had everything under control. But that hint, that he was one of those men who thought women should be happily occupied with small jobs and family, was enough. She terminated with him at the end of that day's session. She didn't tell him the reason. You couldn't be too cautious about burning your bridges in the professional community. Instead, she thanked him and said that she might be contacting him again if other issues arose. He nodded and looked pleased with himself.

The appointment today was with a woman she had found in the phone book under Professional Counselors. Surely a professional woman would understand her concerns. She had turned to the Yellow Pages because asking for recommendations from colleagues would have been too risky, reputation-wise. And she didn't want to ask her primary care physician for a referral, didn't want him sending her to a psychiatrist who'd want to prescribe something. Melanie didn't want more medication. She told herself she simply needed to talk—to talk to someone who would listen to her and who was bound by ethics not to divulge anything. She wasn't as ready as she wanted to be for this first appointment.

The last black spot disappeared from her vision as she set her cruise control on forty-five and passed the city limit sign into Lorenzo. A pall of cotton lint hung over the small town, draped from the sickly trees and the screens and eaves of the houses like widows' veils. She wanted to speed as she passed the cotton gin, situated next to the highway in the middle of town. Instead, she held her breath. The gin pushed bales out the back door, emitted seeds from a huge spout at the side and spewed a lint-filled cloud out the top. How efficient. Thank you, Eli Whitney. How could anyone live here?

She had watched as Jackson's Pond suffered economically after the gin there closed. But Melanie considered its last season, its last gasp and filthy exhalation, four years ago, a personal blessing, although she didn't dare say so publicly. She no longer had to endure allergic bronchitis caused by gin trash three months of every year.

As soon as she resumed her speed after passing through the little town, she steered with her left hand and with her right manipulated the PDA's stylus. She reviewed Today's List for

Friday, December 10, 2004, the one she had developed while eating breakfast at six a.m. She added *?Retirement facility??*

She could accomplish both Numbers 4 and 5 on the list during the meeting this afternoon at the Service Center. They were part of her larger career plans. *Talk to Art Kerry (#4)* would accomplish two purposes. She'd been pleased she thought of the tactic as she did her five-times-weekly thirty minutes on her elliptical trainer this morning. She would see Dr. Kerry at the meeting and inquire about the opening for the Deputy Director at the Service Center. He had sent her an e-mail inviting her to apply for the position. She would manage to talk with him during the break in the meeting and would indicate mild interest, nothing more.

Her boss, Superintendent Owens, would be at the meeting, and if he didn't see her talking to Dr. Kerry, his buddy the District Athletic Director, Jim Parkey would. Coach Parkey never missed an out of town meeting and always spent his time watching the females, no matter who they were or what they looked like. He was a hound, always sniffing around the women. He'd inform Owens of her conferring with Kerry before they were out of the parking lot after the meeting.

Those two had been football coaches together for several years, first in a little town in East Texas and then in Plainview. Owens had gotten some sort of Ed.D., not one that involved much work, Melanie was sure. The School Board hired him, with much fanfare about his qualifications, when the previous superintendent retired three years ago. The board's great find had never even been a principal, much less an assistant superintendent. As a condition of his taking the job, a position of District Athletic Director was created for Coach Parkey. The two always traveled to meetings together, like a pair of overage jocks cruising the main drag.

The fifth item, *Talk with Dr. Carlson*, was aimed at securing an appointment to a commission the Texas Education Agency was forming on elevating the qualifications of teachers across the state. She wanted him to know her name and identify her as a person who would be a good potential member. Networking was the key to getting the people in Austin to see that someone with brains existed west of I 35. After they met she would begin corresponding with him on appropriate topics.

Seeing Lubbock on the western horizon returned her to #1—the counselor. She'd been more careful selecting this one. After eliminating anyone whose Yellow Page advertising mentioned "a Christian perspective," the number left to consider was reduced from twenty-five to sixteen. Then, she ruled out all the names that sounded male. Nine remained. From those, she eliminated the two that mentioned counseling for sexual issues— down to seven. She crossed out one whose ad included a photo— too cute, lots of curly hair, and too young. From the six remaining, she chose the first one who had an opening today, the only time available this month on Melanie's schedule.

Counselor Marilyn Brown greeted her soon after she pressed the buzzer in the outer office, the one above the sign "Press to notify the counselor of your arrival." The inner office was full of books, ferns, and overstuffed floral-patterned furniture—a couch and two large chairs. A person could suffocate in a room like this. Until Melanie sat down in one of the large chairs, she didn't notice the bird cage in the corner. A green parrot cocked its head and peered at her. She quickly completed the intake form.

While the counselor sat behind her fortress of a desk and studied the form, Melanie studied the parrot. "Let's begin, Ms. Banks. May I call you Melanie?"

"Certainly, yes, that's fine." She sat up straight and struggled to establish eye contact with Brown. Struggled because the counselor's gaze had shifted to something on the floor beside her desk. The woman spoke toward whatever it was, "What problem can I help you with today, Melanie?"

Melanie inhaled through her nose, determined to control her reaction. "The main issue I would like to work on is my mother." She had decided as soon as she saw the bird. She'd never mention any other topic in a room with a parrot.

"Your mother?" A snapping sound followed the words. Melanie frowned. *The parrot shelling seeds? What was that sound?* "I notice you're frowning, Melanie. Does thinking of your mother make you unhappy?" Snap.

"Um, no, not exactly unhappy, just concerned. She resists any attempts I make to help her and refuses to act, well, to act her age."

"In what way?" Snap, snap.

"I've tried to help her find other interests besides the Democratic Party now that she's become so disturbed by what she calls apathy in the entire state. At her age, she should realize that she can't change the world, that politics is for younger people. And if they are apathetic, then she shouldn't waste her time caring. And now she plans to go on a cruise. At her age."

"Would you say your mother is depressed? What is her age?" Snap, snap, SNAP.

"She's seventy-four. And no, she doesn't seem depressed. She stays busy. I don't know what she does all day; paints, maybe. She quit coming to church years ago and she doesn't belong to any clubs in Jackson's Pond. She spends a lot of her time on the ranch. She travels out of town to Cattle Raisers Association meetings and until she quit, she was county Democratic Chairperson. But since she quit that, it seems like all she wants to do is—well, I don't know what she wants. But I want her to act normal, not like some woman half her age."

"What would you prefer she do?"

"I want her to be interested in her great grandchildren. Start thinking about changes she needs to make for her long term safety and security—her living situation and her activities."

"Is she unsafe in her living situation? Is her health a problem?"

"Not yet. Eventually it will be. She needs to plan ahead, let me help her. It's a daughter's responsibility."

"Does your mother feel she needs help?" SNAP.

Melanie heard the noise as punctuation—an exclamation point, a comma, a period.

Dr. Brown leaned forward, her fingers laced together, palms outward toward Melanie. She offered her version of a smile, a broad professional showing of teeth. "I can only help the person who comes for counseling. I can help you if you have a problem you want to work on. But if it's your mother who has a problem …" She leaned back, stretched her arms, and several of her finger joints snapped simultaneously. "Then it's your mother I should work with."

Melanie tightened her jaw. She was definitely finished. "Dr. Brown. You're absolutely correct. You can't help me. Thank you for your time. I assume you will bill me." She stood. Dr. Brown stood, pulling on her left thumb until the joint snapped.

Too bad she couldn't tell anyone that story. No one would believe her anyway. She could still hear the sound SNAP, SNAP. And there was that parrot staring at her, like it was memorizing every word she said. If she didn't have so much to do, she'd probably have a good long laugh. At least leaving early gave her some slack in her schedule. She would have to handle her mother without counseling.

Gary's Exceptional Toys had this year's Heirloom Collectible baby doll; it was the only place in town, according to her Internet search. Melanie planned to continue adding each new doll as long as they were produced and to buy each of the older models back to the inception of the series. In time, her granddaughter, Amy, would have a valuable collection, something that would remind her of her grandmother. She hoped that Claire would put the dolls up where Amy couldn't reach them until she was old enough to handle them properly. Now, at age three, Amy's main interest would be whether the doll's clothes would come off. Collectible baby in hand, she stopped at another display. To assure that the Heirloom doll kept her clothes, Melanie selected a less expensive, less fragile, Barbie doll and six outfits of clothes. She imagined her mother would probably buy the child cowboy boots and a cap pistol.

Melanie's own doll collection was one of many gifts from her grandmother. Delia Jackson had not only bought the newest Madame Alexander doll each Christmas from the day Melanie was born but also had hand sewn silk dresses for all of them. The collection contained a doll for every year from Melanie's birth until her grandmother died in 1975. In the interest of keeping the dolls pristine, Delia had given the dolls a room in her house where Melanie could play with them anytime she was there. The twenty dolls now occupied the bedroom at Melanie's house that had been her daughter Claire's.

The meeting with the attorney was brief. Kay Henry, her lawyer, quickly reviewed Melanie's list. She wanted a title search on the ranch property, an analysis of a 1992 version of her mother's will that named Melanie as Executor, a form to assign health care power of attorney, information on the conditions that indicate incompetence to properly manage one's legal affairs, and a review of the terms of management of the trust created for Melanie upon her grandmother's death.

Ms. Henry agreed to have the items ready by the following week. She hesitated and then said, "If you don't mind, can you tell me, is Willa ill?" Before Melanie could answer, the attorney said, "Wait, please, don't answer that. I shouldn't have asked. I don't need to know any more than you wish to tell me. It's just that I admire your mother so. She was a major spark in our little band of Democrats out here during that farce about redrawing the Texas congressional districts last year. I can only imagine how inspiring it would be to have a mother like her."

Melanie smiled her professional smile and made a show of checking her watch. "Thanks so much, Kay. I'll be back next week."

Back at her car, a real half-smile softened her expression. Each morning as she prepared for work, Melanie thought of Eleanor Rigby as she scrutinized her appearance and put on her serious, all-business expression; it was the face she kept in a jar by the bed. But she was still thinking about that parrot—and happy that she would have time now, if she skipped lunch, to visit the retirement facility. She couldn't help but smile.

The visit to Harmony Retirement Village proved fruitless. Melanie cut short the tour and thanked the administrator for her time. She could tell after only fifteen minutes in the place that Willa Jackson would never agree to live there, or in any other similar facility in the foreseeable future. Not that there was anything wrong with Harmony Village; the apartments were very nicely appointed. But the whole arrangement was too neat, too contained, too much a way-station for people who had not only stopped going to a job each day but also had retired from life. No, there would be too many reminders of what Willa could eventually become for her to agree to move to such a place. Melanie decided not to even mention the idea. No need to put her on guard.

To get her mother to leave the ranch, it would have to be to move to a house of her own somewhere. And she had already made it clear that she would never move in to Jackson's Pond. Years ago, she had said, "I wouldn't live in what's left of that shriveling little town for anything in the world." Unfortunately, she was probably correct about the town drying up.

Willa might as well be on the ranch. At least with her there, Melanie would have some idea of where she was and how she was doing. She'd have to wait. Surely before long her mother would admit that she needed her help. Willa couldn't possibly expect that she would be able to go on running the ranch forever. Certainly she must remember the months she had spent nursing her own mother-in-law before she died at the age of seventy-five. Melanie had wanted to help but she had been away at college. Willa had done it all.

Another dose of Imitrex would help. And she still had time to pick up a burger and some milk at a drive through. The headache would win if she didn't eat. She could feel it lurking behind her eye. She stopped on the shady side of the burger joint's parking lot and ate so quickly she barely tasted the food. Her contacts felt sticky when she blinked, the way they did as a headache was developing. She considered switching to her glasses, but didn't. The bifocals betrayed something that her relatively unlined face and trim figure didn't. Too many women were edged out of career advancement because of their age. She didn't intend to let being forty-nine make her a casualty. She had worked too hard to get where she was.

She stood up straight, squared her shoulders, and entered the meeting room. "Good afternoon, Margaret. Hello, James." She greeted each person she met by name; she was very good at recalling names. And she was also very good at putting aside all thoughts except those demanded by the present situation. She had work to do here today. After a brief circuit of the room, she sat through the first presentation, dutifully taking notes. Superintendent Owens would expect her to report on the presentation at the next staff meeting. She simultaneously scanned the mail she brought from her inbox.

At the break, Dr. Kerry approached her and urged her again to apply for the deputy director position at the service center. If she had to, she would go so far as to complete an application, maybe even an interview. But she knew that the only difference between deputy director at the service center and her current job as assistant superintendent would be location— Lubbock versus Floyd County. Without a doctorate, she was destined to be a fairly well paid, very competent "Hey girl" to some man in the top job. Her options for any real advancement narrowed down to either getting the degree or developing state level connections and/or redefining the scope of her current job so that a large salary increase would be in order. Or she could quit. She agreed to contact him before the application period closed.

She sipped water and skirted clusters of school administrators trading gossip. The only thing she gleaned was that the appointment she hoped for to the statewide commission had already been made—some man from Denver City. She tossed her water bottle in the trash and returned to sit through the rest of the agenda.

The meeting ended promptly at four forty-five. A cloudless, faded-denim blue sky had replaced the gloom of the front that had blown through in the morning. Traffic slowed Melanie's drive eastward until she was out of the city limits. The sun glinted in her rear-view mirror, promising a fine display at setting for anyone who had the time to watch. Melanie didn't. She drove with her right hand and pressed with her left on an area at the base of her skull. Her headache had stayed just offstage all day. And she intended to make its exit permanent, at least for tonight.

She needed stress reduction, something to slow the whirling. Her CD of ocean sounds might lull her completely into inattention—not safe while driving at twilight. Instead, she inserted the second disk of the current romance novel she'd been listening to in the car intermittently for a week. A bit of secret guilt attended her pleasure at listening to this trash. She ordered the romances from an Internet site or bought them in Lubbock rather than borrow from the Jackson's Pond library. Romantic heroes and beautiful, resourceful, lusty heroines were inappropriate to her professional image.

Her tolerance for the romance lasted only to the outskirts of Ralls. Without intending to, she had begun replaying the events of the day, comparing results against her plans. By her standards, she'd been less than successful, and there had been a surprise. No, actually two surprises. The only surprises she enjoyed were the ones she planned for someone else.

Dr. Kerry's intense interest in her applying for the job had taken her off guard. The other surprise was that she was too late to affect the appointment to the state commission. Gossip at these meetings was, more often than not, quite accurate. She hadn't moved quickly enough. She'd spent too much time dithering about whether the appointment would benefit her career.

She swerved and barely missed a crowd of tumbleweeds that had stopped their wind-powered travel today at the edge of the highway. No self-respecting West Texas driver dodges a tumbleweed. She'd allowed her attention to wander, had thought the grey clump was a large coyote. She massaged the muscles of her neck. Thank goodness nothing was scheduled for tonight. She opened today's list on the PDA, gave it a brief look, and deleted it with her typical degree of finality but none of the usual sense of achievement.

"Hello, Elsa. And how was your day?" The cat stalked away toward the kitchen as Melanie greeted her. She opened a can of cat food, served it to Elsa, threw away the junk from the stack of mail, and slid off her coat and suit jacket, all within five minutes of entering the house. The light on the answering machine blinked insistently. She turned her back on it and placed the package for Amy on a bookshelf in the living room. Dropping her briefcase and the mail inside her office, changing into a baggy sweatsuit, peering in each closet, checking behind the shower curtains, and returning to the kitchen completed her routine circuit of the house. Nothing here had changed since she left this morning. Except for the light on the answering machine.

She retrieved a small key from inside the butter compartment of the refrigerator. The key fit locks on the two top cabinets to the right of the kitchen sink. She stored Lysol, Comet, and other cleaning supplies behind one of those doors— grandchild-proofing. She unlocked the other door. As deftly as a magician she produced from the cabinet a bottle of Pinot Grigio, a wine glass, an unopened pack of Dunhills and a lighter. She removed the clip that held her hair off her shoulders and severely away from her face. A dark image stared back from the microwave's window, a blond woman with large, long-lashed green eyes who would have been pretty except for her stern expression. The answering machine continued its persistent blinking.

The first message was a hang up. She knew he would call later, until he finally reached her, as he did at least once a week. After listening to the second message, she replayed it. It was the school board president. Dr. Owens was resigning, or retiring, effective January 15. The board president wanted to talk to her about the Superintendent's replacement. He used the words "temporarily or more permanently" and "keep this in confidence for now." Then he recited his home phone number and said, "Please call as soon as possible."

Another surprise. She didn't know a thing about Owens' leaving, whatever they called it—resignation or retirement. She'd thought he had them all fooled. He must have been the subject of the "personnel matters" item on the school board agenda on Monday night. Maybe that explained why Owens hadn't asked her to attend, as he usually did, to quietly hand him notes with answers to any unscripted questions that arose. Her pulse quickened slightly. She was too tired now to plan her response or to be alert for clues. She'd return the call tomorrow.

In her bedroom, out of sight of her grandmother's dolls and away from her own dim microwave reflection, she poured a scant half-glass of wine, lit a cigarette, and settled against the plump cushions on the love seat. She waited for her shoulders to relax, for the ache to disappear from the base of her neck, for the spinning to stop.

She was into her second half-glass of wine and her second cigarette when the phone rang. Without moving from the loveseat, she held the cordless handset to her ear. After letting it ring a third time, she answered. "Yes, I got in a little late. I recognized your hang up on the answering machine." She listened. Then she spoke; she knew he would hear the smile in her voice. "Is this an obscene call?—No, Ray, I'm not going to hang up. Okay, I'm wearing a sweatsuit, not sexy at all. Having a glass of wine. What about you?" She laughed, actually more of a giggle. "That's not too sexy either."—a long pause as she listened, still smiling. "Yes, my hair is down. You would? Right now? Sure, why not? You've seen me before, plenty of times, so you can fill in the details from memory. Hold on a second while I get more wine."

She made him wait, taking a long time to pour the wine and glance at herself in the mirror across the room. "See anything you like?" she asked. She listened for a long time, then laughed aloud. "You never change, do you? Yes, I'll admit it, you do make me laugh, always did." She listened again, her expression gradually becoming serious, not her stern assistant superintendent face, but the face of a pretty woman with sad eyes. "No, I can't meet you in Altus in three hours. I have to be here in the morning. I have too much to do."

Their phone calls and out of state meetings had been their secret for the past seven years. As long as he kept to the agreement, they had fun meeting in places where they wouldn't be recognized. And she had the thing she had missed most as a divorced woman, him holding her as she drifted toward sleep after making love.

He hadn't ever explained how their arrangement benefited him, but he'd been the one who persisted until she agreed to meet him that first time, after avoiding him for nearly five years. And, until the last several months, he'd kept his part of the bargain—not to bring up their past or any possible future for them together. That first "date," they traded reports showing negative lab results for HIV and other sexually transmitted diseases and agreed that condoms would be wise, regardless. When she told him that was one of the conditions of their agreement, he laughed, saying it seemed awfully businesslike, and maybe they should have a notary present.

She heard him speaking, but the words didn't seem to make sentences. "I'm sorry, Ray; repeat that, I didn't hear what you said. Oh, work. Something interesting did happen today." She told him about the call from Mr. Allgren—only that one story. "No, I don't know what will happen, or what I want to happen. I didn't see this coming." She often surprised herself by being honest about her thoughts in these conversations, hiding far less than she had when they were married. "How's life with the governor these days?"

He told her about the governor's most recent public relations disaster. Ray had talked two weeks ago about thinking he would resign as the governor's executive assistant at mid-term, if he could tolerate the job until then.

"Yes, Ray, I'm listening. No, please don't ask me to. You promised me we wouldn't. There's nothing to talk about that we didn't settle a long time ago." The sadness in her eyes had crept into her voice. She watched the ash on her cigarette grow to an inch. The glow at the tip died. She didn't move.

"No, I'm not crying. No, it's okay. Yes, I'll answer when you call. Ray—goodnight, stay safe." She leaned into the cushions on the loveseat and stayed very still for a long time.

She removed the evidence from her bedroom—wrapped the cigarette butts in toilet paper and flushed them, washed the ashtray, slid it under her mattress, and sprayed air freshener until it made her cough. Next, she eliminated clues from the kitchen—

washed the wineglass, corked the wine, and returned those and the cigarettes and lighter to the cabinet.

By nine o'clock she had finished eating dinner—a scrambled egg sandwich, a glass of milk and four carrot sticks. One plate, one fork, one knife, a skillet, and a spatula had been washed and returned to their respective places. All exterior doors were double locked. The coffee pot was ready, programmed to percolate at six a.m. The cat had gone out and was back in.

Melanie turned out the kitchen light and walked toward her bedroom. Part way down the hall, she spun around, as if she had heard her name called, and hurried back to the kitchen. She didn't bother to turn on the light. With a single quick rip, she tore off the sheet labeled December 10, 2004, from the "New Word a Day Calendar."

JACKSON'SPOND GAZETTE
Thursday, June 6, 1946
Jacksons Host Graduation Fete

The 1946 graduating class of Jackson's Pond High School was honored with a party and dance last Saturday evening at the home of Mr. and Mrs. Albert Jackson on the Jackson Ranch.

The event, fashioned on the theme "Academy Awards," entertained 60 guests in addition to the 13 graduates. The Jackson Ballroom was the center of the festivities where The Rhythm Tones, a five-piece band from Amarillo, provided dance music ranging from traditional waltzes and two-steps to jitterbug.

Posters advertising the Academy Award winning films from the period of the honorees' school years decorated the public rooms of the Jackson home; a red carpet led guests to the ballroom; and a pair of searchlights beamed the way to the party site. Six-foot-high golden papier-mâché Oscar statues flanked the entrance to the house to set the stage for a special evening.

Each graduate received individual recognition with a special introduction by the master of ceremonies, Jay Beeler, on hand from WFAA Radio in Ft. Worth. Beeler's jokes and his descriptions of the honored grads, every bit as effusive as those heaped on Hollywood luminaries, kept the evening lively between musical sets. Each grad was likened to some Oscar winning actor or actress and before any of the grads was allowed off the stage, Beeler succeeded in embarrassing him or her with some tale of an exploit from their school years.

This reporter was unable to find any witness who would swear to the veracity of the stories the Ft. Worth radio personality told. But all attested to the fact that the party was a grand one.

Commencement

"Albert, have you spoken to Frank about you two going to Austin to find him a rooming house and complete his application to the University?"

"Not yet, Delia. I'll do it in the next day or two. I've been real busy." He sopped up egg yolk with a piece of toast. A bit of yellow hung in his mustache.

"You recall that I asked you two weeks ago to make a definite plan." She gritted her teeth as he made a slurping sound drinking his coffee.

"I've been real busy."

She placed her knife and fork precisely, diagonally across the top right of her breakfast plate and rose from her seat. He stared at the piece of toast in his hand as if searching for the script, for his next line. Delia stepped toward the window behind Albert. She moved near enough to let him catch a whiff of her perfume.

"I know what will happen if you don't get definite plans made; he'll end up going to Texas Tech. You can't let that happen. He should have a proper university degree, not one from some little college in West Texas," she said.

"Maybe he'd rather go to A & M. He might want to be in the Corps." Albert applied jelly to the toast and took a bite.

"Even that would be better than staying in West Texas. He needs to get away, meet some quality people, see a little of the world, or at least the rest of Texas. He'll come back when he's through with his education, and he'll bring a wife, just like you did." She leaned from behind his chair and kissed him briefly on the top of his head. "And she'll be the kind of wife for him that I have been for you." She closed the door behind her as she went into the kitchen, not giving him time to reply. "Maria, I will have four guests for luncheon at one o'clock. Please make chicken a la king and steam some asparagus. We'll have fresh fruit for dessert. And set out the good china and silver." She had given all the directions she'd intended to for now.

The reflection in her bedroom vanity table's mirror pleased her. At forty-four, she could pass for thirty-five. Her mother's rule—never go outside without a hat and gloves, no matter what the weather—had annoyed her during her childhood in East Texas. But, the first time she saw Albert's sister Geraldine and her friends, she understood. Wind and low humidity and blowing dust and lack of shade had conspired to mark them as something other than Southern gentlewomen. They had the skin of field hands. She vowed to herself then and there that she would never, ever let herself fall into that condition. Twenty-three years later she could truthfully say she had never gone outside in the sun and wind and dust of the High Plains without a hat and gloves. Furthermore, true to her promise, she never missed a night applying moisture cream to her face and neck nor had she ever gone a week without giving herself an oatmeal facial.

Mrs. Pastusek, her favorite teacher at Troufant's Finishing School in New Orleans, taught her students to develop personal goals. Delia had been a star pupil. At the top of her list was "find a suitable husband." Albert Jackson, of Jackson's Pond, Texas seemed to fill the bill. He cut a handsome figure in his Doughboy uniform and overseas cap at the dance in Ft. Worth where they met. His parents had a town named for them and owned a lot of land, both of which increased his suitability, discounting the fact that the land was six hundred miles across the state from her home.

By the time they met, she had been a bridesmaid six times. Then her mother managed to get her sponsored in social circles in Ft. Worth. That was after they agreed that the selection of acceptable bachelors in and around home in Longview and even in Dallas was picked over like last week's vegetables at the produce market. All that were left were too ripe, or too green, or bruised and rotten. "The War definitely reduced the number of eligible young men," her mother told her best friend. "We had to practically move to Ft. Worth in order to find Delia a suitable match."

Her twentieth birthday was on the horizon when Delia accepted Albert's proposal. She had hesitated just briefly, "Why Albert, this seems rather sudden. My, what a beautiful ring." Mrs. Pastusek would have been proud of her.

Albert had looked puzzled. "But I thought that you wanted to be married, and well, now's as good a time as any to get on with things. Do you accept?" He didn't mention the telegram from his father. "Armistice seven months ago. World safe for democracy. Get home now or get a job. Will send no more checks. Signed, C.C. Jackson." She learned of that later. C.C. Jackson had told her the story more than once.

The engagement extended for a respectable six months. After the wedding in Longview, they came to live in the house with Mr. Jackson. Delia immediately cleared the mess that C.C. had made in the three years since his wife had died. She took over as the woman of the house. She did everything she could to endear herself to the elder Mr. Jackson during the five remaining years before he died. One must always be gracious to one's in-laws. And besides, he always seemed rather taken with her, often bringing her small presents from town and complimenting her and telling Albert how fortunate he was to have married a real lady.

Soon after the wedding, she set some other goals for herself. There would be two children; preferably a boy first and then a girl; they would change that ranch house into a proper headquarters; she would be the leading citizen in the town of Jackson's Pond; and she would maintain her own bank accounts separate from her husband's.

She opened her eyes very wide and exaggerated a smile toward her reflection, an exercise aiming to eradicate two tiny frown wrinkles between her eyes. Now that Frank was about to graduate from high school, there was nothing to frown about. She would have the perfect excuse, visiting Frank, to travel to Austin, to get some relief from the sight of this treeless, flat place. She might even go back to Longview to visit some of the girls she grew up with. She may have been the last to marry, but she'd married well, and she had something she was sure that none of them had, money of her own.

And, now that World War II was safely over, things were going to change. No need any longer to play at being frugal, at being one of the folks. First, the party room on the top floor was going to become a proper ballroom. The renovation would be complete in less than three weeks. Next Monday, she had appointments in Ft. Worth to shop for drapery fabric. If there wasn't anything acceptable there, she'd even go to Dallas.

Saturday morning, Delia asked Maria if she'd seen Frank. She hadn't. Albert, reading the *Livestock Weekly*, denied knowledge of the boy's whereabouts, too. She allowed herself only a brief frown. No matter what, Frank wasn't going to give her wrinkles. She'd drive herself to town.

Delia parked her Ford near the trail that was worn from the road to the pond. A movement, or maybe it was a reflection, had caught her eye as she passed going toward town. Curious, she'd turned around and come back to investigate. The public had access to the pond if they needed water, so anyone might be there. But she'd never seen that reflection on any of her numerous trips into town. What could it be? After all, this was Jackson land, even if it was outside the fence; she had a right.

A person could easily see all the way across and around Jackson's Pond from any spot nearby. Except for the slight elevation and a cluster of about a dozen rocks that marked the spring feeding the pond, the bank was no more than a foot higher than any of the surrounding land, more an edge than a bank. Shaped like a long oval, the pond was about ninety feet long and seventy feet wide. Unlike the playa lakes that dotted the area, Jackson's Pond stayed full almost year round. People said it was one of a kind out here. Playas dried up soon after each rain that filled them. Jackson's Pond would overflow and then stay steady. Swimmers said it was at least twenty feet deep in the middle. Lots of people speculated about the origin of the pond, but all agreed that Mr. C.C. Jackson had been smart to acquire it along with all the other acres he'd bought back in 1895.

Delia walked the quarter mile from the road to the pond and stopped in the shade of the two small elm trees near the pond, the only trees for miles. Twice she had to free her hem from tall grass. She could see her son and she saw who was with him.

"Frank—is that you, Frank?" She had warned Albert to tell George Lofland not to let his daughter go off alone with boys, no matter who they were. In fact, she'd suggested that he shouldn't let George renew his tenant lease. They didn't need a motherless teenaged girl living on the ranch. She was fourteen now. In the last year, she'd filled out and definitely did not look like a tomboy any more. Before another year was over that combination of green eyes, black hair, olive skin, and blossoming figure would turn heads. Men never thought about problems like this until it was too late.

"You can see it's me, Mother. Did you want me for something?"

Delia didn't move. She felt a run inching up the back of her nylons, her last pair. There probably wouldn't be a pair for sale anywhere in town. Frank and Willa and two horses were across the pond from where she stood. "Frank, come over here so that I don't have to shout. And bring whoever that is with you."

"Hello, Mrs. Jackson," Willa said when they neared. She walked slowly. Her saddled horse trailed her.

"Oh, it's you, Willa. Are you all right, child? Did your horse throw you?" She didn't wait for Willa to answer. "Frank, is something wrong here?" She reached for his arm with her gloved hand.

"I'm fine, Mrs. Jackson. What—

"Mother, we're both fine. What are you upset about? Why did you stop?"

"I saw a reflection when I passed. And then when I saw people and thought it was you and you were off your horse, I thought you might have been injured." She drew a jerky breath.

"Oh, Mother." He rolled his eyes.

"Willa, take Frank's horse to the barn when you go. I need him to drive me to town."

Frank exhaled loudly as he handed Willa his reins. "Yes, ma'am," Willa said.

"Why did you want me to drive you to town?"

"Standing out there in the sun made me a little weak. And I enjoy your company. We don't get to talk as often as I would like."

For several miles, neither of them spoke. Delia gazed at the wheat fields. With no hail or serious windstorm since the cattle were taken off the winter grazing, the warm March sun had startled the hardy plants into lush growth. Now, in the first week of April, rich green stalks eight to ten inches tall filled the fields. By early June, harvesting would begin.

Albert preferred growing wheat to farming cotton, the other local crop. He actually preferred raising cattle to anything that involved plowing. But he'd created a plan that used the wheat for grazing, haying and producing grain. The land not used for raising wheat was left in native grass or planted with improved grass mixtures, all for grazing. The result, he boasted to her, was that almost every plant that grew on the place was "run through a cow" and, as a result, turned into money.

Delia grew up around her father's cotton farming enterprise in East Texas, although, to be accurate, oil royalties had helped make his land a paying proposition. She was no stranger to farms, but never intended to need to learn the details of operation. That was her husband's job. And she didn't offer any opinions on his management other than the one time she asked if he thought the market for beef would always pay well. He'd looked at her like she'd spoken heresy and told her he'd take care of the ranch, not to worry. She didn't. He put money in the household account to accommodate the large budget she established each year and in the college savings account she had demanded he set up when Frank was born. The arrangement suited her fine. He didn't inquire about the oil royalty money in her accounts, and they didn't discuss his money at all.

Wheat, cattle, and money were all less important at the moment than her new concern about Willa Lofland. She had sensed something in Frank's manner back at the pond—something that was one more reason he must go away from West Texas to college. To be fair to her, nothing about Willa suggested she was a flirt or a tease. She knew that Willa stayed busy helping her father farm. Edna Lofland died when the child was five years old. At the time, Delia thought George might send her to live with relatives. But he'd kept her with him and he'd continued working his tenant acres and helping Albert with the cattle.

Back then, Delia couldn't help wondering if she might be able to do a better job of raising Willa than George could and about how it would be to mother a girl. The stillborn child that Delia and Albert buried the year before Frank was born had been a girl. Not that she could replace Willa's mother, but she'd always wanted a little girl to fuss over. George never asked for help, though, and the only occasions when she saw the child the first year after Edna died were if she drove the three miles down to the house where they lived. She often had Maria make extra cakes or pies she could deliver, just so that she had an excuse to check on the child's progress. How he managed, she didn't know, but the house was always clean and neat and Willa was polite and seemed quite bright, if a bit solemn.

Delia examined the run in her hose. She could tell Frank to turn around and go back to the house. She could change into slacks. But she had never gone into town in anything more casual than a good dress. Slacks or jeans were acceptable for youngsters, but few adult women's figures were flattered by them. Willa, on the other hand, seemed to have been made for jeans.

The day that Willa started first grade, Delia saw her sitting on the front seat of the school bus when it stopped at the Jackson house for Frank. The polite, serious little girl Delia had seen on her visits to the house had been transformed. She was decked out in a dress and patent leather Mary Janes and her black hair was tamed in tight French braids tied with red ribbons. Her smile revealed one missing front tooth. Delia wished she could grab her and hug her. Instead, she waved and Willa waved back, her gap-toothed smile making her face radiant.

Two hours later, Delia drove down to George's place and found him outside working on his tractor. She complimented him on Willa's braids and offered him a deal. Willa could stay at the Jackson house each afternoon after school. "Maria will watch her in the kitchen. She won't be in the way." She pointed out that he had a lot of work to do and that having someone babysit her for the few hours until suppertime would help him out. She could still remember the way he'd looked at her, like he was looking through her for whatever string she was holding behind her back. "It's selfish of me, but I would enjoy having a little girl around now and then."

He pushed his hat back, took out his handkerchief, and wiped the sweat and grease from his face, and said, "I'll ask Willa. If she wants to, she can stay there in the afternoons. Thank you for the offer, Mrs. Jackson."

All her first-grade year, Willa trooped off the bus behind Frank each afternoon. He seemed to take little notice of the child. He'd been far more interested in riding his horse or following Albert around the ranch. At first, Delia spent a lot of time getting Willa to play house or tea party. She even bought a little tea set and several dolls that she kept for Willa to play with after school. One day, Delia brought out the dolls for another of the tea parties. Willa said, "No, thank you. Those are your dolls, so you can play with them. I want to draw with my Crayolas." Before long, Delia had an after school snack with her each day, teaching good table manners, and then left her in the kitchen with Maria. Why, Delia wondered, had she ever thought that a child raised by a man would want to play dolls?

Her first day of second grade, Willa followed Frank, now a fourth grader, off the bus as usual. She went directly to the kitchen table and began drawing. Instead of using children's crayons she now drew with colored pencils. Cookies and milk stopped her drawing, but for only a few minutes.

Near dark, when George came to the back door, she had said, "Wait, Daddy, I'll be right back." She had stood very erect in front of Delia, as if reciting for her teacher, and said, "Mrs. Jackson, I made this for you. It's a thank-you present for letting me stay here after school. I'm a big girl now; I don't need a babysitter anymore. I'll get off the bus at my house." She turned to Maria who was watching from the kitchen doorway. "Maria, I made a picture for you, too."

Delia didn't say a word at first. Both the announcement and the quality of the drawing surprised her. This drawing of a woman and three dolls at a tea party must be the work of a much older person. And why did Willa not want to stay here in the afternoons? She managed a smile and eventually said, "You are very welcome and thank you for the picture." Maria cried and hugged Willa.

All of that was a long time ago. She hadn't seen the child in a dress in years. Willa certainly didn't need a babysitter anymore. But she did bear watching, as far as Delia was concerned.

"Frank, what were you doing at the pond?"

He glanced toward her. She saw a look he'd not given her before, narrow-eyed, evaluative. That look he used sorting cattle—this heifer to breed; that one to auction; that one to the packing plant—a look he'd learned from Albert. "Nothing really. Just talking."

"Son, you need to be careful about being too friendly with her, being unchaperoned. She's becoming a young woman. You being almost a college man, you have to think of her reputation."

She waited for him to say something. He didn't. She rolled down her window a couple of inches and then turned back to watch his profile as he watched the road. He looked exactly like Albert had when they met, lean, strong-jawed, curly-haired. And those times when he smiled, it was Albert's smile, slow, sweet, and cocked up a little on the left. Frank wasn't smiling now. "You do understand, don't you, son."

"Yes, Mother. I understand."

"Speaking of you soon being a college man, your father is planning to take you down to Austin right after graduation."

"He hasn't said anything about it. Besides, we'll be harvesting wheat right after graduation."

"Don't worry about harvest. Your father can hire help, just this once. You must go down there and take care of your application and reserve a spot at a good rooming house."

"If I wanted to go to UT, I could apply by mail. And I could find a place to live when I got there. I need to be here for harvest."

"What do you mean, if?"

"I'm not sure about college. I have to think about it some more."

"Your father lets you get away with that kind of talk, but I'm not going to accept it. You've had plenty of time to think about college. Now it's time to take the necessary steps to get admitted. I don't want to have to repeat myself on this subject."

"Yes ma'am." He continued staring at the road.

George's pickup was parked on Main Street. Delia said, "My errands may take some time. You catch a ride back with George. I feel fine now. I don't need you to drive me home." He nodded as he parked. "Be on time for dinner," she said.

On her drive back to the ranch, Delia thought perhaps she shouldn't have been quite so forceful about Frank's application. Now that he was older, Frank had become a bit less compliant and more resistant to her guidance—more like a man. Eventually, he would do as she wished, she was sure. But, pushing too hard might... Well, she'd have to speak to Albert again tonight. He should be the one to handle Frank's sudden show of willfulness. She had a party to plan.

Thinking about the party put her in a better mood right away. Not only would the party be the first ever in the newly redecorated ballroom, but it would also be her opportunity to repay some long-standing social debts. The guests included the twelve other graduating seniors in Frank's class and their dates and also the graduates' parents. Plus, there were invitations to three couples from Ft. Worth and one from Amarillo who had entertained them when she traveled with Albert to their cities on cattle business. The school superintendent and the high school principal and all eight high school teachers were on the list, too.

The guest she was most pleased to have attending was Ellarene Wisdom. She and her husband and daughter, Elaine, would come from Texarkana as houseguests for the weekend. Delia and Ellarene had been classmates at Troufant's and had corresponded regularly for all the years since. Elaine was Frank's age. By the weekend of the party, she would have been a graduate of her private school in Dallas for a week. Delia planned that Frank would escort Elaine to the party. He shouldn't object; her photographs promised she would be a very decorative addition to the festivities.

Delia sighed as she tried to decide on the best time to tell Frank about Elaine. No need to rush. He hadn't shown any interest in the plans for the party at all. Nor did he seem interested in the remodeling that would create the perfect setting for the gathering. Albert didn't inquire much either. At least he didn't interfere like some husbands would have.

She could only hope that Frank would show some interest in Elaine. Their first meeting might be too soon to expect that. But he would have met a girl his own age with a quality family and who had been exposed to some culture. Not that some of the girls in Jackson's Pond weren't nice enough, or pretty, but none of them had the advantages of private education, some travel, and a mother who had attended Troufant's. She knew he would see the contrast immediately.

If there had been even the slightest elevation or something to break the monotony of the flat landscape, Delia's view from the new French doors would have been perfect. As it was, the sunset provided a fine display. She moved to the second door and looked toward the southeast. She saw Albert and Frank sitting on the tailgate of the pickup, near the barn, both wearing serious expressions. Finally, and it was about time, Albert must be talking with Frank about college preparation. If she hadn't been so busy these past weeks, she would have demanded that Frank complete the UT application. But it looked like Albert was taking care of the matter. As she watched, Frank spit out a wad of tobacco and stood looking at the ground. It wouldn't hurt him to learn that he had to take directions from his parents even if he was nearly eighteen. He was lucky to have parents who were concerned about his future. She watched as he nodded to whatever his father was saying. After graduation and the party, she'd find out the details from Albert. She had other things to attend to now. Everything had to be perfect for tomorrow.

She would have slept late. After all of the weekend's events, she was a bit worn. But the phone had rung no fewer than eleven times this morning. Every call was in response to the party. Several women called to repeat their thanks at having been a part of the event. The editor of the *Gazette* called to check some facts for an article about the party that would run in this week's paper. One of Frank's classmates asked if her evening bag had been found and said it had been the best evening of her life, so far.

Delia sat at her vanity table, brushing her hair. Mrs. Pastusek had tutored them to review their parties and other social events in order to identify opportunities for improvement in the future. She had dictated to the class a list of topics for review that could apply to formal activities such as club meetings and to parties alike. More than twenty years after her days at Troufant's, Delia still found the review beneficial. Her skill as an organizer was well known. She was happy to say that her opinion was often sought for planning social activities and for club work. She had served in every office of both the Garden Club and the Study Club in Jackson's Pond.

Daydreaming wouldn't get things done. She pulled herself away from thinking about the next club year and returned to searching for flaws in the party. She could find none. Albert had looked handsome and played the host with grace that he seldom bothered to exhibit here on the ranch. She received numerous compliments on her dress and her appearance in general. The band played a suitable variety of music and everyone had danced. The ballroom was the topic of much admiration, particularly the French doors and little balconies that had been added to accommodate them. The master of ceremonies had been quite entertaining.

The food was excellent, thanks to Maria. And the girls she hired to serve were gracious and unobtrusive, as they should have been. They circulated among the guests all evening, assuring that both food and drink were available.

With what she thought was a masterful stroke, she made certain that Frank would have no excuse not to escort Elaine Wisdom. Perhaps he wouldn't have thought of inviting Willa since her father didn't allow her to date. Just in case, Delia had ensured that Willa would be otherwise occupied.

The day after seeing the two of them together at the pond, she had hired Willa to work the entire weekend, first to help with food preparation, then with serving and finally with cleaning. There was something about the steady gaze the girl turned toward her when she offered the job that reminded her of George, when she had offered to have Willa stay at the house after school. As if she could see all the way through and behind her. Her answer had surprised Delia. "I would be happy to earn the extra money. I need it for the art class I'll be taking this summer in Dallas."

Even Frank had performed admirably. After being named valedictorian of his class that afternoon, he was the subject of many congratulatory remarks, all of which he accepted graciously. He danced with every female in the room, as she had instructed him back when she had taught him party deportment. And he was appropriately attentive to Elaine Wisdom, who had eyes only for him all evening. Delia wondered why she had ever doubted him. He was a young man she should be proud of, who recognized the value of his parents' guidance. Yes, the party was a major success. She finished applying her foundation and lipstick and smiled again at her reflection.

The three of them had just begun eating dinner. For the past two days, they had been working their way through the appetizers and desserts left from the party. Tonight, for a change, they were having simple food—fried pork chops, mashed potatoes, gravy, green beans, and corn bread. Frank ate as if he had missed a meal or two. "Hungry, son?" Albert asked.

"I'll say. Been busy. Forgot to stop for lunch."

Delia looked away rather than watch her husband gnaw the last bit of meat from a pork chop bone.

Albert said, "No wonder you're hungry. I looked for you after the mail came. I never did see you in the north pasture."

"I worked in the barn all day, on the combine and the tractor. What did you want?"

"Something came addressed to you. It's on the table in the hall."

Frank dropped his cornbread to his plate and left the table. He was back in less than a minute, smiling a huge smile. "Great news. I've been accepted."

Delia said, "That's wonderful, I knew UT would want you, particularly since you were valedictorian. I'm so happy."

"UT might want me, but I don't want them. I applied at Texas Tech. I'm in and they offered me a scholarship. Move in the men's dormitory the last week in August. It's all settled." He waved the letter like a banner.

Albert winked at his son and shook his hand. "Well, look at you, taking care of everything all on your own. And a scholarship, too. We're real proud…" He stopped talking when he looked at Delia's face.

Delia placed her fork and knife precisely, diagonally across the top right of her dinner plate. She rose, without a sound, and left the room.

LUBBOCK JOURNAL
Friday, May 9, 1958
Jackson's Pond Tornado

One person was killed, five Jackson's Pond residents remain in serious condition in Lubbock's West Texas Hospital, and at least twenty others sustained injuries in a tornado that hit the town yesterday. Names have not yet been released.

A very large tornado twisted through eastern portions of the South Plains Thursday evening. Jackson's Pond, 47 miles northeast of Lubbock, took the brunt of the storm which formed from a pair of funnels that spun down from a wall cloud between 6:00 and 6:15 p.m.

According to Civil Defense sources, one of the funnels touched ground briefly outside of town near the Jackson Ranch, ruining fence and killing one steer. Then the two clouds came together and roared into the town.

Jackson's Pond volunteer storm spotter, Stanley Carpenter said, "When a storm starts brewing I'm the one who blows the fire whistle if there's a funnel spotted. Yesterday, we were in the middle of a hailstorm so thick you couldn't see the sky. Next thing you know, the tornado was here. I hardly had time to blow the whistle before windows started popping out from the pressure. I wish I could have known sooner."

Clean up efforts are underway and damage assessments will be completed in the next several days, according to Mayor David Clark.

Spring Storms

Driving with the window open didn't help much. The wind was hot and surprisingly humid, after a long dry spell that had begun in January. You could usually count on at least one good snow in January or even as late as February that would give the wheat a little push before it came out of dormancy. Not a drop of any kind of moisture had fallen for four months.

Frank was having trouble corralling his thoughts. The baby and Willa had been at the hospital in Lubbock for four days; the cattle were going to graze out the wheat if it didn't rain soon; the wheat he planned to take to grain might have to be used for grazing and even then it wouldn't be enough unless the grass picked up and that wouldn't happen until it rained; he might have to sell off some heifers if there wasn't any rain because he wouldn't have feed enough for all of them; the beef market was good right now, but would decline if everyone had to start selling cattle; the baby... Maybe it would rain today; maybe that would be a good sign—that things would turn out all right, after all. Everything might depend on the weather.

Johnny Cash was singing, sounding flat. Frank turned off the radio and stared at the highway, trying not to think about what his wife had said on the telephone. "You can come and get us. There's nothing else they can do here." What Willa said sounded like a complete sentence, but he hoped he hadn't understood. Maybe someplace there would be someone who could do something, maybe it was just that the people in Lubbock couldn't. They would go to Fort Worth or Houston, wherever they had to.

He focused on the horizon. Over in the southwest, not clouds, but something had changed the sky's color from faded denim to something a little different—looked like an eraser smudge on a piece of pale blue paper. There had to be something else that could be done. He was only four months old, that little boy with his mother's black hair, that baby who seldom ever cried. Frank felt the wheel drift off the pavement and corrected carefully, quickly. She would be depending on him. He had to get himself collected.

He'd never heard Willa scream, not even when she was in labor with Melanie. She seldom raised her voice. That day, five days ago, she had screamed. Even though he was in the barn, he heard her and knew something awful had happened. When he got to the baby's room she was holding him and trying to give artificial respiration. She couldn't stop to explain, he knew. She breathed into little George's nose and mouth again and again, little short puffs in perfect rhythm. The baby's left leg twitched. "He's breathing, I think. Wait just one second and let's see," Frank said. He spoke softly, afraid he'd cry.

"He's breathing but he's not opening his eyes, Frank. Something's wrong, bad wrong. We've got to get to the doctor." She flicked twice on the sole of the little boy's left foot with a fingertip, like shooting a marble. "See, he won't wake up. He always wakes up when I do that. Get the pickup; we've got to get to the doctor."

On the way into town, Willa, holding the baby, never taking her eyes from the rising and falling of his chest, explained what had happened. Her voice flat and distant, she said she put him down for a nap after he nursed and that two hours later she had gone in his room to check on him, not because he had cried or anything, just because she liked to look at him while he slept. As soon as she walked in she saw he wasn't breathing. His skin was pale and his lips and fingers had turned blue. There was nothing in the bed, no blanket or pillow that could have smothered him. He was lying just the way she put him down, on his back. He hadn't had a fever or a runny nose or any cough or anything. Nothing was different from usual. Except that he had stopped breathing—and she had not been with him when it happened. She had been sitting down, resting in the living room, drinking a Coke. After she told it, she looked over at Frank and tears began rolling down both her cheeks. "I'm afraid he'll die, and it will be my fault."

He drove with one hand and wiped her tears with the other. Words wouldn't help, he knew. Driving to town usually took fifteen minutes. They were at the doctor's office in ten. He yelled at the office nurse that something bad was wrong with the baby and they had to see the doctor. She didn't question Frank, just pointed to a room and ran to get Dr. Cox.

The doctor put oxygen on little George and checked his reflexes and examined him all over. He shook his head and said that there wasn't anything he could do, that they had to get him to a hospital right away. Frank saw things moving in slow motion. He knew the doctor was talking to him, to Willa, and yelling to somebody else, somewhere. But Frank wasn't really there. He couldn't be. He felt himself watching from low down near the floor in a corner.

Then they were in the funeral home's hearse that doubled as the town's ambulance, with the undertaker's assistant holding the oxygen mask on George's tiny face. And Willa was next to him, holding his hand with one of hers and touching the baby with the other. She was shivering like it was winter and moaning a low sound he'd never heard. Would they ever make it to Lubbock? Or would the ambulance just drive on and on into the setting sun that was shining directly into his eyes and making all these tears fall?

For two days he had paced or sat or stared or held Willa when she was able to be still. George was no better, no different. He lay like a tiny beautiful statue in the child-sized hospital bed. Beside him, an oxygen tank stood like a sentinel. He was fed through a tube taped into his right nostril. Doctors came and went and then they came together, a group of three, to tell them that more tests had to be done to be certain, brain wave tests, deep reflex tests, other things. After they left, Willa said he should call and have someone come get him, go back and take care of things on the ranch, see about Melanie and his mother. She spoke to him from somewhere far away.

He had hesitated and hoped that the relief he felt wouldn't show on his face. Relief only lasted until he got into Johnny Griffith's pickup. Johnny hadn't asked him why when he called and asked him to come to Lubbock. But Frank had to explain, once he was face to face with him. His voice failed just after he began. It was all he could do to try to remember how to breathe. Johnny told him it was okay, not to try to talk yet.

His mother opened the front door on the big house as soon as they drove up. Melanie ran, as fast as a three-year-old can, straight to her daddy. "Hold me, Daddy, hold me."

"She's been asking all day when you and Willa are coming home. What happened, Frank? Why didn't you call this morning? You said you would call. All of my friends and people from church have been asking me, and I had nothing I could tell them."

"I don't like talking about it with everyone on the party line listening in. There's nothing new to tell."

He put Melanie on her feet and she ran immediately to Delia. "Play tea party, Mammaw. Let's play."

"I'll be in the parlor in just a minute. You go and get all the dolls ready for the party. I need to talk to your daddy." Melanie did exactly as she was told. "Frank, I can't help thinking that this awful thing might not have happened if you had moved up here like I've asked you. Besides, that's what your father wanted."

"Where we live didn't have anything to do with what happened. The doctors said crib death has no known cause. The only reason the baby's still alive is because Willa went in to check on him. One minute later and he would have been dead when she found him." Keeping his voice down took all the self control he could muster.

"But, here, if Willa had to rest, I would have been watching the baby the whole time."

"Mother, I came by to tell you that I'm back to check on things and to ask you to take care of Melanie for now. I'll let you know if anything changes. I've got to go."

"Don't you need something to eat before you go?"

"No, mother, I need to go now." What he meant was that if he didn't leave he'd say a lot of things he'd have to apologize for later. Since his father died last July, not a week had gone by that she didn't mention wanting, no, "needing," them to move into the big house with her. He wasn't about to move from the house Willa grew up in. Delia would probably have them sleeping in separate rooms and eating meals on her schedule. She would keep at him about moving, he knew. Today was just one more opportunity she seized on to try to get her way. One more low blow, as far as he was concerned.

Frank managed to get the pickup parked in the hospital's lot. He took another breath of the thick, humid air and made himself go through the front door. As he walked down the hall to George's room, a nurse passed him and smiled a sad-eyed smile and said, "Good afternoon, Mr. Jackson. Mrs. Jackson and the doctors are waiting for you in the conference room right back here."

The conference room, a space holding a table and too many chairs, made him feel like breaking out a window just to get a breath. But there wasn't any window. From here, you couldn't see out. He sat down next to Willa and hugged her to his side. The pediatrician introduced the other two doctors who had been consulted to determine whether complete brain death had occurred. Just as plain as that, no frills, he said that awful thing to both of them. Frank felt Willa's muscles go rigid. She sat up straight and leaned toward the graphs that the other two had in front of them. They explained the tests they had done and how the only reason the baby was not dead was that a part of his medulla still functioned intermittently. He still quit breathing several times a day. The upper parts of his brain, as Frank understood it, were dead. The lack of oxygen when he stopped breathing that first day had caused that to happen. Nothing could repair it. He wouldn't even be able to nurse or take a bottle. The tube was the only way. Vegetative state, they said.

The images that came to Frank's mind, mute potatoes and pale cabbages lined up in tiny cribs, were so horrible he closed his eyes—those vegetables hovered behind his lids, imprinted in his mind. He had to hold onto the chair arms to keep himself from drifting into the corner again. George had been such a perfect baby. Frank caught himself thinking in the past tense. A conference room should have a window.

And then the doctors used the word "options." It boiled down to they could leave him here and let him die slowly in the hospital or take him home and let him die there at his own rate. The questions Frank wanted to ask all sounded stupid as he thought them; he didn't bother to ask. How soon would it happen? What happens in the meantime? Do we feed and change him and keep someone awake all the time to do artificial respiration? Do we just turn our heads and let him go? Who had answers for those questions? Who was in charge?

Willa asked those and other questions, all in a voice so strong he wasn't sure it was hers. And finally, she had no more questions. Frank shook his head, "No, I don't have any other questions." He knew without asking, after the doctors left them alone, what Willa had decided. He wouldn't argue. Either way it was going to be awful. "Frank," she said.

He kissed her gently on the lips. "Shhh. You don't have to say it. I know," he said. He leaned against her and she held him with his head on her shoulder, there in that room with no window.

When the nurse came to ask if they needed anything, Willa said, "Yes, we need to get everything ready. We'll take baby George home as soon as you show us what we need to know to be able to take care of him."

Neither of them spoke on the trip back to the ranch. The air closed around them, even heavier than it had been in the morning. In the rearview mirror, Frank saw that the smudge on the horizon was darker but no larger. He gave up hoping for the rain. Willa held the baby. Sometime near Calverton, she began humming a lullaby.

He didn't ask her, just drove directly to their house and stopped. They could decide later when to get Melanie, when to explain to Delia. Right now, he wanted to be alone with her and baby George. She sat in the rocker in the bedroom, holding the baby. Frank managed to get the oxygen tank in next to the crib. "I wish he would cry, just once more," she said. He put his arms around her and kissed the tiny still form in her arms. Willa rocked and hummed.

Frank stood on the front porch, gazing southwest into the distance. A line of dark clouds was outlined by the sun rapidly falling behind them. His father had done the same; he remembered—stood on the porch and watched the clouds. Often when Frank stood and watched, it was less because the clouds held any interest than because the habit comforted him. He'd imitated his father standing, watching, since he was a child. These clouds kept building, growing, their tops boiling. Willa had stopped humming. The quiet stillness crept out of the house. And the stillness outside fell around him where he stood. The heavy, humid air pressed at his chest. He wanted to run. Then he saw the clouds advancing, bringing the horizon much closer. In the distance, a funnel spun down from the largest cloud and slowly dropped toward the ground. A second funnel formed. Before long, roaring—the sound of a gang of locomotives—replaced the quiet. Willa, holding the baby, came out and stood beside him. He reached for her and they stood together.

The funnels whirled together and became one, heading directly toward them. They waited, not moving. Wind whipped at their clothes and dust blasted their faces. Captured by a barbed wire fence, tumbleweeds, like prisoners, were held to the ground and punished by the wind and flying debris. Frank saw dirt, fence posts, sheets of roofing tin, a dog, all whirling in the great vortex no farther away than the end of the driveway.

Then, as quickly as it had advanced on them, the massive cloud veered and roared away to the southeast. Stillness closed around them again. The baby had ceased breathing. They did not move from the porch. Minutes later the rain began to fall.

Since the day of the baby's funeral, Frank hadn't cried again. That day, at the graveside service, he had stood dry-eyed, masked by sadness, holding his wife, willing her his strength. Afterward, he had taken her home and put her to bed with a kiss on her forehead. When she was asleep, he saddled his horse and rode to the pond and sat on the bank and let himself cry.

His tears were for the baby, for Willa, for himself, for Melanie and his mother, for his favorite dog that died when he was nine, and for every regret he'd ever felt and all the times he'd wanted to cry and never let himself because men don't. He cried until all he felt was empty. Then he washed his face and gathered himself. Willa would need him to be strong. He'd never seen her fragile before.

That thought, that she might break, kept him going. The weeks since May had been a succession of days he couldn't remember. Now, somehow August had appeared.

He could tell it was Willa standing in the doorway of the barn. But he couldn't see her face because the sun was directly behind her surrounding her with a halo and darkening her features. He squinted in her direction and saw her cheeks and elbows and hips, all the angles that weight loss and sadness had emphasized. Willa, up and out of the house. A good sign. For the past three months, she had done the necessary things—put food on the table, bathed and dressed Melanie and kept the house neat, but every action was wooden, every step halting. She never left the house; she haunted the room where the baby had slept, staring at the spot where his bed had been, touching the little dresser that held his clothes and toys. She roamed through the other rooms, and she slept, hours and hours, night and day. There were days when he wondered if she had lost her voice. Her paints lay untouched, the records she had danced to gathered dust on top of the record player.

Frank had done all he could. There had been no harvest because the rain came too late. He had moved the cattle to the grass where they were gaining weight as he'd hoped. When he worked at the house or the barn, he let Melanie follow him around and pretend to help. When he had to leave, he took Melanie up the road to her grandmother's. And at night he held Willa when she dreamed and cried. Now, here she was in the sunshine.

"Frank, there's a couple of things I want you to do."

"I'll do anything I can, honey. What do you need?"

She shifted and took a deep breath, as if she had to gather strength to say what she was thinking. "Tell your mother we'll move in with her. Do it today before I can change my mind. She wants us there and Melanie needs more of a mother than I can be to her."

He watched her take two more big breaths. He didn't question her or disagree. She might be right about Melanie. He wiped his hands on a shop rag. Then he asked, "What's the other thing you want me to do?"

"Put me to work. Hard work. It's the only thing I know to do now."

Saying the words seemed to wear her out. She leaned against the doorframe. He put his arms around her as if she might fall to pieces. Her breathing had gotten ragged. "There's fence work you can start on tomorrow. There's a lot of jobs I've fallen behind on around here. Willa, I need your help." He spoke carefully and slowly, taking his time as he would with a spooky mare. A raven glided toward them and then, with two flaps of its wings, changed direction and lit nearby on the scrawny chinaberry tree. Willa pointed toward the bird. Frank nodded. "Yep, the first one this year."

Frank stood holding her for a few minutes, glad to feel her there. Maybe it was the sun, but he thought that some light had come back into her eyes.

JACKSON'S POND GAZETTE
Thursday, May 18, 1967
Vandals Strike Jackson's Pond

Several sites in Jackson's Pond sustained damage this past weekend in what Deputy Sheriff Henry Collins described as "beyond the usual teenage mischief."

He said, "Some years there will be kids from rival schools, like Paducah, sneak into town and try to steal the statue of the coyote mascot down at the football field. It's not uncommon for some of the seniors to climb the water tower to paint their names and graduation year. Occasionally the cemetery will be trashed with broken beer bottles that were used for target practice with 22s. But that's as bad as it ever gets.

"This is different. Whoever did this was trying to upset people and to tamper with the usual order of things here in Jackson's Pond. There had to be a gang of people involved to do all this in one night without being seen during my rounds."

June's Apparel, Berry's Drug, and the Pass Time Club were defaced with obscene words and drawings. The John Deere dealership had paint damage to a new combine and the windows of all 12 used cars and pickups at Shaw's Ford were completely painted over.

A large peace symbol and the words NO MORE WAR were painted on the water tower and a banner was strung across Main Street bearing the words, "Tell The Draft Board You Won't Go."

No More War

Willa combed through her wet hair with her fingers. Her mother-in-law had been absolutely correct when she said that remodeling the bathrooms would produce "immeasurable pleasure" for them all. Delia was given to such pronouncements, particularly about ideas she had and planned to implement. For Willa, having a shower after all the years of washing her hair with her head upside down over a bathtub was indeed a pleasure. She'd spent all morning in the sun and the dust and she felt gritty, hot, and smelly. And her encounter with Delia when she came in from the barn hadn't helped. Delia had said, "I must talk to you and Frank at dinner tonight."

Willa and Frank were preparing for wheat harvest. If they didn't get hailed out in the next two weeks, June's crop should be one of the best in years. Getting ready meant, among other things, assuring that the combine was in working order—greased, oiled, cleaned, and filled with hydraulic fluid—hot, dirty work. They joked about her ability as a mechanic's helper and in particular her pride in her skill with the grease gun.

She appraised her reflection in the new large mirror. Aside from inch-wide grey streaks shot through her black hair at each temple and a few lines at the corners of her eyes, her appearance had changed little in the fifteen years since she and Frank married. Her streaks first appeared in 1959, the year after they moved to the big house to live with Delia. A recent widow at the time, Delia had wanted them there. They had needed her. When Frank asked if living with his mother had caused the grey hair, she showed him a photograph of her with her mother, taken in 1933, the year before she died. Willa had been five and Edna Lofland thirty-three then. Although the photo was black and white, it showed the same two grey streaks and the contrast between her dark complexion and surprising, light eyes. Willa had inherited those same light eyes too—green, with gold flecks.

Even if Willa could have blamed Delia for her grey hair, she would never have spoken of it to Frank. Having a mother, no matter how demanding, was better than missing one that you could only recall in the way that people hold onto cherished memories from childhood—large and vague and perfect.

Now, there were errands to do in town. She wrestled with the cranky door handle and finally opened the cab door of the old 1950 Chevy grain truck, the one she would use to take the harvested wheat to the elevator. She worked the throttle twice, turned on the ignition, and pressed the accelerator to the floor. It started and idled roughly. After it warmed up and the idle smoothed out, she pulled onto the dirt road. She pumped the brakes. They badly needed repair; several repairs had been put off since last year. The pedal went to within a few inches of the floorboard. For once, she was glad that the land was flat and the roads were laid out square—no curves to make demands on the bit of brakes that remained. She would make the trip into town slowly and cautiously. Paying attention to the road would keep her from thinking about Delia.

Fields on either side of the road showed the result of the past few years' changes in farming in the area. Driving so slowly, she had time to notice the evidence. Natural gas lines had been installed and the accessible fuel made it possible for farmers to operate the high-powered irrigation pumps night and day if they wanted to. Harvesting eighty to a hundred bushels of wheat per acre was almost irresistible to some, regardless of the costs. She passed a huge sprinkler rolling almost imperceptibly on its three foot-high wheels through a lush wheat field, spraying water from three hundred or more feet underground over the grain field and into the air. She downshifted and let the clutch out slowly, reducing the truck's speed to a crawl. A rainbow formed in the spray from the end nozzle as it arced over the wheat.

A new Gleaner combine sat in front of Johnson's barn. Lots of people had bought new trucks and other equipment and implements. Those farmers were doing far better than their fathers ever dreamed a farmer could, if crop yield was the measure of success—or gross income, or number and size of tractors they farmed with, or width of plows, or new cars and pickups, and remodeled houses.

Seeing the opportunity to increase their crop yields by increasing irrigation, many of their neighbors had eliminated their grass pastures entirely. If they grazed any calves on early wheat, it was only for a few months. Then they shipped them off to feedlots to "gain more efficiently" and harvested the wheat when it ripened. The Reeses and several others had plowed up all of their land—land that had been covered with prairie grass for as long as humans could recall. And with massive use of anhydrous ammonia fertilizer, they planted crop after crop, never allowing any land to lie fallow in rotation.

They ignored the lessons of the Dust Bowl; they had access to the immense underground Ogallala Aquifer. Like so many thirsty, greedy kids each putting a straw into a single soda, they began sucking up water as fast as they could. No one seemed concerned that the streams that gushed from the irrigation pipes flowed a fraction more slowly each season. No one called attention to the fact that Jackson's Pond shrank from its banks an inch or more each year. But they did boast of their yields and of their multiple crops and they did polish their new pickups before coming into town on Sunday. They had increased their income and the Jackson's Pond State Bank had been happy to help them increase their debt for new equipment and other operating costs.

Frank's plan was different. The Jacksons made do with older equipment and this old grain truck. He continued and refined his father's approach to operating the ranch. They bred and raised cattle, from birth to sale to the meat packers. And they farmed wheat, some milo, and a rotation of legumes and clover for natural fertilizer. He had sown in improved varieties of grasses among the native grass to improve the pasture on the rangeland acres. Their crops served two purposes—feed for the cattle and, in especially good crop years, extra income for savings. They always rotated the crops to leave a portion of the acres fallow each year. His ideas made sense to Willa. He told her that all the guys who grew cotton and corn laughed and told him he was old fashioned. She told him she thought that those men were working for the bank and the fertilizer company and an early grave.

She passed the pond and made the final turn onto the paved road to town. That pond was where she had first realized how close Frank felt to the ranch, that he didn't think of himself as working the land but as working with the land. Some of those neighbors would have laughed if they had heard. The first time he told her, she had been about fifteen and Frank was nearly eighteen. They often met at Jackson's Pond, always as if it were an accident. Maybe it was accidental for him, but she often chose the pond as a place to paint with the hope that he would find her there even though she dreaded the possibility of his mother's finding them there as she had once before. Willa and her father lived nearby on Jackson land, so she could easily walk or ride her horse there. As she painted, Frank would talk about his hopes, about how he wanted to ranch and farm in a way that respected the land and all the people who had ever lived on it.

He had been on foot, leading his horse, and moving so quietly that she hadn't noticed until he was very near. "What are you painting today, Miss Lofland?" He and the horse were behind her. Frank could see her work on the easel. "That's really something, Willa. It looks like a frame around the wheat fields— the pond, the fence, the horizon. And the clouds look like accessories, like jewelry. Do you see the spirits that are here when you paint?" His voice was earnest, no joking beneath the odd question. She turned to look at him. He blushed. "I mean… Well, I'm not sure exactly what I mean, but your paintings make me think you see things other people don't."

"That's the nicest thing you could possibly tell me, Mr. Jackson—Frank." She smiled a shy smile and cocked her head to look again at her painting.

"Tell me about what you see when you look at those cattle

over there at that stock tank below the windmill." He pointed to six large steers bumping at each other for a space at the tank.

She wiped her brush on her jeans and turned to view the cattle.

"Part of what I see is because of what I know I would hear if I was over there. They make noise when they drink. They sound like old men slurping coffee from saucers, the way they do if there's no woman around to remind them not to. Six guys who grew up together, pushing and joking and doing things that men and boys do. They're not steers anymore, they're males that happen to be dressed as cattle today. That pasture is their territory, the place they own, the way men like to claim places. That's what I see." She dipped her brush in a little cup of water that sat on a rim on the easel. She began painting again. "I think maybe you see things out here that other people don't, too." She hadn't looked at him when she said the words.

They stood for a long time without speaking. His horse stamped at the ground. Frank led him to the edge of the pond to drink. When he came back to the easel, he said, "I do. If you won't laugh, I'll tell you something I see right now."

"I won't laugh. How could I? I just admitted I see things that other people don't and then I try to paint them." She turned to face him; she wanted him to know she was interested in anything he said.

"Well, maybe see is not exactly the word. Like you said you imagined what you hear and it affects what you see—maybe what I feel affects what I see. I've tried to put this in words before, but I'm still not sure I can explain. Don't laugh, promise."

"I promise."

"This is about the land, not just what we can see standing right here, but all this flat land out here. It's plain. But it's beautiful to me. Some days it's so hot and dry, I wonder how I could ever see it that way. Then on a day like today, it's beautiful." He stepped toward his horse and gazed into the distance, at the flat land in every direction. "It's like a woman who seems plain until one day you see a thought spark something in her eye or a memory turns her inward. When that happens, she's beautiful as a sunrise. Like a woman you've known all your life wears denim everyday. Then one day you see her shoulder bare, just her shoulder, and you realize how much more there is under that rough blue cloth." He shrugged and looked at the horse as if he'd just noticed it was with him. His face and ears reddened. He fiddled with the horse's bridle. "That's what I see. That's why I want to take care of this place. I've never tried to explain it to my dad exactly like that, but he knows I understand what he's tried to do. He knows I'll take care of it as soon as I get out of college. Then he can retire feeling good about the job he did."

After leaving the truck with the mechanic, Willa's first stop was at June's Apparel. She stopped outside where June was scraping at the paint on the front window. It was covered with several drawings that might represent soldiers throwing down their weapons. Newspapers frequently carried reports of student protests at universities across the country, even one or two in Texas, such as the recent one at North Texas in Denton. But to find any suggestion of war protest in Jackson's Pond surprised Willa. She had not spoken of her views on the war to anyone except Frank, but had she been asked, she would have agreed with the person who rendered the drawings. The war should be stopped. If she had a son of draft age, she had no doubt that she would encourage him to become a Canadian.

She jerked her thoughts to the present. She had no son now. She had a twelve-year-old daughter who needed her attention and a 32 AA bra. June stopped scraping at the paint and offered to go inside to help her find what she needed. "First one, huh? The little girls all like these that have this little bow. Do you want white or beige?" she asked.

Willa stared at the wispy garment in June's hand. She hadn't needed a bra at all until she was fourteen. But Melanie was developing early. She was going to be built more like Delia, probably shorter than Willa's five feet-eight, and would definitely have a figure sooner than Willa had. "I'll take one of each," she said. There was another stop to make, at Berry's Drug.

She had gotten the only information she had about menstruation from her girlfriends, all of whom started their periods before she did. George Lofland had never mentioned the subject and she'd been too embarrassed to ask him. Her daddy was good about a lot of things, but she just couldn't see trying to get him to explain something that mothers were supposed to tell their daughters. The look on his face the first time she had written Kotex on the shopping list remained in her memory. He raised an eyebrow, looked at her and then back at the list and squinted, like he was looking at something far off, and asked, "Everything okay?"

Melanie hadn't asked for the information or for any supplies, but Willa could tell that she would soon need both. Moodiness, tearful spells, and complaints of vague stomach and back pains all suggested that childhood was soon to be over for Melanie Jackson.

"They grow up fast, don't they." Martha Cooper said the words as a statement, not a question, as she rang up the box of junior absorbency sanitary napkins and the accessory elastic belt. Willa nodded and added three Hershey bars to her purchases. She clenched her jaw. Just once, she'd appreciate some privacy in this town. For Jackson's Pond residents, minding their own business seemed to mean keeping an eye on everyone, drawing conclusions, and passing them along to anyone inclined to listen. She had no doubt that by tomorrow, Martha would have found some opportunity to mention Melanie and the onset of puberty in the same breath to someone. How was it, Willa wondered, that this whole town of highly observant people could have missed seeing who had painted anti-war sentiments all over the town? She studied the figures painted on Berry's window. The artist must be an admirer of Peter Max. Too bad he only had black paint. The figures would have been quite good in color.

The mechanic completed the brake repair in record time. Willa paid and thanked him and made a fuss of hurrying. She knew he'd want to gossip if she would stand still for it. On the way back to the house, she finally allowed herself to think about the thing she had been pushing away all morning—Delia's latest campaign. Willa smiled briefly as an image of her mother-in-law in full military uniform with a general's stars and a chest full of medals came to mind. If ever someone missed their calling, it was Frank's mother. When she had an idea, a desire, a wish, or maybe a whim, she went to work to make it happen. She recruited others to fall in and march along behind her. The women in the Twenty-Three Study Club and the Garden Club of Jackson's Pond marveled at her organizational skills and willingly chose her to lead.

As far as Willa knew, when he was alive, Albert Jackson never disagreed with his wife. Frank and Willa were the only two who ever tested her will—small skirmishes, never full-scale battles, never any lasting damage. Willa had been part of so few she could remember them all clearly.

The first time was when Mrs. Delia Jackson, the woman from the big house, had stopped by their small house. Eight-year-old Willa stood at the stove, cooking supper, barely able to reach the back burner to stir the beans. "George, don't you think Willa works too hard for a child of her age? Her schooling may suffer." Mrs. Jackson handed him the cake she brought. "I could send Maria down to do some cooking and cleaning every two weeks." Willa saw her looking around like she was inspecting for dust on the furniture.

Her father moved the toothpick he was chewing on over to the corner of his mouth and said, "She does work hard and her grades are real good." He discarded the toothpick into an ashtray. "Willa, do you want Maria to come help you clean and cook? It's okay with me if you do."

She shook her head no and said, "Thank you, Mrs. Jackson. But I like keeping house and cooking. And thank you for the cake." Willa stood up very straight as she spoke, but that didn't change the fact that the apron she wore, her mother's apron, still reached the floor. That was years ago, but Willa remembered it clearly.

She tested the brakes again before she pulled out onto the highway at the edge of town. No pumping required. She wouldn't have to feel so uncertain now when the truck held an entire load of 26,000 pounds of wheat. She let herself enjoy the view from the high cab of the grain truck, now that she trusted the brakes. She thought of two other times she disagreed with Delia Jackson. The year her father died.

Delia Jackson had come to the hospital in Calverton the day after George Lofland's heart attack. After visiting briefly with him, she asked Willa to come to the waiting room. "Willa, Frank and our hired man can take care of your father's work until he's better. You just finished college; you need a rest. You should stay here at the hospital with your father."

"I appreciate your offer, Mrs. Jackson, but I can take care of everything." Willa didn't tell her that she and Frank had already talked about how she'd get the crop in. Her father could rely on her; he'd taught her to depend on herself. She would run the combine, and she had hired a man to drive the grain truck. She would fulfill her father's tenant obligation. He never owed anyone, and she didn't intend to be in debt either.

Two weeks later, after George died, Delia appeared at the house, her face solemn. She took off her gloves and sat on the chair near the couch where Willa was resting. Willa saw her look around the way she always did when she came by bringing food, like she might find grime or lint. "Willa, child, you look exhausted. You worked too hard to finish the harvest. Let me take care of the funeral arrangements for you. People all over the county liked your father; they will want to pay their respects. We can have the visitation at our house and Maria will take care of all the food. You shouldn't have to do this alone."

"You're very kind, Mrs. Jackson. But Daddy and I planned everything before he died. We talked about it a long time ago." She saw the older woman's lips tighten. "Visitation will be at the funeral home's parlor. The service will be plain, just the way Daddy wanted, at the little Missionary Baptist Church."

Delia pulled on her gloves and straightened her hat. "Very well. Let me know if there is anything at all that I can do to help."

Willa made the final turn off the gravel onto the dirt road to the Jackson House. A small smile crossed her lips as she thought about their last disagreement. It was the only time she

ever felt she triumphed over Frank's mother. At the time, she had
been too nervous to enjoy her little victory.

No rain fell at all in July of 1952, after her dad died. The grass
crackled as the cattle searched for the few remaining green stems.
Heat mirages made imaginary ponds appear on the horizon. But
even the heat couldn't wilt the excitement that Willa felt the
evening Frank took her to have dinner with his parents. Inside the
Jackson house, Delia had placed large fans on stands in each
room. In the low humidity, the fans actually cooled the spaces to
a tolerable temperature.

Delia had created a cool-looking, festive table on that hot
evening. The good china and silver sparkled against the pale
yellow cutwork tablecloth. Crystal stemware held their iced tea.
Frank signaled Maria to refill their glasses. Then he cleared his
throat and said, "Before we have dessert, I have something that I
want to tell you, something important." He waited until his
mother and father looked toward him. "I asked Willa to marry me,
and she agreed. As of today, we are officially engaged to be
married." He reached for Willa's hand and clutched it. She held
her breath.

Albert Jackson spoke first, "Well, son, that's just great.
Willa, I'm glad you're going to be officially part of the family now,
not just one of the cowboys anymore." He laughed at his own
joke and Willa and Frank joined in.

Delia placed her tea glass on the table, precisely above her
knife. "Well then, there will be lots of plans to make. I suppose
you'll want the wedding to be very soon, so we'll need to get right
to work." Her "we'll make the best of this situation" expression
would not have passed for a smile. The implication of Delia's
statement hung like a storm cloud over the dining table.

After a few seconds, Willa said, "No, there's no reason to
hurry." She paused to drink from her tea glass, remembering every
painful detail of her college roommate Ann Mason's necessity-
rushed ceremony in Austin just after graduation. She drew herself
erect and waited until Delia replaced her fork on her plate. "We
will be married next summer. I've accepted a job in Plainview,

teaching art in the high school starting in September. It's important to me to live on my own for a year before getting married. Frank understands. We will marry next July. School will be out; harvest will be over." She wasn't certain, but she thought she saw Albert Jackson wink at her.

The idea of disagreeing with Delia now made Willa take a deep breath. She owed Delia a lot. When baby George died, Willa had disappeared. Not physically, but in every other way. The only things she had been able to do were to put food on the table for Frank and Melanie and to sleep. Even now, nine years later, she didn't understand what had happened to her. The shape that was left on the ranch had looked like Willa, but it moved automatically, stared into the refrigerator, stood at the stove, ate, unless it forgot, and slept when it was too tired to continue. Willa had departed. That shell stood in for her while she was gone. It did not know how to dance; it could not paint; it seldom spoke; laughter was beyond its ability; and it could feel only emptiness, no other emotion.

Maybe it had been a dream, or maybe it had been real—Frank and Delia's voices talking together in another room sometime in those months. She had heard the words—State Hospital Wichita Falls—shock treatments—profound depression. And she clearly heard Frank shout, "No." The next day she struggled out of bed. She found Frank and told him he had to let her work, that she could do it; that it was all she could do. And without knowing what she was doing, she had given Melanie to Delia.

Frank moved them from the house that George Lofland had leased as a Jackson tenant and where Willa had grown up, into the Jackson house. Delia did all the things a mother would have done for Melanie—dressed her, played with her, comforted her when she was upset—and never once implied to Willa that she was being neglectful. Instead, she had said again and again, "I don't know how I could have gotten along now that Albert is gone, if you had not come to live with me." She ran the household as she always had; she took over and kept them all going.

That absent year, Willa had worked alongside Frank, or alone, at mindless tasks seven days a week. Frank would invent reasons he needed to rest, in hopes of getting her to take a day off. She couldn't.

The next year, Willa returned. That's how it seemed, as she thought of it now. One day she was working, eating, and sleeping and then suddenly, surprisingly, she felt something that had replaced the emptiness. She felt gratitude—to Delia.

Soon, she began to see colors again; she took weekends off from the work of the ranch; slept late on Saturdays; and finally began gaining back the weight she had lost. She got up every morning to have breakfast with Melanie. Delia had her breakfast with them. Willa hoped that Melanie would begin to follow her around, asking her questions the way she did Delia and Frank. But that didn't happen. She had lost her daughter when she lost herself. No, she hadn't lost her, she'd given Melanie away. But Melanie hadn't suffered. She had constant attention from her grandmother; she had a gentle and loving father; and she had a mother.

For the next seven years, Willa worked to win back her daughter. She asked Frank to hire part-time help so that she could be with Melanie each afternoon and on weekends. She began to paint again and did all she could to interest Melanie in art projects. When Melanie was eight, Willa returned to dancing three times a week. The dancing woman she saw in the upstairs ballroom mirror was the wiser version of the girl who had taken ballet classes in college. Melanie did not reject her, but neither did she seek her out. Melanie played dolls with her grandmother and stuck by Frank's side anytime he was in the house. Now, soon she would longer be a child.

In all the years they lived no together in the big house, there had never been a real argument. Willa waited and observed her mother-in-law's tactics. If Willa offered Melanie a picnic at Jackson's Pond, Delia presented an alternative—a trip to Lubbock to shop. When Willa proposed an afternoon at the movie, Delia suggested they bake Melanie's favorite cookies. She always included Willa in the preferred activity. Delia seemed to know what the little girl liked best. As recently as this past Christmas, Willa and Frank's gifts to the child took second place to the newest Madame Alexander doll from her grandmother.

The only time that Delia remained uninvolved and silent was when discipline was required. That she left to Willa and Frank. Recently, those occasions had become more frequent. Disrespectful language, a messy room, and homework not completed had become weekly events. Frank or Willa meted out punishment consistent with the infraction. Usually they sent her to her room or withheld television time.

Last week, for the first time, Delia interfered directly. Melanie had lost her television privileges for a full week for refusing, in a passive but effective way, to clean her room, the only chore required of her.

"Mammaw, tell her that I have to be able to see American Bandstand. It's not fair." Willa heard Melanie whining to her grandmother. When had Delia gone into the child's room?

"You straighten your room like you're supposed to, and I'll speak to Willa about it. Here, I'll help hang up your clothes."

In a few minutes, she heard Delia say, "Melanie, have you thought any more about going to Camp Waldemar? I think it would be a very good experience. Just think, a whole month with no chores, lots of other girls from different places, and all the exciting activities."

"You know I want to, Mammaw, but I know they won't let me. They never let me do anything. Will you talk to them? Please, please."

Willa flinched at her daughter's tone. She was determined to respect Delia; she owed her that, and more. She was equally determined to have a parent's influence on her daughter. She bit her lip and left the house. No sense turning this into a battle.

That evening after dinner, Delia asked them to come to the front parlor to talk. "Frank, I would like to give Melanie a special present. But I feel that I should have permission from you and Willa." Willa and Frank were sitting side by side on the sofa, but

Delia spoke as if Willa were not present. She watched Delia's face and hands as she explained a list of advantages to Melanie's attending Camp Waldemar in Hunt, Texas, more than four hundred miles away from Jackson's Pond—a rehearsed performance if she'd ever seen one. How could they object? It would be an opportunity for Melanie to meet and become friends with girls from quality families—one of her favorite phrases. Delia didn't mention cost. To her, cost was not an issue. No expense was too great where Melanie was concerned. Willa knew her mother-in-law would play that ace only if they objected.

Frank looked at his mother for a long time before saying anything. "You've already told her about it, haven't you?"

"Well, yes, I did mention that a month at a good camp would be a wonderful experience for her."

"You should have talked to us first." His voice sounded odd, flat. He knew his mother better than anyone. "We'll discuss it and let you know."

Finally, she turned her gaze to Willa. "You'll need this brochure. A decision will need to be made this week if she's to get in this summer. The camp is very popular and girls whose mothers attended there are given first choice." Willa resisted an urge to apologize.

She pulled the truck into the barn. Delia's "talk" tonight would be about the camp. Willa still didn't know exactly what to say about it—so far from home—Melanie's periods about to start—her fits of mood—Delia's persistence. Frank didn't want to let her go and she wanted to say no, outright. But she didn't want to upset Frank by disagreeing directly with his mother and she definitely didn't want to get into a battle of wills with Delia. He should be the one to tell his mother no.

Willa found Melanie in the house, watching Bandstand. She calmly reminded her daughter that she was not permitted to watch television until the next week. The soon-to-be-teenager turned the set off with a dramatic flourish, flounced from the room, and slammed her bedroom door. An hour later, she refused dinner, saying she wasn't hungry.

They began the meal without her. Delia said, "I'm sure you have discussed the camp and we can talk about that later. But first, there's something else I want to mention. And before you ask, Frank, yes, I have talked about this with Melanie. She's very interested." She paused and called Maria from the kitchen to bring more butter.

"You may have heard of the Hockaday School in Dallas. Maybe you met some girls at UT who attended there, Willa. Frank you remember Elaine Wisdom. That's where she attended."

Surprised she'd been included, Willa felt her muscles tighten. She swallowed the chicken she was chewing and sharpened her attention.

Delia launched into a long explanation of her plan for Melanie to board at Hockaday beginning in September. Another well-planned presentation, Willa was certain. She and Frank both listened respectfully. Their food remained on their plates. Delia paused from time to time to continue eating. She commanded the situation with point after point about the school's long history, the quality of its educational program, and the opportunities for Melanie to be surrounded by girls from quality families. And, to top it off, she repeated that it was a girls-only school. Stabbing the air with her fork, she said, "You can't be too careful about allowing her around boys. Look at those thugs in Jackson's Pond. You know what damage they've done to the town."

"Are you finished, Mother?" Frank asked.

Willa looked at her cold mashed potatoes and pushed her plate away.

"Yes, I am. Thank you for listening." Delia smiled widely and began eating her apple pie.

"We'll discuss it and let you know." His voice was controlled, just above a whisper.

Frank and Willa were in the only place in the Jackson house where they could talk privately, their bedroom. Frank jerked his boots off and threw his socks at the wall. "My mother! She never changes. She's using the school thing to try to force us to give in about the camp. She knows we won't let Melanie go away to boarding school. It comes down to whether we'll give in on that or the camp, or fight her on both."

Willa felt her jaw muscles tighten. If Delia wasn't Frank's mother, she would have told her long ago exactly what she thought of her methods. It wasn't that she didn't appreciate all that Delia had done for them, for Melanie. Usually, Willa could overlook the offhand remarks that suggested Delia, not Willa, was the expert in all matters Melanie and the controlling way that she got Frank to do whatever she wanted. But tonight she had reached her limit.

"What do you want to do?" She straightened the bedspread and picked up his socks.

"I want to move out and run our own lives and be in charge of our own family," he said.

Willa heard resignation in Frank's voice. The same tone she'd heard last summer when drought had forced him to give up on the wheat and plow it under—like he's had to swallow a dose of something bitter. An old man's voice, worn down by contending with forces of nature beyond his control. Weather was one thing; his mother was another. Willa wasn't going to allow her to wear Frank down and destroy their family.

He fell back onto the bed and stared up at the ceiling. "I guess the only thing to do is let her send her to camp."

"Melanie needs to be home this summer. She's starting puberty—moody, not understanding how her body feels, all that. She needs to be here with us, not off with strangers in a strange place." As she talked, her pulse throbbed in her neck. Not this time; she wasn't going to give in just to get along.

"Dad always said the best way to deal with Mother was to let her do what she wants and then stay out of the way."

"No, Frank." She threw the words at the wall, heard them rebound and fill the room. She turned to face him. "Not this time. She's not sending our daughter to camp *or* to Hockaday. I'm not going to give Melanie away again."

He stood, barefooted, and looked at her as if she had spoken in Greek.

"I mean what I say." She tossed him his socks. "Get your boots on. We're going to settle this now."

She heard Melanie's radio playing a Beatles song as they passed the closed door of her room. Willa stopped in the living room doorway. "Mrs. Jackson, we've decided," she said.

Delia looked up from the *Jackson's Pond Gazette* briefly. She remained seated in her chair, the upholstered wingback that looked like a throne. She returned to the paper, as if interrupted in the middle of something important. Then she said, "Frank, did you read about the vandalism in town?"

Frank opened his mouth, then shut it and stared at his boots.

Willa said, "We've decided. Melanie isn't going to camp."

Delia folded the paper and laid it on the coffee table. She switched off the reading lamp, rose from her chair, and moved toward the doorway. "I think it's time to go to bed. We can talk about this tomorrow after we've all rested," she said.

Willa didn't move from the doorway. She stood erect, fully three inches taller than Frank's mother. Delia stopped.

"No, this is final. She's not going. There will be no further discussion," Willa said. She avoided looking at Frank.

"I see. Since she'll be going to Hockaday in September, you want her here for the rest of the summer. That's understandable," Delia said. "I know she'll be pleased once she gets over the disappointment about camp." She showed Frank a big smile; it faded a bit as she looked toward Willa.

"She's not going to Hockaday, either," Willa said.

"Frank, make Willa be sensible about this."

Willa said, "I am being sensible. She's our daughter and we decide what she will do."

Delia's smile disappeared. She retreated to her chair. "If it's the money, don't be concerned. I intend to pay. It's a further investment in her future. With that taken care of there's no reason for her to be denied a quality education. You can't appreciate how important Hockaday can be in her development. It's unfortunate you didn't have a similar opportunity."

Willa almost laughed. She'd wondered when Delia would pull that card from her sleeve.

"She's not going. That's final. We'll tell her in the morning," Willa said.

"Frank, you and Willa need to think carefully about making decisions like this without consulting me. We're a family. And after all, you do live in my house."

Frank looked directly at his mother and said, "It's time we moved back to our own house anyway. We won't discuss this again, and we'll be out of here by next week," he said. Willa moved closer to him and reached for his hand.

If the words had been visible, they would have looked like a handprint on Delia's face. She shrank back into the chair. Minutes seemed to pass. She took a tissue from the box on the end table and dabbed at her eyes, not looking toward Frank and Willa. Their silence magnified the sound of her irregular breathing. Willa held tight to Frank's hand, silently urging him not to back down. She wanted to say something, something hateful like, "It's your play, Delia." But she'd said enough, all that needed saying.

Delia stood again, took a deep breath. She said, "I'm sorry it's come to this. Please don't move out." She spoke directly to Willa.

Willa looked at Frank. As far as she was concerned, it was up to him, now.

"Mother, it wouldn't have happened at all if you had stayed out of it, not talked to Melanie until you'd talked to us," he said.

Delia nodded, still not looking either of them in the eye. "I may have overstepped. If you stay, I promise it won't happen again."

For a second, Willa felt sorry for this woman who seldom had to apologize.

"We'll stay. We don't want trouble, but no more talk of sending Melanie off, ever," Frank said. "We're going to bed now. There's lots of work tomorrow."

In their room again, neither of them spoke for a while. Frank quickly stripped down to his underwear and got in bed. Willa put on her gown. She sat on the bed and stared out the window at a large cloud passing across the moon. "I'm sorry I lost my temper. I didn't mean to start a war. I just want her to stop running our lives. Hope I didn't upset you," she said.

He pulled her to him and held her close. "You didn't. I should have put my foot down a long time ago."

JACKSON'S POND GAZETTE
Thursday, March 20, 1975
Hayes Haven Motel To Close March 31

Jackson's Pond's only motel will close its doors March 31, 1975. Mr. Hayes said, "Business has been slow since 1957 when the highway was rerouted and bypassed town. We would have had to close sooner if it hadn't been for the trade brought by the auction barn and the truckers during cotton and grain harvests.

"Our last guests were here in early December. There was a big party at the Jackson's and several people from out of town stayed with us. But since then, we have not had any occupants at all. We hung on as long as we could."

Mr. and Mrs. Hayes will continue to live in the owner's quarters of the motel, their home for the past twenty-eight years. But the large neon sign on the Haven will go out on March 31.

Not Ready

Delia Jackson's left leg wouldn't move. She tried again; she couldn't feel it and it would not move. "Maria, help." That's what she tried to shout. All Delia heard was, "Maaa! Maaa" in the voice of someone she didn't know, a not-quite human voice. The headache that had been dull and small on the right side, coming and going for three days, throbbed now, as if her head might split.

Her bedroom chair where she'd been sitting—she was certain she had been—loomed above her. She shifted the parts of her body that would move—her head, her trunk down to her hips, her right arm. Now the chair came into view again, above her right arm. With her arms—no, the left one moved, but only like a log, unconnected to her intention—her right arm, she pushed herself up, raised up on her elbow. Her right leg. Yes, that was her right leg that moved. The room shifted around her; nausea rolled up from her depths. A roar in her head. She let her arm relax and felt the rug meet her back. Several determined deep breaths kept vomit from rising. Don't move. Wait. She said aloud to the chair, "Am I dying?" Actual words came out this time. She tried shouting, "Maria, help, help!" The voice sounded human, but not hers. Then a whisper. "Please God, don't let me die yet." Definitely her voice.

Foul odor covered her face. Frank with manure on his boots again? Something on the rug. She tried to push herself away from the smell. Now it was on her hand. Panicky tears rolled from her right eye. Her pulse sounded in her ears, too fast.

Moving, floating, maybe—nothing she could see. "Open your eyes, Delia." *What man is speaking to me in that tone?* "Open your eyes, Delia."

"I'll vomit."

"If you don't move, opening your eyes won't make you vomit. Now, open your eyes, I must examine you." *Dr. Steele.* "That's it. Now, do each thing I tell you. First, squeeze my fingers, take both my hands with yours and squeeze. Good. Now tell me if you feel sharp or dull and where you feel it when I touch you." She saw him at her feet now, touching her right foot. "Close your eyes again."

"Foot, sharp.—Knee.—Big toe.—Heel, dull."

"Very good. Now where? While I'm touching you, tell me your name and where you are."

"Something big, dull, shin. Nothing now." She stopped speaking, then remembered, "Delia Jackson. My bed." The words came out clearly, no slurring.

"What town? Now shrug your shoulders and let them down. Okay. Now, make a frown. Stick out your tongue. Wiggle it from side to side. What town are we near?"

"Jackson's Pond."

"What is today's date?"

Couldn't think. "Wait.—1974, December. Friday."

"Now, I'll shine this light in your eyes, first one and then the other. Okay. Now, watch the point of the light. Follow it with your eyes without moving your head."

He told her to move her right leg and then her left. She didn't try.

Eyes open again. *Dr. Steel.* She said, "Hit my head? What?" A woman standing behind the doctor—Willa, her face solemn, eyes large.

"You may have fallen, but I believe you fell because you had a stroke. Your blood pressure is quite high, particularly for a seventy-two year old woman. Willa told me you had a headache for several days, intermittently. Is that correct?" She nodded, slightly. The movement made her headache worse. "We're going to take you to the hospital in Lubbock. If everything goes well, you will be back home soon."

"Won't go."

"It's necessary. You need constant observation and I want a consultation with a neurologist, Dr. Tipton."

"Private room." The idea of sharing a room with a stranger nauseated her worse than the headache, and nearly as much as the fear that made every breath ragged.

Eyes closed. Stinging in her arm, needle. "This will help her rest." Drifting. Moving. Someone holding her leaden left hand. She opened her eyes. Willa. Stars outside a tiny window.

A man's voice—Frank? "I'll be right behind y'all. Soon as I tell Johnny Griffith what needs to be done about the cattle in the morning."

"Be careful driving. I love you, Frank." Willa. Beside her, holding her hand.

Delia almost surrendered to the cloud that offered to take her and her headache away. She allowed herself to drift. Woke again as the hearse began to move. The funeral director drove slowly to avoid the ruts in the dusty road.

"Good morning, Mrs. Jackson. I think you're awake. Are you?"

"Yes." She searched the pale green ceiling, the green walls, tried to focus, to find her daughter-in-law who still called her Mrs. Jackson after all this time. "Tell me."

Willa said, "You've been in intensive care, sedated. You've slept most of three days. You're in the hospital in Lubbock. You had a stroke."

Delia remembered her stubborn left leg. She concentrated on it. She felt it move, saw the sheet twitch. "Can I get up? Can I walk?"

"Not yet."

"Will I ever?" She had to know, even if she was afraid of the answer. Dying would be better than being an invalid.

"Dr. Tipton said as soon as your blood pressure is well-controlled, we can begin physical therapy and you should be able to walk. We will have to work hard at the therapy, but you should recover."

"Who found me?"

"I did."

The odor, she remembered. "Had I...? Her voice trailed off. She stared at the ceiling, looking anywhere but at Willa, the person who had found her helpless.

"Had you what?"

She fussed with the sheet and spread until they covered her entirely, except for her head. "Soiled myself." She would not be an old woman lying in her own filth.

"Don't worry. I found you. I cleaned you before the doctor saw you."

"I'm sorry." She turned her face away.

"Don't think about it. No one knows."

"You do."

"No one who matters."

Delia closed her eyes, hoping to sleep and to wake up at home.

She only had to ask once, on the day that she woke up determined to be herself again. From then on, without being asked, every morning and evening, Willa handed her the jar of moisturizing cream. Days before she could tolerate looking at herself in a mirror, Delia carefully applied the cream to her face, neck and hands after Willa bathed her and again before she went to sleep each night.

From the first day in the hospital, Willa had bathed her. How did she know, Delia wondered, that she hated the thought of a stranger touching her even if it was a nurse she would never have to see again? During the bath one morning, she said, speaking each word slowly, "Willa, there's something I want, no I need, you to do." Her voice was her own now. But sometimes she had to search for words she wanted to use.

Willa continued gently drying her left arm, the one still weak. "What is it you need?"

"I need you to never call me Mrs. Jackson again. Call me mother or call me Delia." She stopped talking and studied the puzzled look that crossed Willa's face. "You're the only daughter I have."

"You have Melanie."

"She's your daughter, yours and Frank's." She used her right arm to lift her left as Willa helped her into a fresh bed jacket. Willa didn't speak.

It seemed to Delia like a long time passed before Willa said, "Since she was three, you've been more her mother than I have." She uncovered the sluggish left leg, placed a towel under it, and bathed it, gently. "Calling you Mrs. Jackson has always been my way of showing respect. But if you prefer, I'll call you Delia and consider it my privilege." She smiled and then gently applied lotion to Delia's pale, soft skin.

Delia watched Willa's hands. Even though Willa had worked outdoors with Frank every day for years, her hands were soft and graceful, a lady's hands. Willa emptied the washbasin and straightened the bed. Delia couldn't form the sentence. She wanted to tell Willa she had always hoped she would love her like a mother. She said, "Thank you, Willa, for everything." Delia studied Willa's smile. She saw it as a gentle expression of the sort reserved for loved ones and small children.

"You are more than welcome. Rest now. We start your therapy this afternoon. Hard work," Willa said.

Physical therapy was the hardest work she had ever done. Every day in the hospital, Willa forced her through the exercises the staff taught her. And she reported Delia's progress to the doctor. Willa also reported the things that Delia was supposed to do but didn't— like bathing herself, taking a nap, eating the hospital's meals, and using the four-pronged cane to steady herself between the bed and the chair. Delia preferred to lean on Willa.

Delia asked the doctor each day when she could go home. "Soon," was the only answer he gave. But yesterday, after three weeks that seemed like three months, he said today would be the day, December 23.

And now she was home. The house needed her attention. "Willa, you must get Louisa here at once, she's been slack with the cleaning since I've been gone. I knew this would happen. People always take advantage."

Willa said, "You need to take your nap now. You can worry about the house later; it'll still be here."

"I don't think anyone put water in the Christmas tree stands. See, there are needles on the floor." She stopped the wheelchair by clutching the wheel with her right hand. "No, don't take me to my room yet."

"Your blood pressure has to be checked. Doctor's orders."

"The doctor has been in charge long enough. I'm home now." But she released her hold on the wheel and let Willa roll the chair to the bedroom.

She had thought that the physical therapy in the hospital was the most difficult thing she would have to do, that the worst was behind her. But tolerating the continuing routine of increasing exercise was nothing compared to her frustration at allowing others to be in charge in her house.

She still had difficulty sitting in a straight chair, so she took her meals in the recliner in her bedroom. She knew that Willa and Frank had abandoned proper decorum. They ate in the kitchen, like hired help. And the food—Maria must have had a stroke herself. Nothing she cooked tasted right. No seasoning—and even the beef tasted wrong.

Delia was glad the holidays were behind her. Of course, she had made all the preparations early, in November, because of the party she'd given on December first. All the presents had been wrapped and meals for the month had been planned. But having Melanie home from college during the holidays proved to be a strain. Her granddaughter hardly took time to sit and talk with her; she was so busy paying attention to her boyfriend. When she wasn't gone with him, she was chattering about him—Ray this, Ray that. She didn't seem to understand that Delia needed her attention too. You'd think now that she was twenty, she might be a little less self-centered.

Home, in her own territory, even though she was not yet fully in command, Delia designed a plan for her next three months. She would recover completely; she would walk unassisted, and she would drive her car without supervision. No plan succeeds without accomplishment of small goals. She recalled that lesson from her days at Troufant's Finishing School. Each day, she would focus on a single goal. The doctor had said six months' recovery. According to her plan, it would be no more than five. Two were already gone, wasted, she thought, with self-pity and weakness. No more.

She marshaled her strength each morning and reviewed her achievement each night. The day her calendar showed February 7, she told Willa, "I've been slack with my exercise, I will walk farther each day and will increase the distance each week. And more repetitions of the balance exercises. I hate this cane."

Willa raised her eyebrows briefly, then said, "Would you like me to make a chart to record each day's progress?"

"That's a very good idea. Thank you. I'd also like you to put vitamin capsules on the shopping list."

Willa nodded and said, "The doctor will be impressed by your determination."

"It's not the doctor whose opinion matters to me. I won't tolerate being an invalid."

On the first day of March, she surprised Frank and Willa by arriving in the dining room for breakfast. "It's spring and I intend to get out, to start having visitors." It was time for things to get back to normal.

"You're ahead of schedule—only three months. The doctor predicted six. And…"

Delia interrupted, "Willa, can you see that lampshade over there. It's crooked."

Willa inhaled deeply and straightened the shade. "I'll be in our room. If you need me, just call."

A few days later, Delia issued instructions to Louisa and Maria on several subjects, and had Maria help her to the front porch. She sat in a rocker and watched Willa paint. She stayed there nearly two hours. At first, she was interested in the process of Willa's watercolor work. Several times she made a comment and Willa answered without turning away from her easel. By the time she asked for help getting indoors, she was a little miffed that Willa couldn't take the time to chat with her, now that she was back to normal.

Willa helped her settle in the bed for her nap and started toward the door. "Willa, if anyone calls tomorrow, tell them I'll be having visitors before long. It would be nice to have someone to talk to." By dinner time, Delia had to admit to herself that her "normal" day had tired her.

She was certain that her long absence from the activities at church and at her women's clubs had created much speculation. Gossip fueled the engine of social life in Jackson's Pond. Not a death or birth or illness, not a social event nor a rumored dalliance escaped notice. By the time April first arrived, Delia felt ready. She announced to Willa, "Today, I'm putting that cane away. If it wasn't metal, I'd burn it. My balance is as good as it ever was." She was herself again, able to walk without assistance and to manage the house. She planned to return to services at the Methodist Church in two weeks. But, before that, she would permit people to pay their respects in person, in small groups, and if things went as she expected, to marvel at how good she looked.

Until yesterday, she didn't even take phone calls. She entertained herself each evening reading the notes Willa took from the callers. Daily messages—from the Methodist minister offering his support and prayers; questions from the Study Club about a change in the program schedule; a request for approval of a substitute for her as representative at the bridge club, "just until you are better," a report that the Garden Club was replanting the iris beds on the town square—those and many more verified she had not been forgotten.

"If these are a bother to you, I can tell them they should make these decisions on their own," Willa had said.

"No, they rely on me for leadership. Many of these people haven't any idea how things should be done, how the rest of the world conducts itself. It's my responsibility."

From the day Delia returned home, Willa took dictation each morning—thank-you notes, correspondence, lists of groceries and other items to purchase, and household assignments for Louisa and Maria. She sorted the mail and prepared checks for Delia's signature. As Delia improved, Willa became more her secretary than her nurse. The one aspect of Delia's care that she continued was delivering medicine to her on schedule, three times daily.

At first, Delia took the pills without looking at them. Three weeks ago, she asked what each pill was and its purpose. Willa called the drugstore and returned with a written list of answers about the medicines. After she read the information, Delia said, "From now on I will be responsible for my own medicines. Just put them and the information over there on the dresser. You have done enough for me through all these weeks. I'm not an invalid, so I shouldn't act like one." She didn't mention that she also planned to stop taking the afternoon nap the doctor had prescribed. It slowed her down, left her feeling lethargic until bedtime. She didn't have time for that.

"I did as you said. When Mrs. May called this morning, I told her that you were ready to have visitors. She's bringing four of the women from your Sunday School class at two o'clock. And James Reese will be here at three," Willa said.

"What does he want?"

"He said, 'Please tell Mrs. Jackson that I would like to stop by for a neighborly visit.' And he mentioned he's a deacon at your church."

Delia smiled and raised an eyebrow. "Deacon, my foot. He uses that to prey on widows, offering to buy or lease their land—'just to help out.' He doesn't know, the only thing out here still in my name is this house. He tried to buy that north half-section that joins his from Albert every time the price of cattle went down. If Albert were alive he'd get a laugh out of Reese visiting. The last time he was here was after Albert's funeral. I can hardly wait to see how he gets around to offering to help out. He's always fancied himself a big operator. He's more than fifteen years older than Frank and still trying to buy up land."

"Maybe he thinks that deacons get to take it with them when they die," Willa said.

Delia laughed. She hardly recognized the sound. "You're probably right."

Melanie had come home each weekend since she returned to college after the holidays. This weekend, she talked about her plans for the summer. She and Delia spent one long afternoon together in Delia's room and another out driving on the ranch. Delia's earlier irritation with her faded. Even though she talked about her classes and her friends and her professors and, of course, her boyfriend, she focused on Delia's interests, too. She wasn't self-centered; she was young and her life should be larger than the ranch and her family. The only concern that remained for Delia was that boyfriend. With two years before she would complete college, Melanie should be meeting and going out with several young men, not just one.

"Are you two serious?" Delia asked.

"Well, I don't date anyone else, but Ray and I aren't engaged or anything."

"I should hope not. You have many things yet to do before you think of marriage. Tell me about his family."

Melanie's glowing description of Ray's family—only child; beautiful, charming mother; handsome banker father; beautiful house in Amarillo—didn't do anything to put Delia's mind at ease. Her granddaughter showed every sign of serious infatuation. The possibility of something spoiling Melanie's future still hovered even when Melanie described her plans to become a school counselor. A dull headache began at the base of Delia's skull. She took an aspirin immediately after Melanie left to return to Lubbock. Thirty minutes later, the pain was gone along with worries about Melanie. Her granddaughter had a level head. She wouldn't disappoint her.

Eight o'clock. Had she failed to set her alarm or turned it off? Delia hurried toward the bathroom. She had a Garden Club meeting in town this morning at ten-thirty. Today was going to be her first day to drive to town. Five months since her stroke, she now felt sure enough of her concentration and reflexes to take the car farther than the mailbox. She had practiced each day for the past month by driving to get the mail, backing up, turning around, and driving back. She was ready and eager to be rid of the last reminder of her period of infirmity. She stopped on the way to the bathroom to collect her pills. She left one bottle unopened, the tranquilizer that she identified as the one causing afternoon fatigue. She stopped taking it several weeks ago. She substituted an aspirin now and then, if she felt the day's strain causing a tiny headache to develop. Doctors didn't know everything.

The club meeting took longer than expected because the hostess prepared an elaborate lunch, complete with a May Day theme, in Delia's honor. When she called home to explain her delay, Willa mentioned that Melanie would be coming to the house around two p.m. Delia was a bit surprised. Melanie seldom left Lubbock during the school week.

When Delia arrived home, Melanie and her boyfriend were in the dining room talking with Frank and Willa. Without being asked to join them, Delia sat down at the head of the table. She called Maria to bring her a cup of tea. "I see that you all have coffee already."

Frank said, "Mother, Melanie and Ray have come out to tell us that they're engaged."

"Engaged? When did this happen?"

"Last night, Grandmother. We wanted to tell you all right away."

Tiny frown lines creased Melanie's forehead and Ray looked very serious. Delia looked at the four of them—Willa with her always calm exterior; Frank, a replica of his father, a half-amused expression on his face; and the two tense young ones. She prolonged the silence by taking a drink of her tea. "I suppose you aren't here to ask permission," Delia said. "I do hope that you will wait until Melanie graduates to marry. Ray, when do you graduate?"

"Like I told Mr. Jackson, I graduate the first of June."

Before he could say more, Melanie said, "We plan to marry that day, Grandmother. It will be just perfect to have it in Lubbock before all of our friends leave."

"I see. Then I suppose it's all settled, isn't it? Is there anything that you wanted to ask me, anything I can do, or has all the planning been taken care of?"

"I want you to be there and be happy for us. That's what I came to ask you." Melanie reached across the table to grasp Delia's hand. "Please, Grandmother, be happy for me."

"I'm sure I will be eventually. This has come as such a surprise that I need time to think." She placed her teacup noiselessly in its saucer, rose, and went toward her bedroom without saying more.

The next morning at breakfast, she said, "What is Melanie's hurry? It wasn't a month ago that she was talking about graduating and traveling and assuring me that she and Ray weren't serious. Isn't there anything we can do? That you can do?"

Frank said, "I talked with them both about how they would manage things after the wedding, like where they would live, Melanie's college, Ray's work. They seem to have thought about all of those things. Willa asked them both if they shouldn't give it a little more time."

"They're determined to marry—with or without us," Willa said. "They believe they're in love."

"What about wedding showers, an engagement party, or at least a wedding reception? Have they considered all of those things that should be done?"

Willa shook her head and shrugged. "They weren't concerned."

Delia pushed her breakfast away, untouched. "I'll be having visitors this afternoon, Marjory Carroll and Sarah Bean. I don't intend to mention any of this to them. We'll let Miss Melanie take care of her own announcement."

That afternoon, after her visitors left, Delia went to her room for the first nap she'd taken in several weeks. She heard the door open. "I'm awake, Willa. Did you want something?"

"I wondered if you're feeling all right."

"Just tired. I'll be fine."

"A nap is always good. Call me if you need anything."

A pain above her left eye stabbed Delia into consciousness. She opened her right eye. Not in her bedroom. Pale green ceiling and wall. Hospital green. No, not again. Please, not again.

Delia could hear them talking outside her door. The words were muffled—"not able to predict—observe—more bleeding—nursing home—full time nursing care." She knew. Another stroke. Large this time. She might never be able to walk or talk again.

She tried to make words; a croaking sound from the back of her throat was all that would come. Willa, Frank, and Dr. Baker appeared at her bed seconds later. She appealed to Willa with her eyes and hoped she understood.

"Dr. Baker, when we are able to leave the hospital, we'll go home. And when you call for private nurses, get them only for nights. At the ranch. I'll do the rest," Willa said.

Delia saw her son pull Willa close to his side and hold her tight.

Delia exhaled and closed her eyes.

JACKSON'S POND GAZETTE
Thursday, May 19, 1989
After 50 Years—Final Edition
With this edition, the *Jackson's Pond Gazette* ceases publication after fifty years.

"I would love to continue publishing the *Gazette* as a weekly, but doing so is financially impossible," owner/publisher Homer Huckaby said.

"I have enjoyed being able to report on the activities in Jackson's Pond for all these years. Being the local newsman gave me a first-hand view of the town's development and the lives of its citizens. I had hoped that when I retired, my son, who has worked with me for the last 28 years, could continue as publisher. But advertising revenue and the subscription sales have dwindled as businesses have closed. After the high school closed, without any local sports to cover, our content shrank.

"All the social and service clubs except the Lions have ceased operation as their membership aged and died, so the clubs are no longer a source of news or information. Altogether those factors convinced us it was time to put the paper to bed permanently."

The paper's archives will be housed at the Texas Tech University Southwest Collection in Lubbock.

Elevator Will Remain Closed

Jackson's Pond's only grain elevator will remain closed. Alton Harboe, Owner and General Manager, said this week that he has been unable to find a buyer for the elevator that has operated here for the past 35 years, 24 of those under his ownership.

Harboe said, "I had hoped we could find a buyer who could afford to truck grain to the railroad. But no one made an offer. I am very sorry that our move to Clarendon will leave Jackson's Pond without local elevator service. But, it was move or starve out."

The nearest elevator is at Four-Way, 15 miles west of Jackson's Pond. Management at Four-Way said they welcome area farmers with this season's harvest.

Evaporation

He hadn't been certain ahead of time what he was going to do, but when he went in for coffee at the City Café Thursday morning and saw Junior Reese sitting at the front table with a couple of the locals, Frank sat down at the counter and waited. One of the guys with Junior was telling a long-winded yarn about a spray plane flying under a high tension line about a hundred feet off the ground and then losing power and stalling and leveling off and flying straight down the highway and losing power again and diving directly into the cab of a cattle truck. "Yessir, they was steak all over that highway. I seen it myself." When the guy finally took a breath, Frank stood up and said to Junior he wanted to talk to him, outside, now.

Junior picked up the check for the coffee drinkers and waved it at them and said, "I'm buying." He counted three ones from his money clip and stacked them on the check in the middle of the table. He said, "Sure, Frank, I'll be right with you." Then he laid a quarter off to the side of the check, a tip.

"Ready to talk about that section up south of my place?" Junior asked, wearing his shit-eating grin.

Frank hadn't stopped at the café to talk about land, but he did have something to say to Junior. Getting a rise out of Frank Jackson had never been an easy thing to do. But Junior Reese had managed to do it. Since his father's death, Junior had taken up where his old man left off, trying at every opportunity to get Frank to sell him the Jackson's north pasture, just the same as he had done with other owners on his land's west and north borders. He had taken his most recent run at Frank about six weeks ago.

That evening when Frank told Willa about it, he had imitated Junior's "big operator" style of talking. "'I'm just outgrowing what I have here. I need to enlarge my operation again and you're not really using that section, just letting grass grow.' That's what he said, not two minutes after he'd said hello. Said it like he'd just been waiting for me to meet him there at the post office to make me an offer and sure I wouldn't refuse. Probably had the contract drawn up and in his pocket, right next to his sharp pencil. Offered me a hundred and a half an acre. Said, 'I'd probably have to re-drill that little well you water them cattle from' like that explained the price he offered." Frank stopped his story and shook his head like he couldn't get over the man's gall.

"I'd sooner donate it to Boy's Ranch than sell it to him, if I ever thought we would get rid of it," Frank said. Then he leaned back and laughed and told her that he guessed Junior needed him—the one person around who wouldn't roll over whenever he flashed money and his big shiny smile. "It'll help him build character."

Then, about three weeks ago, Frank and Missy, a red heeler that had ridden everywhere with him in his pickup since she was a stray pup, had been checking that north pasture. They'd been up there about thirty minutes. He was driving slow and letting Missy chase jackrabbits, having a good romp in her favorite hunting spot. Missy came running toward the truck from the north fence line. She stopped, suddenly, and vomited and then squatted and had loose bowels. She managed to get to the pickup and tried to jump in, but her back legs wouldn't work. Before Frank could get out of the pickup, he saw her try again to get in and fall and stay down, twitching and drooling. Frank picked her up like a limp baby and drove as fast as he could to the closest vet's, just outside of Jackson's Pond. All the way he wiped tears out of his eyes and talked to her, telling her to hang on, she'd be okay.

The vet took about two minutes to check her and give her a shot with a big needle. Coyote bait—the vet told him someone had put out an organophosphate poison for coyote bait, probably on raw meat. Said that if he hadn't gotten her there, she would have died in a few minutes because it affects the nervous system. He'd said to leave her overnight, so he could give her an IV and several more shots to try to clear the poison from her system. If it worked, she might live over it.

The vet called the next morning to say he was sorry, that he'd been up with Missy all night, but she hadn't made it. She'd been too far gone when Frank got her there.

By the time he went to pick her up to bring her home, Frank figured out that Junior Reese had done it. He put out that poison in his own field across the fence from Jackson land. And for no good reason except maybe to get back at Frank—coyotes didn't eat wheat or cotton. Nobody on the Jackson place would have done it. That left Junior. And he'd done it on purpose.

Frank didn't tell Willa all the worst of how Missy had died. He just said she'd gotten into some poison and was too far gone when he got her to the vet. And he didn't say a word about how he'd cried more than any normal man would or how it still gnawed at his stomach if he thought about it.

"Junior Reese did it." She said it as a fact, not a question, with a frown and her mouth tight. Then she went and got the shovel and they buried Missy, wrapped in her favorite horse blanket, the one Frank let her ride on in the pickup seat.

A couple of the coffee drinkers were idling on the sidewalk just outside the café door, near Frank and Junior. Frank didn't care if they heard. In voice that sounded like it came from the bottom of some deep well, he said, "Junior Reese, you better not ever let me see you again near my fence line or anywhere at all. You killed my dog for no reason. If I ever see your face again, I'll kill you with my own hands." Junior's grin disappeared. He stared at Frank for a couple of seconds, like he might not be sure of what he'd heard. He slid a look at the idlers who had both backed toward the café door. Then he found his pickup keys and walked fast toward his new green pickup. The two at the café door watched Frank, and Frank watched Junior speed away down Main Street. Frank didn't go back in for a cup of coffee. He drove to the cemetery and parked and stared off into space for quite a while before driving slowly back to the ranch.

Melanie brought Chris and Claire out Friday afternoon to spend the weekend. She and Ray were going to Lubbock for the weekend. She'd mentioned they needed some time away to talk. Willa had raised her eyebrows when she told him what Melanie told her on the phone. Chris, a tall, strong thirteen year-old was going to take Willa's place as his helper for two days. The boy was good help and loved being on the ranch.

Eight-year-old Claire would get a dancing lesson from her Gran and a chance to stay up late and watch the Cosby show. They were no sooner out of the car than they were ranch-ready, Chris standing next to Frank and Claire upstairs in the ballroom getting her pink leotard and ballet slippers. She usually wore them the entire time she was at the house. Frank sent Chris to the barn to saddle their horses, telling him they'd check fence in a little bit.

Melanie followed her parents to the kitchen for iced tea. As soon as they sat down, she asked, "Daddy, is it true, what they say you did?"

"What are you talking about?" her mother asked.

Melanie looked at Frank, "Did you actually threaten to kill Junior Reese?"

Willa looked over her bifocals at Melanie. She didn't say anything for a few seconds. "Where did you hear that?" Frank didn't say anything, watching the two women talk about him as if he was not present.

"Last night Ray told me he had heard it at the insurance office, overheard two people talking, and when they noticed he was there they changed the subject. Then this morning, Mary Lee Hester asked me about it in the teachers' lounge. Even Chris asked me; he said Bobby Jay Spring had heard his father telling his mother. You can just imagine what people think." She spread her hands wide and shook her head. "It's all over town by now."

Before Frank could answer, Willa said, "It wouldn't have to go far to be all over town. If you've got any sense, you wouldn't care what a bunch of pissants in that little fart of a town think or say. If he did threaten Junior, it's no worse than he deserved." She gave Frank a nod to confirm her statement.

"Mother! Please don't use such language. The children might hear."

"You mean don't say what I think? What do you care what people gossip about? No, don't answer that. I know where you learned that you should care about the right people's opinion. Your grandmother would be upset by this, wouldn't she?" Willa smiled a half smile, her raised eyebrow telling that there was no pleasure in it.

Melanie looked at her mother. Then she said, using her school counselor's voice, "Now mother, don't get upset with me. I'm only concerned about the children. They could be the ones to suffer if our family behaves badly." She looked at him again. "Daddy, did you do what they said?"

He cleared his throat, but Willa didn't give him time to answer. She said, "Let me tell you something. If all that matters to you is what people think, you should spend your time with them, the ones who want to be in charge of other people's lives. Did you even wonder if it was true, or why your daddy might have threatened Junior? Did you tell Mary Lee and Ray and Chris that he's a good man who wouldn't harm anyone unless he was provoked? Or were you too embarrassed?"

Melanie started to sniffle. "I didn't mean for you to get upset with me."

"Don't start with those tears. You know they don't work on me." Willa poured the last of her tea in the sink and rinsed the glass.

"What made you do that, Daddy? Did you mean it?" She had stopped sniffling.

"Junior killed his dog, poisoned her. Just because he owns a bunch of land and is on the school board he thinks— Oh, that's it." Willa tossed the dish towel toward the cabinet and missed. She sat back down across from her daughter. "I'm sorry, Melanie. Your daddy wouldn't want to affect your job. That's the trouble with living in a little town. It's like a small pond. Junior thinks because he's got the loudest voice, that makes him a big frog. In the real world, he'd just be a tadpole." Frank laughed and patted Willa's arm.

Melanie said, "I'm glad you can laugh about it. It's not funny to me."

He said, "Honey, you know I'm pretty level-headed. But once in a while, even a level-headed person needs to let people know that he won't be taken advantage of. I promise I won't shoot anyone. And Junior's too fat to strangle. Something else'll come along in a day or two for people to talk about and this will be old news." He knew Melanie would worry more than a day or two. She was that much like his mother.

Frank checked the cinches on both horses Chris had saddled, and searched in a box of hammers and pliers for his fence tool. "Good job of saddling up. I'll be ready to go in a minute," he said. He looked up from the tools and caught Chris standing back watching him, like he was measuring to see if his dimensions had changed. "What are you thinking about? You're awful quiet."

"Just wondering."

"About what?"

"If you really would kill Junior Reese if you see him ever again."

Frank snorted. "I might want to. I'd be tempted. But I imagine my better judgment would keep me from it. Guess it would all depend. "

"On what?" Chris was back at his usual place, standing right next to his granddad.

"Whether he ever did anything else that was wrong, that affected me. Say, maybe if he did something that hurt you or your sister. You know, something serious. What made you ask?"

"You know, people in town talking."

"The most important thing you need to know is that people in town are going to talk, no matter what. If it wasn't me, they'd be talking about somebody else. You can't ever let what people might say about you decide what you do or think or how you are. You have to decide for yourself what's right. Remember that, son."

"I will, Granddad." Chris' forehead wrinkled, the thirteen year-old concentrating on a serious subject.

The following Saturday morning, Willa and Frank lingered over second cups of coffee after breakfast. Neither had mentioned the Junior Reese incident again. Apparently neither Melanie nor her family had suffered as a result of it. She hadn't mentioned it either, and she surely would have. "Looks like Jackson's Pond is close to shutting down entirely. You always said it would completely evaporate and blow away one day. Says here this is the last edition of the *Gazette*," Frank said. He folded the paper and handed it to Willa.

"No great loss." Willa unfolded the final edition and tore it with a flourish into four long strips. She winked at Frank. The things that passed for news in that paper had been their joke for years. "In case you missed it, an article here says Harboe's elevator won't open this season for wheat harvest," she said. She handed him one of the strips.

"I was expecting that. Guess we'll have to use that elevator at Four-Way. Be a thirty-four miles round trip for us." He sighed as he read the article and then wadded the strip. "We'll need two trucks or we'll never get it all cut and hauled. I've got half a mind to just hire it custom cut and save us the trouble." He knew he wouldn't do it, even though he was already tired before they started. He loved combining his own wheat.

Now the wheat looked ready. June 1. Each day for the past five days, Frank had watched Willa walk out into the middle of each of the four quarter sections where she pulled exactly three heads from the knee-high stalks around her. Just the way she learned it from her father, she did the same thing in each field. One head she rolled between her palms and looked at the kernels that spilled out. She counted them and checked the shape. The second stalk, she did the same and compared what she saw with the first. She chose two kernels from the third head, bit each of those in half. Today she said the kernels were plump, the shape of a long oval. Few were shriveled or misshapen. Those that she bit were firm but not brittle and exuded nothing milky or the consistency of soft dough. She told Frank she thought it was ready. "You're the boss," he said. He tested the wheat every day himself, but every year he waited until Willa said it was ready. He'd done that since their first harvest back in 1955. At the elevator, the moisture tests on the wheat they took in always proved her judgment correct— they never had payment docked for a load being too wet or too dry. "We'll start right after we check the combine one more time. Your truck ready?"

Willa nodded. In the winter, they'd bought a used 1980 model Chevrolet grain truck with a dump mechanism that emptied the bed. They got it at a farm auction when Jacob Havlicek had to sell out his place and start working for hire. She had driven it on several test runs and practiced operating the power take-off that lifted the bed. She would drive that truck and Havlicek would drive the one they leased for the harvest. Johnny Griffith would drive the tractor pulling the grain cart alongside Frank as he ran the combine. They were ready.

Everything was going fine. The first three days they stayed at it until dark. They finished the first field and had moved to the second. After eating the lunch Mrs. Havlicek brought to the field, Frank climbed back into the cab of the combine. He cranked it up and in a minute, shut it down again. "Something's wrong with the raddles and the straw walker's not working at all," he said. He climbed down and he and Havlicek started taking things apart, looking for the problem.

He shouted, "Johnny, get my tool box out of the back of the pickup. It's too heavy for Willa to carry." Johnny was standing about four feet away. He wrinkled his brow and moved fast, for him. "Willa, get up in the cab and get the Gleaner manual. Never mind. Damn it, I left it in the barn. Go back and get it. Now." He could see on her face that his tone surprised her, but he didn't have time or energy to waste on courtesy.

Four hours and a lot of sweat and cussing later, with a sixty mile round trip to the Allis-Chalmers parts store by Willa in between, the Gleaner vibrated and clanked to life. Wheat moved up and into the bin and straw blew down and onto the ground, forming rows that marked the machine's progress up and down the field. Frank drove as fast as the machine would tolerate, determined to make up for the delay. He yelled at Johnny, who couldn't possibly have heard him from inside the tractor cab, to keep the grain cart positioned so he wouldn't have to stop. More than once he avoided Willa's eye when she waved at him on her return from the elevator.

Around seven o'clock, with at least an hour and a half of light left, she stepped directly into the path of the combine. She stood completely still with her hands on her hips, looking straight at Frank as he and the Gleaner came toward her. He braked and shut down the header and the cutter bars. He pushed open the cab door and yelled, "Have you lost your mind? I could have run over you. It would serve you right for being stupid. I haven't got time for any foolishness. I've got a lot of wheat to cut."

She yelled back at him, over the noise of the Gleaner's engine. "It's time to stop. All this wheat will be here in the morning. You've worked hard today."

"I'll have to work a lot harder to catch up. Now get out of the way, dammit."

He could tell he'd made her mad, cussing at her. Well, by God, he didn't care. This wheat had to be in the elevator and the sooner the better. He started the header and the cutter bar and checked to his right, intent on turning to make another round. He looked left and she was on the top step, opening the cab door. "I swear if you don't get down this minute, I'll knock you down," he shouted.

"You do and it'll be the last time you knock anyone down." She yelled just as loud as he had, then elbowed her way in front of him and jerked the key out.

Everything stopped—cutter bar, header, lights, engine, everything.

Frank stood up. Both legs threatened to buckle. He sat back down. "Okay, you win. Are you happy?"

She didn't respond. Her boots clanked on the steps as she left the combine, and Frank, and stalked to the grain truck.

He knew she was right; he was tired from the work and the heat, and though he wouldn't admit it out loud, from his age and all the years of work and that pain that had started down low in his back and made his legs weak. A sixty-year-old man shouldn't try to harvest wheat non-stop from morning until dark the way a twenty year-old could. If he didn't stop now, he'd start making mistakes and something else would break down or somebody would get hurt. If he told the truth, he was glad she stopped him. Even though it was still daylight, he might not be able to stay awake and upright long enough to eat supper. He'd have to apologize in the morning. Right now he didn't have the strength.

One week later, on his last pass around the field, Frank waved at Willa to come to the combine. "Want to take a victory lap around this field, Miss? I don't usually hang out with women who drive big trucks, but I'll make an exception for you."

Willa climbed the four steps to the cab and sat on the armrest of the driver's seat with her hand on his back. "Finished cutting six hundred and forty acres in ten days. And we'll have it all in the elevator before dark if everything goes our way. Good job, Mr. Jackson." She kissed him on the cheek. "I wish you'd go in and rest after you get this to the house. Johnny and I can finish buttoning everything up. And I'll bring in the weigh tickets as soon as we get back from the last trip to the elevator. You can calculate the yield and sleep late in the morning."

"Not too late. We've got the straw to deal with. Now that your truck driving job is finished, are you looking for work driving tractor?"

"I've got a painting to finish, but I'll be happy to sign on as a part-timer. I think you ought to hire Mr. Havlicek to help, too." Frank nodded and coasted to a stop. "Thanks for the ride, fellow. I hope you'll pick me up again sometime." She added a big wink.

He caught her hand as she started out of the cab. "What about a real kiss for the combine jockey?"

He decided to put Havlicek to work running the plow on two of the fields and Johnny baling the straw on the other two. He had cut the wheat so the straw was left long on those two in order to make more straw. The cattle might need that for dry matter next winter. Johnny rolled his eyes when Frank told him to drive the baler, but he didn't complain. He only asked, "Who's going to check the cattle?"

"You'll still be doing the cowboying too. Check them in the morning before we start. It'll be too damp to bale before ten, I imagine."

Later that day, Frank, Havlicek's fourteen year-old son, J. D., and Chris started loading the oblong bales that the baling machine deposited at intervals around the field. Frank stood on the hay trailer and looked out across the field. The bales made him think of beads from a broken necklace, strewn around by some giant hand. He got down and showed the boys how to toss the seventy-five pound bales onto the trailer so they would stack. When he tossed the second one, he felt a pain shoot from his back down both legs. His face must have shown it, because Chris asked if he was okay.

Frank nodded, "Just pulled a muscle in my back. Do both you boys know how to drive that old tractor?" He pointed at their old John Deere tractor, a model that had no cab, only a canopy over the driver's seat. They both nodded, looking serious, like they might not be certain they could do the job. "Well then, you take turns, one hour each. One drives, the other tosses bales. Okay?" He started to leave, then turned back. "Be sure you drink enough today. It's going to be hot. Do you have plenty of water and bug spray?"

"Yes, sir."

"If I don't see you before, I'll be back at lunch time. Don't try to work too fast, just keep at it steady. I don't want my best help to wear out on me." The boys traded high fives, like big-time basketball players, and got to work.

He couldn't get out of bed the next morning. Willa told him to stay put or he'd make his back worse. She left and came back an hour later to report that he was expected at the doctor's office at ten; that Johnny, Havlicek and the boys were all underway; that it was going to be another hot, dry day; that late evening thunderstorms were predicted, and that she would be out near the barn painting. She'd seen two ravens this morning and hoped to put them in the painting she had started.

"Right now the best thing you can do for your back is take this to relax your muscles and this for the pain." Dr. Baker held up two prescriptions he had written. "Get them filled and go home to bed. You can get up and go easy tomorrow. I'll call you if the x-rays or blood tell me anything else. I believe it's a sprain and muscle strain."

Frank did as he was told. Each of the next two days he made the rounds to get everyone started and then went back to the house to bed. By the second day, he felt lots better, but slept for hours, awakened only by occasional brief coughing spells. Willa woke him around six that evening. He was relieved to find that he could walk without pain. After supper, he asked Willa if she wanted to go for a ride. He had an urge to watch the sunset with her beside him. He also wanted to check the grass pastures. They were getting dry fast. He wouldn't mind if it rained tonight, even if the straw wasn't all loaded.

Chris jumped into the bed of the pickup and Willa and Frank got in the front. He drove south to begin a tour of the property. Neither of them said anything, just riding along looking at the land and occasionally watching the sky. Frank patted Willa on the knee. "Thanks for keeping everything running, honey. I guess I needed the rest." She scooted across the seat to sit next to him.

When they reached the north grass pasture, he parked near the stock tank. The sun had set, leaving only a pink glow showing behind the clouds. Lightning played in the distance toward the west. "Quite a light show tonight," he said. "I recall my daddy telling me that displays like that are one way God reminds us who's in charge." The fence shone in the fading light, a steady line punctuated by cedar post exclamation marks. "Willa, remember what I said. No one is ever to sell this grass." She nodded. He took a deep breath and turned his attention back to the sky. "I hope those clouds have something in them besides electricity." Some of the cattle raised their heads as thunder drummed in the west. They stopped grazing and began milling, closing the distance between cows and calves.

Willa suddenly sat up straight, and pointed southwest toward a glow on the horizon. "Is that a fire out there?"

"Damn, I think it is. It's pretty far off." He sat forward and scanned the horizon. Then he spotted a second fire. The lightning was starting them. He knocked on the back window. "Get up here, Chris. We've got to get back to the house and call the Fire Department."

He wasn't the first one to call, the operator told him. They'd already blown the fire whistle in town. But the trucks hadn't left yet. "You know it takes a while. There are just six young men volunteers now and all the rest are older and well it just takes them longer than it used to. I've called Four-Way and I'll go ahead now and call Calverton, too."

He and Willa and Chris stood on the porch and watched. It was all they could do for now. That and hope the wind wouldn't push any of the fires together into larger blazes. The little groups of volunteers and their tank trucks could be located by their flashing emergency lights as they sped across unpaved county roads. It looked like two fires erupted for each one they extinguished. Things were getting worse; the fires were closer now, probably not more than five miles from the porch.

Frank said, "I ought to go and help. They don't have enough people to get this under control, not with this wind and lightning." He looked at Willa and Chris, then nodded his head as if he'd come to some conclusion. "Come to the barn with me." They all ran. Frank threw two shovels and a pickaxe and some rope into the back of the old four-wheel drive pickup he used in mud or snow. "Listen, I'm going straight west, to whichever fire is closest to our fence line. Willa, call Johnny and tell him to pull his horse and trailer up to the north grass. You and Chris meet him there. Tell him to open the gate onto the field south of the grass and drive those cattle onto that wheat stubble and push them toward the tank on the east side. Chris, you can drive our pickup, and Willa, you drive Johnny's and help him keep the cattle bunched up if you can. Take these wire cutters. Tell Johnny if a fire starts near you, cut the east fence and run them in that direction and all of you get away any direction you can. Don't let anybody get hurt."

Frank and three men he had joined digging a trench along a fence line were working fast, without talking. They succeeded in stopping one small blaze and moved north along the fence after a second line of flames sprang up about a quarter mile away and advanced steadily in their direction. Lightning continued etching patterns across the huge clouds and thunder followed each display.

They'd been working nearly an hour when the wind shifted again, this time from due west, and picked up to about twenty-five miles an hour, in gusts. None of them said anything about the first drops that fell. But when it turned into a real rain, Mark Wiggins looked up and yelled, "Thank you, Jesus." They continued digging, but stopped when water started collecting in the trench. They leaned on their shovels and watched as the fires died out, one by one. "Well, I guess that's it for tonight," Wiggins said with a little salute. "I'm going back to my recliner."

Johnny, Willa, and Chris were sitting on the porch steps when Frank limped from his pickup. He asked about the cattle. "They're on the wheat stubble and grazing like they were happy to get a change of diet," Willa said.

"Whew, we were lucky," Frank said. He sat down carefully; he felt fragile.

"I been waiting to tell you," Johnny said. "You know that piece to the north and west of here that belongs to your friend Junior Reese? Well, let's just say the wheat there ain't going to need to be harvested this year. A bolt of lightning lit up the sky and then a big gust of wind come up and turned the whole damn field into a bonfire, just about four or five minutes before it started to rain. Course, that put it out."

"Well," Frank said and stared off into the rain. "All I can say is, it couldn't have happened to a nicer guy."

The sun was up when Willa leaned over him and said, "Frank, I'm going to be outside doing some things. Sleep some more. You need it. You tossed and coughed all night. Must have been a lot of smoke with that fire. Just yell if you need anything."

At ten-fifteen, the phone rang. He had trouble waking up until Dr. Baker said, "Frank, I'm glad I got you. Are you feeling any better?"

"I was till I pretended to be a firefighter last night. But I've slept late, just woke up. I'll be okay."

"Can you come in the office this morning?"

"Aw, doc, I'll be okay. I don't think I need to come in."

"I need to talk to you. It's important."

Frank wanted to say something, but didn't know what—maybe words to convince the doctor he was okay. "Something that won't keep and you don't want to talk about on the phone? If you're trying to scare me, you're doing a good job." He tried to laugh like it wasn't true. No sound came out.

"I'd rather talk to you here, Frank. See you in an hour."

Frank told Willa the doctor had called. Told her it was just routine follow up and she didn't need to go with him. Dread was his uninvited companion.

"Come over here and look at these x-rays. You'll get a better notion of what I'm talking about. Soon as I saw these and your lab tests I called a specialist at the med school in Lubbock. See here, these big round spots on these vertebrae that look like they've been punched out. Those are tumors. You must have been having a backache for a long time for it to be this far along. What other symptoms have you been ignoring?"

"Nothing I couldn't put down to age and mileage." He stared at the bones shining white, with holes that made them look like lace on the black background. He was tempted to ask the doc if he hadn't mixed his x-rays up with someone else's, but he knew better.

"We're ninety-nine percent sure it's bone cancer," Dr. Baker said.

"Is it serious?" Stupid question. He didn't know what else to say.

The doctor stared at the x-rays again as if they might change if he watched long enough. His frown told Frank the answer. "We need a couple more tests to be absolutely certain. And then we need to start you on treatment."

"I have to get harvest finished. I'll come back for the tests after that."

"You shouldn't wait, Frank."

Frank watched the doctor's eyes. "Well, I appreciate your advice and I understand. I won't take too long, but there are some things I need to do. Meanwhile, I'd like this to be between us. Understand?"

"Willa will have to know. You'll have to be in the hospital for some of the treatment."

"Not till I get things taken care of. Then I'll tell her and come back for whatever you have to do to me."

"If I can't convince you, then at least until then don't do anything strenuous. Get as much rest as you can and take those pain pills. There's no sense you being in pain."

Frank shook the doctor's hand and moved toward the door. He turned back and said, "One other thing. Could you put my chart where no one else can see it? I don't want this spread around."

Dr. Baker lifted the chart from his desk, opened the top drawer, and put the chart inside. "It will be here until you come back. Make it soon."

Frank couldn't seem to put enough pressure on the accelerator. The pickup crawled along the road toward the pond. The few miles from town back to the ranch stretched to the horizon and beyond, it seemed. He stopped and turned off the ignition. The pond waited for him, as it always had when he needed to be alone to think.

He sat on the bank, near the water's source, hoping for the right words to come, the sentences he could use to explain to Willa. She was his to take care of. How could he tell her what he knew, had known since before the doctor gave it a name?

If the baby had lived, he'd now be old enough to know

what to do, to carry on and see after his mother and the land. Frank had never told Willa how every year he had seen their son grow, marking each of his birthdays, his graduations, him learning to ride a horse, to drive a pickup, to buy cattle, putting together all the things a boy did to learn to be a man out here. How he talked with him and told him the same kind of stories his own dad had told him, and when he felt foolish for doing that, how he told himself it was okay to love his son and to be sad because that boy never got the chance to grow up and tend a part of the earth.

He turned his gaze to the pond, its shrinking diameter, the mesquite invading on its east side. Maybe he'd go saddle his horse and ride back out here this evening to watch the sunset. He stood, slapped the dust from his Wranglers, and headed toward the pickup and the hardest job he'd ever have to do.

She didn't break into tears; she didn't wring her hands or run away. When Frank repeated the doctor's words and told her about his plan to get everything in order on the ranch before he would go back, Willa shook her head no just once and put her arms around him. She said, "Frank, we have to go back tomorrow and start whatever has to be done to treat this. I can take care of what needs to be done here. I've had the best teacher. But I don't intend to live without the only man I ever have or ever will love. So you have to get well, starting tomorrow morning."

There wouldn't be any use arguing; she was right. Using the work on the ranch as an excuse didn't accomplish anything. The determination her face showed him she would prevail in any test of wills on the subject. She did promise she wouldn't say anything to Melanie until after they knew exactly what they were dealing with. "No sense in getting her upset, and the kids. Until we know something for sure," he said.

The rest of the day they spent making lists. She'd kept the books all along, so there was no need to go over anything financial. They were in good shape. Instead, they listed all the chores that had to be done to finish up after harvest—plowing, storing seed wheat, moving cattle from one grass pasture to another, keeping weeds under control until planting in early

September. And after that, lists of things to be done for planting wheat again in the fall, to be done after the wheat was in the ground, just in case, to get ready for winter—checking on the progress of the pregnant cows, moving the bulls to a different pasture, patching fence, maintenance on all equipment, and a long string of other items. Watching Willa, listening to her, he saw that working, doing what needed to be done, helped her stay steady. And watching her, answering her questions, holding her hand for a second now and then, all those things helped him finish out the day. By supper time, he felt calmer. They sat together on the porch and watched the sunset. That night, Willa beside him in his dreams and next to him the several times he woke helped the hours pass.

They saw Dr. Baker together the next morning. He got to the point immediately. "You'll see the specialist at the med school tomorrow. I got in touch with them to save an appointment as soon as I knew you were coming in here this morning. We'll know by tomorrow afternoon just what we're dealing with. You need to start thinking about whether you want to go to M.D. Anderson Hospital in Houston or stay in Lubbock where they would use the Anderson treatment protocols for whichever type of tumor it turns out to be."

Frank looked at Willa. He didn't want to leave, but maybe it would be easier on everyone if he just went down there and then came back when he was well. Maybe so, but he knew he was kidding himself. He'd stay in Lubbock, close to the ranch. "Here's where I need to be."

"We'll draw some more blood and take skull and chest x-rays now and you'll be able to take them with you when you go to Lubbock tomorrow." Doctor Baker had his head down, writing on a lab order sheet. Without looking up, he said, "You might as well pack a bag. They'll want to put you in the hospital when you get there."

Willa drove toward Melanie's house instead of immediately going back to the ranch. He switched on the radio; the announcer seemed to be speaking a foreign language. He turned it off. He cleared his throat. When she looked his way, he said, "You're right on two counts."

"I am?"

"Uh, huh. It's the right thing to do to go by Melanie's. And I don't want to. Good thing you didn't ask." Telling their daughter would be admitting the doctor was right.

When Willa stopped the pickup, neither one of them moved. She sat staring straight ahead, hands still on the steering wheel. He touched her shoulder, felt the texture of her denim shirt between his fingers.

Without looking at him, she said, "I haven't said anything to you. I hoped they'd work everything out, but I don't know. She hasn't said much, but I know Melanie and Ray are having trouble. This could make her unravel completely. Sometimes she's not as strong as she acts. Let me tell her. It'll be easier."

He touched her cheek with his forefinger. She turned to him. The sadness in her eyes didn't match the firmness of her jaw. "I'll do it," he said. She nodded and opened her door. He got out on the passenger side, and they walked to Melanie's front door.

Melanie opened the screen, a small frown on her face. "This is a surprise. Come in. Have some coffee?" The house echoed as they walked through the hall and living room on the way to the kitchen. "Chris and Claire went with Ray to Lubbock," she said.

She pointed to the kitchen table and said, "Here, sit. It'll just take me a minute to make coffee." She cleared some books and papers from the table. "School work," she explained.

Unlike her usual quick efficiency, Melanie got the coffee started and the cups and saucers on the table only after spilling water and making three trips to the pantry, first for coffee, then a filter for the Mr. Coffee, and finally for napkins. None of them said anything until she sat down. She smoothed her hair back and redid the elastic at the nape of her neck. "What brings you to town this morning?"

The aroma of the coffee made the room almost pleasant. Frank turned his empty coffee cup so the handle faced west rather than east. "Thought we'd better let you know I'm going to have to go to the hospital in Lubbock tomorrow morning," he said.

Melanie looked at her mother, then immediately back at him. "Why? What's wrong?"

Willa got up and brought the coffee pot to the table and poured for the three of them. Melanie pushed her cup away. "Daddy?"

"My back. Dr. Baker says I have bone cancer, and I have to have more tests and begin treatment right away." The last two words came out weak. He took a sip of his coffee, scorching his tongue.

"Mother, why didn't you tell me?"

"We didn't know until today." She fixed her gaze on him.

Melanie said, "You should have a second opinion. Baker's not a specialist. You should go to Houston, to M.D. Anderson. He could be completely wrong." Her breathing had gotten ragged. Reminded him of a calf separated from its mother for the first time. She said, "I have a lot of questions."

He nodded and said, "We don't have any answers yet. Baker gave me the choice—Houston or Lubbock. I decided. I'm staying out here, close to home. It'll be okay. We'll go first thing in the morning and we'll let you know soon as they decide on the treatment." He drank some more coffee.

Willa followed suit, took a couple of drinks, and then said, "I guess we should get back to the house. Get ready for tomorrow."

Melanie said, "I don't know what to say, what to do." She was near tears, he could tell.

He said to Willa, "You go ahead and get the pickup started. I'll be out in a second." She'd understand.

"Come here, honey. Don't be upset. There's nothing you can do right now. It's all going to be fine." He hugged Melanie and patted her back. She hadn't seemed so small in his arms since she was a little girl.

"Daddy, I couldn't stand it if something happened to you." She had started crying, but quietly, like she was already weary of tears before she started.

"I intend to do everything they tell me so I can get well.

No need to think about me dying or anything else drastic, you understand?" She nodded, her face against his shirt. "Listen, don't upset the kids until we know more. Just tell them I had to go have some tests." She nodded again. "Okay then, I've got to go now. We'll talk to you tomorrow."

In Lubbock, they had an answer almost immediately. It was worse than Frank had been willing to think about. The cancer had already spread all along his spine, his right hip, and both lungs. Willa said that when she called to tell her, she'd had to talk Melanie out of coming to Lubbock immediately. They finally agreed she would wait until the weekend so Claire and Chris could come with her.

The day after he went to the hospital, he had his first radiation treatment. The afternoon after that, he started having diarrhea and couldn't eat. No matter what medicine they gave him, nothing stopped the constant nausea and weakness. They explained it, or tried to—the radiation had to be strong to combat the widespread tumors. Anything strong enough to kill cancer cells was strong enough to make him very sick.

He tried not to complain and he'd be damned before he'd cry, but more than once he had a hard time assuring Willa that he'd be okay. She didn't believe him, he could tell, but she never let on. They spent the long days at the hospital lying to each other that way.

Melanie brought Chris and Claire to visit his fifth day on the radiation. He'd just made another trip to the bathroom and had to lean on Willa getting back to bed. Melanie opened the door and then stopped dead still. She stood like she was rooted, nothing moving except her eyes. He knew he didn't look good, but if what he saw on her face was any measure, he looked really bad.

"Move on out of the door, Melanie, so I can see my favorite grandkids. Come on in, everybody," he said. Hugging the kids and smiling took the rest of his strength. He half-fell back against the pillows and tried to make it look intentional. Willa fussed with the covers and raised the head of the bed, clenching her jaw the entire time.

Melanie hung back near the foot of the bed. Finally, she said in a voice he remembered from her childhood, "Why didn't you tell me you were so sick?"

"I wasn't until they started curing me." He tried for a laugh and hoped it didn't sound as hollow to his daughter as it did to him. Chris' eyes widened; Claire grabbed Willa's hand and crowded next to her legs. He said, "I was just about to ask your mother to go down to the gift shop and get me a mystery to read. Why don't you two do that and let Claire and Chris keep me company?"

Willa promptly grabbed her purse and urged Melanie out of the room. As soon as they were gone, he beckoned and both kids hurried to him, one on either side of the bed. Holding a hand of each of them, he said, "That was an excuse to get those worry warts out of here. You two can help me a lot while I'm working on getting well."

He squeezed Claire's hand, and said, "You both need to help your mom and gran until I get back home." He looked directly in his grandson's eyes. "Chris, you and J. D. will need to help keep the ranch running. Your grandmother's in charge. I'm counting on you."

"Yes, sir," Chris said.

"When will you be well?" Claire asked.

"Can't say, sweetie. Soon as I can. Let's see what's on the television." Claire occupied herself with the remote control. But Frank could see Chris ignoring the television, watching him.

After that, when Melanie and the kids came, he and Willa both put on their "everything's going to turn out fine" faces until they left. He'd asked the doctor to order that there be no other visitors. He didn't need people trooping through shaking their heads and looking gloomy.

Three weeks later, and twenty pounds lighter, so weak he could barely walk, Frank heard a positive word from one of the doctors. "We're going to let you rest for five days and then start some chemotherapy. Today we need to run some tests to see what the radiation has done."

That evening Frank asked Willa for the first time how things were going at home. She told him everything that had been taken care of and what was left to do. "Looks like I've just been kidding myself about being necessary out there. You've got it all under control. Doesn't surprise me a bit," he said. The smile he tried was a pretty weak version.

He immediately hated he'd said it because she began crying and couldn't seem to stop. "No, I don't have it under control. I'm trying so hard to do everything the way you would, but I need you back home," she said. And that started her crying again. "I don't even have myself under control. I can't stand seeing you this way."

He hugged her to his chest and patted her back. After the crying settled down, he said, "My hair'll grow back when they quit poisoning me. Then I'll look better."

This time she understood he was kidding. He knew because she said, "Just when I was thinking how sexy a bald man can look." She wiped her eyes and blew her nose and stood up straight.

The doctors reported some progress with the primary tumors, but said the growth of the lung masses had accelerated. Willa said nothing, her lips grim and her back stiff, like she was ready to fight for him. "Time for the chemicals, right?" Frank asked.

They didn't wait, started the chemotherapy the next day and the same cycle of side effects began again. Only worse. The third day, he had a spell of coughing. First, it was a dry hacking; then deeper spasms that racked his chest. More medicine, oxygen, antibiotics. Too sick to get out of bed. And Willa now sleeping on a cot next to him every night, only going home to check on things and keep Johnny and Havlicek moving on the work that had to be done. When Melanie visited, Frank didn't have the strength to put on a front anymore. She told him she loved him and left crying every time.

He woke, coughing, in the night. A light came on over his head. Someone, Willa, talking, not making sense. He couldn't get a breath. And couldn't stop coughing. Blood sprayed on his hand when he pulled the oxygen mask away. Had to get a breath. He struggled to sit up. More blood. Vomit and more blood. And so much light. Felt himself falling and couldn't stop. Can't get a breath. Coughing. So much blood.

Screaming. Willa; she never screamed, not even in labor. Reaching for her to pull her in the light where he could see her. See the baby he knew she was holding. "We'll get him to the doctor, make him breathe," Frank said. Willa's screaming faded and dark settled around them.

Floyd County Register
Centennial Edition
Memories of Jackson's Pond
Thursday, May 2, 1996
by Ellen Nelson, Features Editor

"I proposed to my wife at the Pond. It was a romantic spot back in 1954," said Joe Arnold.

That pond, Jackson's Pond, from which the nearby town took its name, is today far smaller than in 1954 and even smaller than when it was the primary landmark on the southern boundary of the C.C. Jackson homestead in 1895. Mr. Jackson initially watered cattle at the spring-fed pond when he established his ranch.

Melanie Jackson Banks, great grand-daughter of C.C. Jackson, said, "The original fence was placed north of the property line to give public access to the pond soon after the town of Jackson's Pond developed. Until the mid-1950s my grandfather left the fence where his father had placed it. The state highway was built then, farther south, and there was no longer a need for public access. The traffic bypassed both the pond and the town of Jackson's Pond.

"After the highway was completed, Grandfather Jackson fenced along the actual property line. Since that time, the pond has been closed to the public, except for special occasions."

Former Editor of the *Jackson's Pond Gazette*, Homer Huckaby said, "Our files contain many stories of social events at the pond. I'll bet everyone who grew up in Jackson's Pond has some "pond" story to tell. And I don't mean just the ones who were youngsters before the place was fenced off. Sneaking into the pond after dark was almost a requirement for completing your teen years in this town even into the late 1960s. All that had to be stopped when juvenile delinquency became a problem in the Viet Nam years. The sheriff began patrolling the area and kids found other things to do."

The pond's past is part of the memory of many Jackson's Pond residents. But what of the pond's future?

County Extension Agent Tim Haws explained. "Many playa lakes dot the county during rainy periods and dry up very quickly after the rains. The only source of the playas' water is the rain. But Jackson's Pond is the county's only true pond, one with a constant source of fresh water from an underground spring.

"Ponds age and eventually dry up as their water source declines. With the drop in the level of the Ogallala Aquifer, the source of Jackson's Pond's water declines also. When that happens, the vegetation in and around the pond changes. You can see that the water line is several feet farther down than it was a few years ago and that there are fewer mossy plants and more native grass moving in toward the water. Small mesquites are also taking hold. Before many more years, this pond will be only a memory."

Opportunity

"He's been my best friend nearly all my life," J. D. said. "Don't ever use that word around me again. Not about anyone and certainly not about Chris. What have I ever done or said that would make you think it was okay to call Chris a queer?" J. D. would probably have decked Tiffany if she'd been a man. His father had always said that narrow-minded people needed to be put in their place.

It was plain to him from the look on her face that Tiffany wasn't accustomed to having her prejudices pointed out to her. She probably wouldn't have looked more surprised if he had slapped her. If he wanted to, he could erase that look with an apology. And he thought for a second about doing it. But, dammit, she'd been crowding him lately—actually, for almost the entire seven months they'd been dating—hinting about getting engaged. He didn't have anything to apologize for. She had just shown him something about herself that all her blond hair and fancy clothes couldn't make up for. She was as bad, or at least as unthinking, as any other bigot. And he wasn't about to give in and go to Hereford with her to her family's Christmas.

Silence blanketed them as they sat parked in his pickup in front of the Lubbock house she shared with two of her sorority sisters. She blinked several times, like she might be trying to tear up. Then she sniffled, loudly, and said in a little-girl voice, "J. D., I'm sorry I upset you. All I was doing was trying to find out why you'd rather visit Chris and his boyfriend in Austin instead of coming home with me for Christmas. I didn't mean anything bad about your friend."

He knew she was lying. He said, "Tiffany, I thanked you for the invitation, but I told you I already made plans, and I'm not going to change them." He softened his voice—no sense in making things worse. "It's nice of your parents to invite me. Please tell them I appreciate it."

"Daddy said he had something he wanted to talk to you about. He liked you when he met you at homecoming. He was excited that you'd been in Saddle Tramps like he was when he was at Tech. He said he thought you knew a lot about raising cattle." She flipped down the mirror on the visor, reapplied lip gloss, and practiced a sweet smile at her reflection. She aimed the same smile at J. D. and said, "I think he wants to offer you a job in his feedlot operation when you graduate."

"Did he say that?"

"Well, not directly, but he asked me what you plan to do after graduation."

No telling what she had said to her parents about him being prospective husband material. On the other hand, Bobby Frank Carroll did operate several of the biggest feedlots in the Panhandle. So maybe he should talk to him again. But not at Christmas. He'd promised Chris. Besides, it would take him a while before he could tolerate being around Tiffany for any length of time.

Growing up, he and Chris had been like the brothers neither of them had. J. D. was two years older. From the first year they worked together on the Jackson Ranch, when Chris was twelve, he worked hard to learn everything J. D. had learned from his own father and from Frank Jackson and Johnny Griffith, the cowboy. He even started chewing Red Man like J. D. and his Granddad Frank did. J. D. never missed a chance to kid Chris about the time he forgot to spit and swallowed a lot of tobacco juice. He'd puked all over the tailgate and on his own boots.

At school they ran with different crowds. Chris spent his time with people from speech and drama and the band; J. D. hung out with the Ag types. After Jackson's Pond High School consolidated with Calverton, they rode the school bus together, and they worked side by side on the ranch most weekends. It didn't matter to either of them that they had different interests; they agreed on important things, like the fact that most adults would never understand either one of them and that Chris' grandmother Jackson was the only exception to that rule.

J. D. had been the one who bought Chris his first beer and offered him his first joint. They both got in trouble for fighting after school, for different reasons. Chris understood that J. D. couldn't tolerate being confined, and J. D. accepted that Chris' adolescent infatuations were with boys instead of girls. "Don't worry too much about it. Just be who you are and be careful," J. D. had told his friend. When J. D. graduated, he had worried that when he wasn't there, Chris would be mistreated by some of the redneck types in school. But Chris took care of himself just fine. It only took a couple of fist fights with local shit-kickers before he and the two black guys in his class established that they were not to be messed with.

A few days later, after he'd thought about how to avoid the topic of an engagement, J. D. took Tiffany out for tacos. He said, "Tiff, I've been thinking about your dad wanting to talk to me. If it's okay with him and with you, I could come up to Hereford in January, the weekend before the next semester starts."

She brightened up the hangdog expression she'd been wearing like he'd said some magic words that changed her entire face. "Yes, that would be just perfect. Mama will want to have a nice dinner for you. So plan to spend the night."

He nodded. "Okay. But tell her not to go to any trouble on my account." Just great. A family dinner. But it wouldn't hurt to talk. Right now, he didn't have any other job opportunities waiting for him after graduation.

Last summer Chris had come to Lubbock, but not to Jackson's Pond. When he called J. D. to tell him he'd be there and that he had a surprise, he said, "I told you when I left after high school that Jackson's Pond had seen the last of me. Gran and Claire are going to meet me in Lubbock. They'll tell Mom they're going to shop for Claire's school clothes and stay overnight. If you could come, it would be perfect."

"You aren't going to see your mother?"

"Not this time. Maybe later. I don't want to spoil my trip by having to listen to another one of her 'you're involved with the wrong kind of people' rants. She just doesn't get it. She doesn't want to know me. She wanted a rancher for a son and got an artist instead. I'm an embarrassment to her."

J. D. couldn't imagine how Chris felt; his own dad and his mother, before she died, had always told him they were proud of him. He did understand Chris' not wanting to engage in useless arguments. Chris wasn't going to change, and J. D. would be surprised if Melanie Banks ever did. Chris' dad was another matter. A lot of Ray Banks' work as District Liaison to the local State Representative required him to be in Austin. When he and Chris' mom divorced in '92, he'd moved down there, and Chris said they saw each other frequently.

This trip there had been no pretense. J. D. and Willa were flying to Austin the day after Christmas to see Chris. Everyone knew the trip was J. D.'s present from Willa. As soon as they landed, J. D. remembered why he preferred the High Plains to places like Austin. Everything here seemed offensively green, even in winter, and too close.

Chris met them at the arrival gate. He had grown since last summer. As they hugged and clapped each other on the back, J. D. saw they stood eye-to-eye now. Chris must be getting regular meals. "I'm so glad to see you both. Gran, is Claire okay? She didn't call me this week like she usually does," Chris said.

"Melanie actually let her go out on a date last Friday night. Maybe that had something to do with it," Willa said.

Chris cocked an eyebrow. "Uh oh. Tell her I expect her to call me on Wednesday nights no matter what she's doing on the weekends."

J. D. watched the two of them, both looking so happy. As they chatted he wondered for a second when Claire got old enough to date. He hadn't paid any attention to her when she was a little kid and hadn't seen her in at least a year, except at a distance, riding with Willa in a pickup at the ranch.

Chris stowed their bags in the trunk of his not so new Chevy. "We're going to the house to relax a while and then we'll go out to Sixth Street tonight. Joe Ely's playing." Before he closed the trunk, he looked again at the bags. "Gran, did you bring those paintings? I've already talked to Arthur at the gallery and shown him the slides you sent. He wants to meet you. Act surprised when he offers to represent you."

"They're right here." She pointed to a portfolio under the coat draped over her right arm.

"You never give yourself credit for being a fine artist. Just wait, one day our work will be hanging side by side. You'll pave the way for me."

She hugged Chris. "I don't think you need me paving the way. But your Gran thanks you, sweetie."

Chris parked in the driveway of a small cottage-style house on a quiet street in an older section of Austin. The houses nearby all appeared to have been updated and had small neat yards. He said, "Well, here we are." But his face showed something more; this was home and he was proud of it. He hurried in front of them to the door, mumbling something about the bags could wait. First, they had to meet Andrew.

"Gran, J. D., this is Andrew Mullins. Andrew, this is Willa Jackson, soon to be a famous watercolorist, my favorite woman in the whole world. And this is J. D. Havlicek, my best friend, the person who taught me how to fight and how to drink beer and who always understands me."

Andrew said, "He does know how to make an introduction, doesn't he? I'm so glad to finally meet you both." Andrew was Chris' equal in size and probably about his age or a bit older. Immediately, J. D. felt comfortable in his calm presence. He was the person Chris had told Willa and J. D. about last summer, that they were buying a house together. Chris had said then, "This is for good. He's the one."

Until now, J. D. hadn't realized he'd been worried since then that maybe Chris was being taken advantage of. But, he could tell Chris had grown up a lot; he could take care of himself.

Andrew went to bring in the luggage while Chris showed Willa and J. D. the rest of the house. Chris' comments about the work he and Andrew had done together remodeling it assured J. D. even further. His friend had found a true partner.

When they returned to the living room, Willa held her arms wide, then said, "Come here, all three of you. I'm so happy and proud for you all—Chris and Andrew for finding each other and for creating a lovely home. And you, J. D., for being almost ready to graduate." Her three-part hug made J. D. feel like a little boy, one who sometimes missed his mother. "Now," she said, " I'd like to freshen up before we go out."

Willa returned a bit later, ready, she said, for an evening on the town in Austin. She pointed to the tall-topped ropers she wore with her full-skirted, calf-length denim skirt. "I expect someone here to join me on the dance floor," she said. "Are you boys ready?"

The place on Sixth Street, the Roundup, was a yuppie's idea of a West Texas honky-tonk, done up for the holidays with a Christmas tree on one side of the tiny bandstand. The tables didn't have any beer stains on them and the chair legs were all the same length, but Joe Ely and his band sounded the same as they did in a real joint in Lubbock. Surprisingly, the dance floor was large; apparently the owner wasn't relying on beer and liquor alone to maintain the crowds. Chris and J. D. watched as Willa and Andrew did the cowboy two-step, circling counter-clockwise around the floor along with lots of laughing college kids.

"Your gran's quite a dancer, isn't she?" She had danced with each of them and with at least three other young men. "I knew she did ballet every week at her house, but I didn't know she did a fancy two-step," J. D. said.

"Yeah, she looks like she's having a great time. Before he died, she and Granddad would dance in the living room." J. D. saw nostalgia bring sadness to his friend's eyes. "She hasn't had a partner for a long time now," Chris said.

An appointment with the gallery owner for Willa and a trip to see the offices of the newspaper where Chris worked part-time filled the next day. Chris blushed when someone they met in the newsroom referred to him as their best photographer and said when he graduated from UT some out-of-state paper would hire him away. The next day, while Chris and Andrew were at work, Willa and J. D. played tourist at the State Capitol building and spent the afternoon at an art exhibit at UT.

And then, the third day after they arrived, J. D. and Willa boarded the plane for Lubbock, promising they'd be back soon. J. D. watched from his window as the landscape below gradually changed from dense cedar-green hills to flat brown plowed ground waiting for crops. While they were in Austin, he'd been able to push Tiffany out of his mind. But as they neared Lubbock, the lingering aggravation about her and her none too subtle hinting about an engagement began again, like a low-pitched buzzing in his head.

He shouldn't have dated her as often, but seeing just one girl was so much easier than dating around. And at first, she'd been fun, always ready whenever he called and always looking great, fetching lots of sidelong looks from his friends. Maybe it was his fault for not making clear that he didn't have marriage in mind, not before he was thirty, anyway. But, hell, why should she assume he did? He never led her on and they had never gotten any more involved than some steamy groping.

But he had done one thing right. Before she had a chance to surprise him with some fancy Christmas present and get in more hints about expecting a ring in return, he handed her a professionally gift-wrapped package one afternoon at a restaurant. She looked a little shocked when she opened it—a pictorial history of Texas Tech—but she recovered pretty soon. "What a nice surprise," she said.

He figured that's what they'd been taught in her sorority to say when they found something objectionable, like a turd floating in a fancy punchbowl. He said, "I'm so glad you like it." He'd practiced sounding sincere.

Not long before they were scheduled to land, Willa said, "J. D., tell me what you see in your future. What would you like to be doing this time next year?"

He thought a while before answering. When he did speak, he continued looking out the window. "What I see is one thing and what I'd like to be doing is something else. What I'd like is to build up an operation of my own—cattle, supported by enough farming to keep them in feed, raising natural beef. But my dad told me, years back, the reason he sold out, equipment and all, except for the quarter section where our house sits. He said he realized he was never going to get out of debt for all the loans he'd had to take for operating money and the payments he had to make on the land he was trying to farm. He said that anyone who got in over their head like he did was just asking to die young and leave his family in debt."

He paused and took a long, deep breath, then turned from watching the land below and smiled a wry smile. "That hundred and sixty acres is all we own. And you know how many cattle that would support. Not many. So what I guess I'll do is get a job somewhere, with a regular paycheck and maybe keep a few head out at Dad's place, just to feel like I'm still doing something real."

"Do you have any prospects yet?"

"I'm supposed to talk to a man at Hereford next week. He has feedlots."

"Bobby Ray Carroll?"

"Uh huh." He shook his head as an image of Tiffany intruded. "Any advice, Mrs. Jackson?"

She laughed. "Sure. My first advice is to call me Willa. You've known me nearly all your life, so I think it will be okay. Second, don't rush into anything. Opportunity comes in lots of forms and often in surprising ways."

"I'll keep that in mind." He thought about easy, too quick, choices and about how a person's options can get narrowed down before he knows it. It was like a calf being pushed into a squeeze chute, going in expecting to be a bull all his life and coming out a steer. "Yes ma'am. I sure will," he said.

Dinner with Tiffany's parents at their house outside Hereford was finally over and J. D. was smiling. He hadn't intended to. Tiffany asked, "What's making you smile?" She arranged herself on the couch like a queen too long away from her throne. Seeing her here in her family's house, with her parents, proved all he'd thought. She was spoiled and proud of it.

"Oh, nothing much, just thinking about that cherry cobbler. Someone here is a mighty good cook."

With a smug little smile, she patted the place next to her. He ignored her signal and sat in a chair across from her. She put a tiny pout on her lips for a second and then said, "That's Louisa. You didn't see her because she stayed in the kitchen. She does all our cooking. Mama hasn't had to cook in years, not since daddy got into feedlots in a big way."

J. D. hadn't been smiling about the pie. He'd been imagining what her mother would have done if he'd tracked manure in on the dining room's white carpet and put his elbows on the table. Or if he'd said, "Horse shit" when her father, old 'Call me Bobby Ray, son,' had told him to make himself at home and dig in. That was right after the grand tour of their house, the one Bobby Ray described as eight thousand square feet, not counting the landing strip out back. The house sat a quarter mile downwind from the feedlot Bobby Ray pointed out, as if J. D. couldn't locate it from the smell. Bobby Ray explained that the lot was kind of dinky compared to the rest of his operation but that he kept it open for sentimental reasons. "Yes sir, that's where I got my start. I worked there five years as a pen rider when I was in college. And then I bought the whole son-of-a-bitch when I graduated."

After dinner, Tiffany's father seemed to be on the verge of telling a lot more, but her mother dragged him off to their media room. J. D. was kind of sorry to see them go. Now he'd have to talk to Tiffany. Pretty soon he relaxed because with Tiffany he didn't really have to talk. All he needed to do was pretend to listen. The girl could say more about less than anyone he knew. He paid just enough attention to be sure he didn't say "Uh, huh" to something—like an engagement.

The next day, he could tell Bobby Ray saw himself moving in to close the deal. They had toured what seemed like every inch of Deaf Smith County and parts of Castro and Parmer. Bobby Ray talked even more than his daughter. J. D. strained to follow his running commentary as they drove through his feedlots and across a lot of territory in between. The man talked about the ration he fed, about his long-range plan for a methane-converting power plant, about how he custom-fed for a lot of old boys but how at least half these pens were full of his own cattle. "See, within my overall operation, I've got a second one. I suppose your professors would call it vertically integrated." Without much of a pause for breath, he explained how he bought truckloads of number twos from Central Texas—"doesn't matter what they look like—they all look a lot the same after they're butchered"; get 'em straightened out, take a little death loss—"I don't pay much for 'em to begin with, so I can afford it"; and then put them in a set of graduated pens, changing their ration and their location as they gained weight. The only thing that stopped his mouth was that they had arrived back at the first lot, the one near the house.

J. D. looked toward the house at his pickup—decided Bobby Ray would probably catch him if he made a run for it. He had been close to vomiting the whole day. Cattle standing around on hills of manure, others edging each other out for a space at the empty feed bunks, and others walking the perimeter of the pens like listless prisoners in an open-air jail had turned his stomach. It wasn't the smell; it was the whole idea.

J. D. ate beef like everyone else; he knew that a lot of cattle were fattened in feedlots. But most of those lots were clean and the cattle were treated humanely. It wasn't the beef industry that had made him squirm and check his watch all day. He had seen feedlots before, but never where the deads were stacked up like firewood, or where the manure hadn't been cleared out of the pens in months and the cattle stood and bawled constantly. Bobby Ray had his operation spread out in a bunch of poorly maintained lots in places far from the main highways. J. D. was pretty sure he didn't want anyone looking too close.

And now old Bobby Ray was getting to the point, finally. "I wouldn't want you to think I'm offering you anything I wouldn't lay out for any other smart young man about to graduate from Tech's Ag college. But you do get the first opportunity at the job I have in mind. That's because Tiffany tells me you two have been dating for quite a while. I take that as a recommendation. My daughter's a good judge of character."

He promised to be back in touch with Bobby Ray, said his goodbyes and thank-yous to Mrs. Carroll and Tiffany, and made an excuse about being needed at home, all in the space of about twenty minutes after they got back to the house. Seventy miles per hour didn't seem fast enough as he headed out of Deaf Smith County. Before long, he came to a halt on the side of the highway, spraying gravel as he hit the brakes. He hadn't gotten far from Hereford but he had to walk around. The inside of the pickup cab was pressing against his chest. He couldn't get a good breath.

He didn't have to think about it at all. His body told him. As soon as he got back to Lubbock, he'd type out a nice letter to Bobby Ray and Mrs. Carroll. In whatever decent words he could dredge up, he would say thanks again for the dinner and say not no, but hell no, to being manager of Bobby Ray's feedlot—the one closest to the big house. He'd figure out later how to avoid Tiffany until she found her another prospect. Her daddy said she was a good judge of character.

Finally, the end of the semester was in sight. Two more weeks and he'd never have to sleep in this cell of a dorm room again. He'd only tolerated it for four years to save money. Going home to work most weekends had made it easier. But when he was here, he felt surrounded.

He rearranged the four stacks of paper again. They made little mounds around him where he sat in the middle of the bed. Each stack represented one of his job offers. None of them was bad. He should be grateful. Some guys didn't have any offers yet. The papers were beginning to get dog-eared from all his handling. He'd read and reread them again and again. He had tried being logical, listing the pros and cons of each job. They were all entry-level—assistant County Ag Extension Agent; Level I Soil Conservationist; Sales Representative Trainee for a veterinary supply company; Assistant Agricultural Loan Officer at a small bank in Nocona. Pay was okay and pretty much the same for all of them if you figured in benefits. And when he quit being logical, he couldn't imagine himself doing any of those jobs.

He was pretty certain what his dad would say—get something secure; take the County Agent job; it's steady and has a good retirement. Guys in his class were all looking for prospects of quick advancement; they pushed him toward the sales job. He stared at the piles.

Chris probably would be out on assignment. J. D. dialed the newspaper in Austin where he worked, anyway. When Chris answered, hearing his voice made J. D. feel better. When he explained his situation and asked his friend's opinion, Chris said, "This is a switch. It's usually me asking you for advice."

"I hadn't needed much until now, buddy. Don't give me any crap, I'm serious. I need to know what you'd do. You've already got a job and have plans for the future, and you're not even out of college yet. I don't have a clue."

"I'd do what Gran always told me. Be still and wait."

"That's it? You mean don't take any of those jobs?"

"Will you starve if you don't?"

"No, I can move back home."

"When something seems right, you'll know. That's what I'd do. Listen, I've got to go photograph a bloody six-car wreck, but call me tonight if you want to talk some more. And J. D., thanks for asking me."

J. D. lay back and stared at the ceiling, trying to be still.

He woke up and wondered where he was—he must have dozed off. He closed his eyes again and covered his head with a pillow. A parade of J. D.s marched behind his eyelids—J. D. the County Agent, herding a bunch of 4-H kids around a livestock show ring; J. D. the junior loan officers shuffling papers; J. D. the salesman smiling and making deals to boost his sales figures. He threw the pillow across the room. He sat up and in one quick motion pushed all of it—bank, soil conservation, the whole mess, onto the floor. He pulled his boots on and headed to his pickup.

The last time he had been to the pond was early last September. In those nine months, the water had receded nearly another foot. Damn, one more thing changing. At least watching the sunset would make things clearer. This was the place he often came to think.

He heard a pickup stop on the road. Claire waved from the passenger seat. Willa was the driver. They walked together to where he sat, near a mesquite at the pond's edge. Watching them, he thought Claire could have been a young copy of Willa, complete with long legs, slim figure, green eyes and black hair, but missing the two wide streaks of grey that had been in Willa's hair as long as he could remember. Neither of them asked what he was doing. "I'm glad we saw you," Willa said. "If you have time, I'd like you to come up to the house. I have some things I need you to look at for me."

"I'll be up after sunset, if that's okay."

She nodded, but her eyes searched the perimeter of the pond. "It makes me sad to see this pond. I can hardly make myself come here anymore except when I paint it. Those paintings will be the only way for me to remember it when it's dry and gone."

J. D. didn't know what to say. He looked toward the horizon and thought again about things changing.

More than the view and memories brought him here this afternoon. He'd put off talking to his dad as long as he could. All the way out from Lubbock, he'd tried to come up with a way to explain why he wanted to move home instead of taking any one of those perfectly good jobs.

Trouble was, every reason sounded, even to him, like an excuse for being lazy or scared. Jacob Havlicek had never been one to tolerate excuses. J. D. left the pond and drove past the Jackson place and six miles farther north to where he knew he would have to face his dad. Maybe disappoint him.

He found his dad in the barn, hands covered with grease, straw hat pushed back, sweating, sitting on a stool and staring at their old Chevy pickup. "Hope you came out here to fix this," he said. "Otherwise, you can just go on back to college."

"Need some help?"

"Need a new pickup, looks like. This one's just about done for. Can't buy a good vehicle these days. It's only been two hundred eighteen thousand miles and already give out completely."

"What's wrong with it?"

"Could be the mechanic. I'm sick of screwing around with it. Let's go in and drink some tea." As they approached the back door, he asked, "What are you doing out here today? I thought you'd have something to do at school right here close to graduation."

J. D. got out ice and the jar of tea his dad kept in the refrigerator. They sat on the front porch. "Well," said his dad. Sounded like a statement, but J. D. knew it was a question.

"I need some advice." J. D. told him about the job offers and the particulars of each one. His dad nodded and didn't say anything. J. D. could see that he wasn't going to make it easy for him. "What do you think about those jobs?"

"They all sound like pretty good offers for a new college graduate, but then being a farmer, I never did have a job with a steady wage. You might be asking the wrong guy." He bit down on a piece of ice. "What do you think of them? I thought that's what I paid all this tuition money for, so you could get the work you want and be secure."

J. D. hemmed around a little bit and then said, "They all pay okay and have benefits. You're right, they'd be steady and I did learn things in my classes that prepared me to start out in any one of these jobs."

"Then I reckon you're going to have to play one and look at the others, just like in dominoes."

He made it sound simple. But, dammit, deciding wasn't that simple if you didn't want any of the jobs. "But…"

"But what? Just like everybody else, you have to just stand up and get on with it. You've had four years to get ready, to finish growing up. So now it's time to act like a grownup."

J. D. didn't want to ask the next question. "Can I just come home and help you out for a while? I'll find something I want before too long, I'm sure."

Jacob Havlicek put his tea glass on the porch rail and sat forward, put his elbows on his knees and his head in his hands. "Son, there's nothing I'd like better than to have you come out here and just take over so I could rest. But the fact is there ain't nothing much to take over. If you hadn't worked summers to help pay for your school; if we had a debt, one of us would have to give up eating. A quarter section of this kind of land will just about support me, if I don't get any extravagant ideas like getting a new pickup. Sorry, son, there's nothing here for you."

"I just don't think I could stand to take any of these jobs. I'd be miserable doing anything that keeps me indoors even part of the time."

"Sounds like an excuse to me." His dad had his head up now and sounded like he'd had about enough. Next thing you know, he'd either get up and walk off or start cussing and fuming.

"I know it does. Maybe it is. I wouldn't expect you to pay me or anything. Just let me help you and maybe get some day work somewhere around here till I get an offer that I think I can stand to take."

His dad stood and opened the screen door. "Tell you what, you come out here and work this place and I'll take a four-year vacation. Hell of a note if you ask me. A college education and offers of jobs and you don't want any of 'em."

J. D. knew when to keep his mouth shut. He followed his dad inside, keeping his head down.

"Oh hell, go ahead and move your stuff back out here. At least I'll have company to eat with. Maybe you can get that pickup to run."

He could barely hold himself back from hugging his dad. "I'll do my best. Thanks, Dad. I appreciate this. I'll find a job before long." He told him he needed to head back toward Lubbock and he'd see him on the weekend. He didn't bother mentioning that he'd stop at the Jackson place on the way. Relief should feel better than it did right then, but at least he could breathe.

Two ledger books, a fat manila folder, and a map lay spread on the dining room table. Willa told him about the contents—the records of the Jackson cattle herd since Frank took over from his dad; the crop records from the wheat fields for the same time; the financial records for the place for the past two years, and the map of the current acreage plus the Wheeler's half-section due east. After he looked briefly through each of the ledgers and the folder, she told him she wanted his opinion on whether it was reasonable to consider increasing the herd over the next three years by forty more registered cows and one more good bull and leasing that east three hundred-twenty acres from Les Wheeler for additional grazing. "I'm interested in getting Natural Angus Beef certification and marketing through that outfit in Childress. I'll be in the front room if you have questions. Stay as long as you like. If you're not through when I go to bed, just lock the door when you leave. We'll talk tomorrow," she said.

She returned a few seconds later. "In case I didn't say it, I appreciate your doing this. You know the place and you have a good education. I'll value your opinion."

He couldn't figure out why he felt a blush rising up from his neck.

He was still studying the ledgers when Willa came into the kitchen the next morning. He had stayed at it all night. She had trusted him enough to ask his opinion; he wouldn't give one based on a less than thorough review. Sometime in the night he had made coffee. And more than once he wondered at her trusting him for advice.

"I didn't mean for you to wear yourself out."

"I didn't notice the time until the sun came up. You have really complete records, just the kind they tell us in school a good rancher should keep, but no one actually does. I think your idea is a really good one. There are a few more facts I need to be certain, but from what's here, it looks like this could pay off down the road. Of course, you know it'll take a few years to do more than break even."

He drank coffee and shuffled the papers back into the file. He could feel her studying his face.

"I keep my personal funds separate from the ranch," she said. "I won't have to worry about my old age on account of money. But I'd rather not lose money by making these changes. Breaking even would be sufficient if we can benefit the land and raise good cattle."

The additional information he wanted was about the beef marketing company in Childress. She got another file for him and said, "I'll be gone until after noon. You get some rest and we can talk again then."

He nodded without looking up from the file.

He drove toward his dad's house, intending to rest and explain why he was still in the vicinity. Jacob Havlicek respected Mrs. Jackson. He'd be proud she asked his son's advice. But he wasn't at the house. So J. D. rested until near three o'clock. He couldn't sleep for thinking about Willa's plan. He gave up trying and drove back to the Jackson house. He found her in the kitchen.

"Let's talk," she said. "Sit down." She poured coffee for them both and sat across from him at the table. "I'm glad you think my plan is a good one. Changes would keep me interested in staying on the ranch." She stacked the files and folded the map.

He nodded and swallowed hard. The idea had come to him as he drove the six miles from home. Apparently this was his time to learn how it feels to beg. First his dad and now Willa. "Mrs. Jackson," he began.

She shook her head. "Willa."

He corrected himself, "Willa, if you do decide to take on this plan, do you intend to add some help?"

"At least one full-time, a hands-on person with management ability. Yes, I know we didn't discuss how adding that person would affect the costs. But there's no way for me to do it otherwise. One cowboy, one part-time hand, seasonal help, and me wouldn't be enough."

He tried to sound like a disinterested party—like a consultant. "Yes, I agree." He stared at his coffee cup. "Well, you probably know this already, but if you decide to make these changes and to hire someone, I hope you'll consider me for the job."

"Your dad told me the other day you had four offers already, and didn't you also look into something with Bobby Ray Carroll?"

"I did, but his operation isn't something I'd want to be a part of. And those other jobs… Well, let's just say I'd like to be considered if you are willing to look at someone as young as me, with no management experience." He must have drunk too much coffee; his heart rate seemed to have doubled.

"I intend to decide pretty soon. I'll keep your interest in mind. But I have to tell you I don't know if it would be fair to you. Most young men want to get away from home and to get something secure. This isn't very far from home and you can tell from all the things you reviewed, it wouldn't be entirely secure."

He stood up and held out his hand. "I understand. Just keep me in mind. And thanks again for asking my opinion." She shook his hand, and patted him on the back. He got to his pickup and hoped that his pulse would get back to normal. He headed back toward his dormitory in Lubbock. He'd had all the excitement he needed for the past two days.

Friday morning, before class, his telephone rang. Willa asked if he would stop by if he was coming home that weekend. He told her he'd be there around six that evening. He had trouble paying attention in class.

She offered him iced tea and a sandwich. He took the tea. Without any small talk, she said, "You probably know why I asked you to stop by. I've decided. I'm going to lease that land and start the beef herd development we discussed. Would you be willing to take a job working for me being the manager, that pays seventeen hundred a month to start plus free rent and utilities at the tenant house? I'll pay half of your health insurance, too."

He sat very still, to keep from shouting, "Would I?" Instead he said, "I appreciate you considering me. I do have one question. What is the opportunity for advancement?"

"If, after a year, we agree that we can work together and you see a future in it, then we'll set up an annual bonus based on the profits, and eventually I would want to have a partnership arrangement."

For a second, he had trouble believing what he'd heard her say. But unlike Bobby Ray, she was someone whose word a person could trust. If she said annual bonus and eventual partnership, she meant it.

He didn't hesitate any further. "There's nothing I'd like better. I'm available anytime after next weekend—as soon as graduation's over. When do you want me to start?" He already knew the first thing he was going to buy—a new pickup for his dad.

FLOYD COUNTY TRIBUNE
Thursday, September 23, 1999

<u>Public Notice</u>
JACKSON'S POND
CITY COUNCIL MEETING
Monday, November 1, 1999
7:00 p.m.
Jackson's Pond City Hall
Agenda
1. Call to order
2. Invocation
3. City Manager's report
4. City Tax Office report
5. Old Business
    a. Request for County funds for a new tank truck for Volunteer Fire Dept. (action item)
    b. Approval of agreement with County Commissioners for EMT services location in Jackson's Pond (action item)
6. New Business
    a. Report of Economic Development Board
    b. Proposal to enter contract with Landfill Technologies for a contract landfill on city property—
(first reading-no final action)
7. Information items
    a. Citizen input on Landfill Technologies contract
    b. Public information from Texas Wind Turbines Coalition representative regarding wind farms.
8. Other items from the floor
9. Adjournment.

Surprises

Mike knew he shouldn't be surprised, but that didn't stop the feeling—something that made him blink and stretch his neck and take a deep breath. How could a place that had been peopled by friendly giants when he was a boy—tall men with large plans, gentle women with watchful eyes and hopes of bright futures—have become so small? Small in every way. Where there had been two streets, four blocks long each, lined with businesses and, on Saturdays, people shopping, getting haircuts, leaning against their pickups talking about the weather or politics, now only eight businesses and city hall remained. And the people—where had they gone when the shopping and visiting stopped?

Stopped. That's what he did. He willed himself to stop remembering and to focus on the three men approaching him. After his earlier brief tour of Jackson's Pond, the twelve minutes it took to see what was left of it, he'd been surprised also by the fact that the City Council's meeting room contained about forty people. Most of them clustered in groups of three or four. The majority were men around his age, in their fifties and sixties, and a few women who were already seated and quiet, except for two who were standing. One was in her twenties and the other could be her mother, maybe her grandmother. He thought he knew the older woman, but couldn't be sure. Maybe they represented the trash company.

One of the men who zeroed in on him offered a handshake and immediately announced his name, Junior Reese. In a short exchange of pleasantries, he told Mike that he remembered him from school. Reese took his time, looking around as if to make sure that others saw him claiming the right to be the first to greet the outsider. His manner suggested he owned something.

The other two introduced themselves as Tuff Johnson and Freddy McClendon. "You ought to remember me, Mike. My dad had the feed store you used to walk through on the way home from school every afternoon," McClendon said.

"I remember the smell of the feed store, Freddy. I loved it. That's why the detour every day," Mike said. He wouldn't have been able to pick Freddy out of a lineup on a bet. The other one, Tuff he'd called himself, got right down to the usual questions. Not the sort of questions used to fill the air at class reunions, but the ones about why Mike was interested in Jackson's Pond for a wind farm—the same questions in every town. What do you want? What's in it for me?

Tuff's version was, "Did they send you because you grew up here? You know, ha ha, thinking we'd mistake you for a local."

Mike felt pretty sure that Tuff hadn't always been a local; at least he hadn't been in school when Mike was, as far as he could remember. Surely he'd have remembered a guy who called himself Tuff. He'd have had to earn that nickname. There would have been stories about riding bulls and broncs or winning fist fights. Mike eased into a posture that reflected Tuff's—the cocked hip, a thumb in his belt, sidewise glances at his two pals when he had delivered his "ha ha." Mirroring was so much a part of Mike that he was no longer conscious he did it. But after all these years, he could tell by responses, verbal and not verbal, whether he blended in with the people around him well enough for them to hear whatever message he wanted to convey. He also dressed with an eye toward blending in. Tonight his costume included starched, creased, slightly faded Wranglers, a white shirt with no tie, a navy blue blazer with plain buttons, and black ostrich boots (belly, not full quill—didn't want to be too well turned out). His belt matched his boots and the buckle was plain silver. No hat. Nothing he wore was new. A 1998 Chevy pickup with a crack in the windshield furnished his transportation.

He said, "I consult for the Texas Wind Turbines Coalition. My job is to provide information to people in areas that could have potential—lots of wind—ha ha—for turbine placement."

McClendon said, "I'm a little disappointed. I thought you might have brought money."

Mike smiled and stepped to his left; he often did that when he changed the subject. This time his sidestep had another purpose. He wanted a better look at the older of the two women across the room, the ones still standing. "Sorry, they don't furnish me a checkbook, just a slide projector. Will you excuse me? I see someone else I know over there."

As he sidled closer to the tall woman, he pretended to study the agenda he found on a table outside the meeting room. Within six feet of her, he knew. Her profile convinced him. He had drawn that face all over his book covers as he stared at her across classrooms from the first through the eighth grades. She was Lofland—L, and he was Ward—W, so they were never seated next to each other. She was the first girl he'd ever had a real crush on. It lasted for a long time. The fact that his pulse was racing now made him wonder if it ever went away.

"Willa? Willa Lofland?"

She turned to face him. "Yes?" She stared at him with a tiny frown. Then her eyes began to sparkle. "Mike Ward! What in the world?"

"I'm on the agenda."

"Which one are you—trash or wind?"

She laughed when he rolled his eyes and said, "I guess that depends on who you ask." He gave her the abbreviated version of his job and reason for being on the agenda.

She shook her head. "I don't want to discourage you, but this place is… let's call it insular. I guess you've been to a lot of places and seen this…"

"Whatever happens, it's not a problem. I'm just here to provide information." He couldn't stop staring at her; she really hadn't changed in any important ways.

The young woman standing with her said, "Gran, I'm going."

"Oh, Claire, I'm sorry, I should have introduced you." She introduced Mike and her granddaughter and said, "Mike, if you don't have to leave after, let's have a cup of coffee. We can catch up."

He watched as she and her granddaughter took seats beside a tall, good-looking, young man. He was the one he'd seen standing across the room watching while they talked. The granddaughter could have been the same girl he'd had that crush on so long ago, same profile, same long legs, green eyes and black hair. He sympathized with that young man. The boy was done for.

Mike talked with several people who hung back after the meeting adjourned. He took time to listen carefully to each person—they always preferred private conversations—and to give his usual well-practiced factual answers, without any hint of attempting to sell the project. That would come later. He memorized each of their names. A good memory was one of his assets.

He waited a few minutes after the last person in the group that had gathered around him moved away. He never left until every question had been asked and answered. Now he couldn't see Willa in the meeting room. Had she changed her mind? Had he misunderstood her invitation? He stepped outside and his smile returned, this time feeling genuine. She was waiting for him out front.

The only place they could get coffee after the meeting was the Allsup's convenience store on the east side of town. The City Café closed at six. She said if he didn't mind a little drive, he could follow her out to the ranch. He didn't mind a bit.

All the way to the ranch, following her pickup, he wondered. About a lot of things. Mostly about her husband. He'd heard, years ago, that she married Frank Jackson. That explained where she lived. He remembered the Jackson place, that big house he'd never been inside or even seen up close.

He'd lived in town. His dad had grown up in Jackson's Pond and ran the family dry goods store. According to family tradition, Mike had been sent to boarding school for his high school years. At San Marcos Baptist Academy he'd grown from a self-conscious boy with feet and hands too large for his body to a well-coordinated, curly haired, young man known for his sense of humor and for being the smartest guy in his class. From there he'd gone to A & M and studied engineering. Once he'd left Jackson's Pond, he had no desire to return; certainly no wish to sell dry goods. His father sold the store in the early fifties and moved to Central Texas. So there was no reason, until now, for Mike to return. That didn't mean he hadn't thought, occasionally, about the girl who occupied his thoughts constantly back then when he should have been diagramming sentences and memorizing historical facts.

Had Frank Jackson stayed home tonight? Was he still alive? Mike's wondering had him so preoccupied that he nearly missed seeing the pond. Funny, he didn't remember the fence being on the south side. And apparently that body of water, like the town itself, had shrunk.

Rationally, he knew that part of his reaction, his sudden sense that he'd had it all wrong for all these years, that the town and its people were not as large as he had remembered them, was a product of being disappointed with the difference between a child's view and his view of the same scene as an adult. As his size changed, his perspective had changed, too. That didn't mean he was wrong back then; he was a child. And it also didn't mean he wasn't correct now. If tonight's meeting was any example, Willa's comment about the town—insular, she'd called it—was accurate. He had heard undertones of suspicion in many of the questions he fielded.

The Texas Wind Turbines Coalition had sent him here precisely because he had grown up in Jackson's Pond. The company president had explained that the area was an important target for setting up the first wind farm on the Texas High Plains. The one they developed down near Abilene was running smoothly and now they were ready to expand.

That first one had been developed without much opposition, largely due to the support of influential people in nearby Abilene. The company planners thought that Lubbock, the only nearby urban center, was too far away to create any positive pressure for acceptance in the ideal area for the High Plains operation. They needed the buy-in of landowners whose holdings lay within a ten mile strip along the edge of the Caprock. The dramatic difference in the terrain, the change from the mesa-like High Plains to the Rolling Plains a thousand feet below, created velocity changes in the wind currents that swept across the area. That wind would assure that the giant turbines would turn almost every day of the year. It should out-produce the Abilene operation by thirty percent. People's reactions at the meeting gave the engineer lots to think about.

But the engineer-like thoughts of turbines and wind currents and potential resistance to the project did not account for his twisting the rearview mirror so he could check his reflection and pat down his curly grey hair. And the engineer in him would never have smiled the goofy smile that the sixty-nine year-old fool in the mirror was wearing.

Claire and J. D., the young man Willa introduced as her ranch manager and cattle partner, made a foursome at the kitchen table. Over coffee and cookies, they talked for nearly an hour about the meeting.

J. D. said, "I can't, for the life of me, understand why they wouldn't want the revenue for the city. That piece of land hasn't had anything on it since the tornado in the fifties. Nothing but metal scraps and junk nobody claimed after the wind dropped it there."

"And what difference would it make if the trash is bulldozed up into a big hill over the years and planted in grass? It's not as if it would spoil a view of anything," Claire said.

"Mike, what do you think, as an engineer?" Willa asked.

He took a sip of coffee, noticed his collar felt tight. He reached to loosen it but picked up a cookie instead when he noticed J. D. watching. He said, "I agree with Claire and J. D. The regulations they operate under assure it's a safe method of disposal. Trash has to go somewhere. Jackson's Pond might as well have the revenue."

Willa told them the overwhelmingly negative response to the landfill proposal didn't surprise her. She said, "Anything not local is suspect. You heard Poor Boy Holt ask why the Federal Government wants to put trash in our back yard. He sees a government conspiracy in everything. And probably isn't alone in that."

They stared at their coffee cups for several seconds. J. D. said, "A trash mountain would sure beat having a prison on that piece of property. Every little town in West Texas seems to have a prison these days."

Mike said, "These cookies taste like ones my mother used to make. Chocolate chip but with some secret extra ingredient." Willa smiled, but didn't say anything. J. D. was back to studying him again, he could feel it. "I noticed that Junior Reese and Tuff had plenty of questions for me, but were silent on the subject of trash."

"That's a little odd, too. They both have houses in town," Willa said.

They all considered their empty coffee cups again. Mike never had been comfortable with the way people out here would pause for long periods during conversations, as if pondering what had been said and rehearsing what they'd say next. Interrupting silence was as impolite as interrupting a sentence. He stirred his remaining coffee. Claire pointed to the clock on the cabinet and said she had to get to bed.

They all stood and took their cups and saucer to the sink. J. D. shook his hand and said, "Good to meet you. Good luck with the wind turbine project." J. D.'s handshake and the accompanying smile both seemed brief to Mike; he'd shaken lots of hands in his time.

After Claire followed J. D. to the door to say good night, she returned to tell Willa she'd be gone early in the morning. "Clinical in Lubbock at six forty-five, so I'll be off in the dark."

Willa explained later that Claire was in nursing school and would graduate with a junior college degree next May. She said she expected Claire and J. D. would get married then, maybe sooner, even though her mother would probably disapprove.

Mike watched Willa as she talked. A half smile softened her face. He had noticed it earlier when she talked with Claire and J. D. That smile kept the acute intelligence in her eyes from alarming whoever had her attention—him in this case. She changed the subject from Claire to her husband, Frank, mentioning that he died several years ago.

Mike nodded and told her he knew from experience how hard the first few years were after losing someone you loved. He responded before he thought. He had used the same phrases he often did when talking with widows, the ones who would assume that his wife had died. Divorce, years ago, ended his only marriage. He should correct himself, backtrack, so he could be completely honest with Willa. He wouldn't want to risk her seeing through him and finding he'd misled her.

But he said, "I'm sorry you had to go through that, Willa." He'd get back to full disclosure later.

"Several people I've loved have died. It's a part of life. I never will like it, but I'm better at accepting it now," she said.

She poured more coffee. Mike took a drink and saw the hand that replaced his cup in his saucer shake a little. His hand. He took a deep breath and waited until the feeling passed. He was the one the guys at Texas Turbines called "Slick"—the one they relied on to set it up so they could get their land deals at prices favorable to the company. Good thing they couldn't see him now. He'd better get himself under control.

"Tell me about your life," she said.

He told her about consulting with the wind company, part-time. Then he leaned forward and said, "That keeps me up to date with engineering, but I'm thinking about quitting after this job and spending full-time on my little ranch. It's between Windthorst and Fort Worth. I've started a little natural beef operation…"

Willa's face brightened at the mention of his cattle interest. "That's what J. D. and I are doing. We need to talk more about this. Do you have to be somewhere tomorrow?"

He could feel his goofy grin starting again. He couldn't help it. "No, Jackson's Pond was my last stop on this trip."

She showed him the guest bedroom and pointed to where the towels were in the bathroom. Outside the bedroom, in the hall, she said, "I'm glad you're here. It will be such fun showing you the place and talking cattle with you. Get a good night's sleep. We'll keep you busy tomorrow." Then she kissed him on the cheek and moved quickly down the hall.

He watched her walk away, a young woman's walk, no hint that she'd seen sixty-nine years. The last thing he remembered before falling asleep was that silly smile on his face.

Mike got up before he heard anyone moving around in the house. He reviewed the county maps he'd laid out on the bed. Other documents listed each land owner, his (or her) acreage, and the most recent tax appraisal on their property—all public information supplied by the county tax office. Another printout showed the Federal payments made to each landowner in the past three years from the USDA along with some not-public pieces of information about the status of several landowners' loans with area agricultural lenders. Texas Turbines was connected; they had information that they acquired legally and some that they got in other ways. He didn't want to know how. Texas Turbines always supplied the facts; the rest was up to him.

He'd made a mistake mentioning cattle last night. As soon as Willa and J. D. started showing him theirs, he'd either have to sidestep or admit he only had three hundred twenty acres and thirty cows. Well, truth could sometimes be a powerful weapon. He folded the maps and locked them and the other Texas Turbines materials in his suitcase. Telling at least some of the truth could be useful.

Near seven o'clock, J. D. knocked on the back door and then walked on in. He raised an eyebrow when he saw Mike sitting at the table with Willa, but he only said, "Good morning."

Willa invited J. D. to sit down and have some breakfast and explained that she promised Mike a tour of their cattle operation. J. D. nodded.

They ate in silence for a few minutes. Then Mike said,

"Willa, J. D., before you show me your place, I need to tell you something." They both watched him silently. "I know your operation is about ten times the size of what I've started. I'm just small time and won't ever be any more. I'd feel bad if you thought otherwise."

J. D. stirred his coffee and said, "Well, Mr. Ward, I imagine you know a good deal more than the size of this place. Your company wouldn't send you out without plenty of information." He put his spoon down and looked directly at Mike and said no more.

Mike didn't respond.

Willa gave him a long look and then said, "That doesn't mean we're not eager to show you what we're doing. You're an old friend and I'm happy to see you. Relax. J. D. has read a lot about wind energy. We're hoping you can fill us in on real experience, especially how landowners are affected."

He made a sound that passed for a laugh. "You've taken me by surprise. That doesn't happen too often. But to tell you the truth, I'm a little relieved."

Willa's half smile disappeared. "Relieved? Why?"

He matched her serious gaze. "It's a relief to know I won't have to be careful about how much to let you in on. You're both obviously way ahead of what most people know about wind energy. I'll tell you all I know—good, bad, and ugly." He watched for a clue from either of them. Nothing. He drew a deep breath. Never play poker with these two. He made a show of finishing the last of his meal. "Okay, I'm ready when you are."

They took the pickup, Willa driving with Mike in the other front seat. J. D. rode in the crew seat, turned sideways to accommodate his long legs. Beginning with the north pasture, they proceeded slowly toward the south, discussing land, cattle, breeding practices, and prospects for marketing natural beef as they covered the acres between the boundaries of the ranch.

As they neared the pond, Mike said, "I'm impressed. Really impressed. You have a fine operation here."

"It wouldn't have been nearly as far along if J. D. hadn't agreed to work with me," Willa said.

Mike studied the way the two of them spoke of their plans

and the current status of the ranch. They each listened carefully to the other and, if their opinions differed, discussed ideas as collaborators, not as employer and employee. A team.

Texas Turbines' land men hated dealing with teams. Give them a big solo operator or a widow anytime. And even worse than teams, they disliked making deals with groups, like the consortium arrangement those guys in New Mexico had put together. He wasn't sure he agreed with the "one owner at a time" strategy. But he hadn't tried to explain to the Texas Turbines group that doing some community organizing could be useful in the long run, could save time and maybe money. The Turbines guys were corporate types, all bent on making deals, looking to win. To them the whole business was a game, or a war to be won.

Mike told J. D. and Willa that the Jackson grassland was ideally situated for the proposed project and that the turbines could coexist with the cattle without problems.

Willa glanced across the cab at him. "Do you have research data about cattle and turbines?" she asked.

Mike looked out the window as they passed the pond. "I remember this pond being a lot larger." He wished he'd sat in the back seat of the crew cab. It was easier to think, to stay ahead, when Willa's eyes didn't interfere. "Not with me. I can get it for you."

She showed him that half smile. "You're right. It's less than half the size it was when you left here."

They rode in silence the rest of the way to the house. Willa drove the way farmers and ranchers out here did—on the dirt road's crown, the rise in the middle made by the county's road graders—taking her half out of the middle, making better time, and raising less of the powdery dust that piled up nearer the ditches. Watching in the side-mirror, Mike saw their wake, a plume of beige rising behind them.

"One more cup and I'll hit the road." The three of them sat at the kitchen table. Willa and J. D. asked about Texas Turbines' next steps. He explained that he would write a report on the reaction to his presentation and his recommendation about whether to proceed with seeking contracts with landowners, based on that response. A contracting agent would be sent and talks with individual landowners would begin. "I'll be recommending that they send someone as soon as next week, if possible. This is a good time of year. People have time to talk—no harvest going on." It would all take a while. The best he could tell, there were sixteen parcels of land, some with multiple owners and undivided interests from inheritances. The whole land acquisition process could take months, if the company decided the project was a go. He knew that this project already was Texas Turbines' highest priority and that his report would reinforce their interest.

He didn't mention that his report would also recommend strategy—he wouldn't bother recommending developing a single standard contract. That wouldn't give the corporate types the thrill of the game of making deals. His recommendation would focus on who should be approached first. Word of the first deal, particularly the dollar amount of the annual payment per acre, would inevitably get around and everyone else would try to turn that knowledge to their own advantage. The company relied on his ability to read people and to gather information at least as much as they did on his skill at making the public presentations.

During breakfast, he'd managed to confirm his notion that Junior Reese would want to be able to feel he was the biggest winner, and that Tuff Johnson was more talk than action. That made Tuff a candidate for the first contract. Mike asked J. D. and Willa if they had any suggestions or warnings about any of the others he had talked with at the meeting.

He'd had to laugh when J. D. described Freddy McClendon as a man who carried a list in his pocket everywhere he went, always checking things off, who probably had the same thing for breakfast every day and a bowel movement at the same time every morning. Mike relaxed a little; maybe J. D. was a little less wary of him than he'd seemed earlier.

Willa told a story about the Warrens. Mike had talked to three of them last night. Old man Warren, Louis, originally owned a lot of the acreage on the west side of the project area. Several years back, he started parceling it out to his three boys. Some they owned together, some individually, in a sort of checkerboard arrangement. The old man wanted to be sure there was never any one of them who would get in better shape than either of the others, she said. He fixed it so they'd always be fighting over something. Now Louis spent his time running things as an Elder at the Baptist Church and keeping those boys of his under his thumb even though not a one of them was under fifty years old. She also said that, unlike their old daddy, the Warren boys drank a lot of whiskey. And they tended go to bed at dark.

Mike said, "So the moral of that story is to deal with the Warrens as a group and only in the daytime?"

"Absolutely. And even though his name doesn't show on any deed, Louis will have to be part of making the deal."

"Anyone else I should know more about?" He sat back in his chair, fiddling with a toothpick—like he was just passing the time with this conversation, not developing strategy, estimating probabilities. J. D. and Willa consulted each other with a look and then both shrugged. Willa shook her head.

He didn't decide until he was loading his suitcase into his pickup. "Willa, I'd like for you, and you, too, J. D. to see Texas Turbines' operation down near Abilene. You can get answers about cattle and turbines directly from some of the landowners. You could see how everything is working out down there, say this weekend, maybe?" He held his breath and shoved his suitcase around.

With no apparent hesitation, Willa said, "I could get there by one o'clock on Saturday."

"That's great. I'll buy you dinner out at Buffalo Gap."

"Uh oh," J. D. said.

"What's wrong?"

"If you take her to dinner, she'll expect you to take her dancing, too. I won't be able to come. You'll be on your own. I remember taking her dancing in Austin. She wore three of us guys out."

Mike relaxed. "Well, I guess I'd better start thinking about dance halls, see if I can find one that has a resuscitator." He couldn't believe his good luck.

Back home, on Wednesday morning Mike started the day early, working on his report. He finished it and printed a copy. He leaned back in his desk chair, closed his eyes and put both feet on the desk. A flow chart moved across a screen he saw in his mind—possibilities, results following action. He'd wait. If things went his way this weekend, before long, he might be able to send the turbine folks his resignation letter. He stood, punched the fax machine's speed dial #1, and fed the report into the machine. He had plans to make.

They met late in the afternoon at the hotel in Abilene where Mike had made reservations for each of them. They checked in and agreed to meet in the lobby in twenty minutes. They would go to dinner at the combination restaurant and dance hall near Buffalo Gap.

Mike and Willa returned to their table after dancing. They had ordered a light meal and didn't linger over it. They had danced the past three numbers and without saying so, Mike was glad she was ready for a rest.

"Did I tell you that you're the prettiest rancher I've ever seen?" he asked. That much was true. Willa had changed out of the Levi's and chambray shirt she'd been wearing when they'd visited the wind farm and talked with landowners. She fit right in; she talked with them like one of the guys. Now she sported a long denim skirt, white blouse and turquoise jewelry, and of course, her boots, navy blue with turquoise tops stitched in navy. Her black hair shimmered. The single streak of grey over each temple emphasized her green eyes. Definitely not like one of the guys.

He'd "lightly" romanced several widows since he'd been working for Texas Turbines, all in the line of duty. And another woman who lived near Albany occupied him for a while, mainly because he'd liked the way she looked. Trouble was, she didn't have much land and had less money than he did. And she wasn't really too smart.

But none of those women affected him the way that Willa did. With her around, he felt fourteen again, only required to imagine and hope. Three of those widows ran their ranches on their own and could carry on interesting conversations on a variety of subjects. But not a one of them also painted beautiful watercolors and attracted admiring glances on the dance floor.

"I'll bet you tell all the cowgirls that." Willa said it with a smile. "I think I'll sit out the next one and catch my breath."

Just then a thirtyish cowboy in a black hat approached and asked, "Sir, do you mind if I ask your partner to dance?" And off she went. He watched her and recalled his amazement at how she had painted the two small watercolors of the turbines this afternoon. Her painting made it seem as if the giant machines grew naturally from the landscape and complemented it. She understood. And she could depict it. That was when he knew.

He couldn't help the feeling in his stomach or wondering if his palms were going to start sweating. They reached her hotel room door. "Willa, I haven't had such a good time in years. Can we do this again, soon?"

She looked at him with that half smile. "I'd like that a lot. Thanks for a really fine day and evening."

For once, he didn't stop to think. He pulled her to him and kissed her. She leaned into the kiss and didn't back away. He eventually took a breath. "Willa..."

She held up one finger and smiled. "Wait here. I have to leave early in the morning, but I want you to have one of the paintings I did this afternoon. She closed the door behind her and was back in less than a minute. "Thanks again, Mike. Call me when you want to get together again. Good night."

Never had he been told no so gently and felt so good about it.

By the time Thanksgiving passed, they had met five more times. Once when he passed through Lubbock on a flight to Denver, another time in Abilene for a full Saturday and part of Sunday, twice in Amarillo for dinner and dancing, and three times she had driven to Fort Worth to meet him there. In fact, she always drove to meet him; said she preferred to have her own transportation.

Between those times, they spoke often on the phone. She had a way of encouraging him to talk about himself, something he seldom did with other women. He found himself replaying their conversations in his mind, recalling the first time she spent the night with him, thinking of his delight and surprise at her ability to find humor and beauty in almost everything she saw, and smiling at the way she would get agitated and talk back to the Republican political ads on television

Then, one day, he caught himself reviewing his imaginary flow chart, the one that marked progressive steps in disarming a widow. He told himself he didn't feel that way about Willa; this was different. But if that was true, why did the flow chart reappear? She was perfect for him. And it didn't depend on getting her signature on a contract. He didn't care; well that wasn't true; he did care if she signed. The corporate types who had met with her and J. D. had told him two weeks ago that they were on their list of those likely to sign. That would make her place even more valuable. That would be good for her. And maybe it would be good for him. "You are one calculating bastard, Mike Ward," he said to his reflection as he shaved.

Anxiety. That was probably what was making him imagine flow charts. They were his way of making sense of disorder. And his mind had been a model of disorder lately. But this weekend, he had to decide. Hell, he knew he'd already decided, if he was the least bit truthful with himself. He would ask her to marry him. The only question was when. He did need to choose the best possible time. He had to be sure just how to ask her so that if she said no, he could still have a chance; so that he wouldn't be told no and goodbye, but just no, not now. He turned sideways to check that his abdomen was still relatively flat. Then he checked his smile and patted down his wiry hair.

He'd offered to pick her up at the airport if she would fly in to DFW, but she had, again, said that she preferred having her own transportation. Fort Worth suited both of them better than Dallas. This weekend they planned to visit the Amon Carter Museum, have dinner downtown, and then decide the rest as the evening progressed. He'd told her to meet him for lunch at Joe T. Garcia's, the Mexican restaurant they both enjoyed, down near the Stockyard district.

He had a surprise planned for tomorrow. In one of their many long talks, she had told him that she really loved seeing stage productions, especially musicals. Touring companies were adequate, she'd said, and she usually saw a couple of those each year in Lubbock or Amarillo. He planned to surprise her with plane reservations to New York City for the two of them and tickets to a Sunday performance of *Chicago* on Broadway. How could she say no? He planned to tell her over an early breakfast tomorrow morning—room service, another surprise.

She walked into Joe T's right on time at one o'clock. After they ate, he asked her to follow him downtown to the Worthington where he'd already checked in, separate rooms, the way she preferred, even if she stayed most of the night with him. She rested alone for an hour and then they visited the museum. He spent more time watching her enjoy the art than he did paying attention to the paintings. They ate dinner that night at Del Frisco's. They had excellent steak and talked about the Jackson Ranch's recent success at the bull sale they hosted, their first.

He couldn't have been happier. The flow chart never entered his thoughts when Willa was in his arms in his hotel room that night. What could be wrong with loving a woman who also happened to be beautiful and financially secure? Sometime in the night, his final step became clear to him—the timing. He would propose just after the theater, before they flew back from New York.

The waiter set up the room service breakfast, complete with the mimosas he'd ordered as the crowning touch. They were both ate quietly, as they usually did. He liked that she didn't chatter like some women, first thing in the morning. She finished eating before him and sat back, holding her glass up to the light. The mimosa cast a glow around her face. Beautiful, he thought.

He knew he should get to the point quickly this morning. She'd packed her bag last night, and said she had to get started back toward home before noon.

"Mike, I need to tell you something."

"Me, too. You go first."

She looked away, then returned her full focus to him. "I haven't been entirely honest with you." She softened the harshness of the words with a gentle smile. "We've been, at least I have been, having such a good time these past few weeks that I've kept something from you. Now, it's time I told you."

"Willa…"

She didn't give him time to finish. "You need to know that nothing more can come of us than friendship." She spoke in a low, clear tone. She didn't avoid his eyes. "Spending as much time as we have together may have implied something more to you than could ever be. I'm sure it has."

"At least let me tell you…" He couldn't recall a contingency plan; he didn't have one.

She raised an eyebrow and paused. He didn't speak.

"Tell me what?"

"Let's not decide anything right now. Please." A flash of himself in a high school football game, scrambling to find an open receiver, being sacked, occupied him. Finally he said and knew it was lame when he said it, "We should talk."

She stood, holding her glass. She looked through it again, into the morning light. "That wouldn't be fair to you. There are lots of widows with land just waiting for a man like you." She looked directly at him in a way that made him feel transparent. "I learned a long time ago it's best to leave a party while it's still fun. So it's time now for me to go," she said.

Before he could protest, she took one final sip of the mimosa, then moved quickly away from the table, picked up her bag, and walked to the door.

"But, Willa…"

She raised one finger. "You don't have to worry. We will sign the contract. And I've had a wonderful time. Thank you."

Then she was gone.

FLOYD COUNTY REGISTER
Thursday December 23, 2004
Jackson Receives Art Award

Willa Jackson, Floyd County artist and rancher, has received the Texas Watercolor Society's annual Best of Show Award for 2004.

President of the Society, Donald Thomas, in a press release dated December 20, stated, "Ms. Jackson placed in the top five each of the past two years. This year, her painting was awarded first place unanimously. The judges commented particularly on her bold use of color and unique composition.

"Her vision translates to use of strong hues and to combinations of subject matter that manage to be both familiar and realistic and yet somehow surreal. Perspective is also unique; in the painting that received the award, the viewer has a simultaneous sense of distance and immediacy."

The winning painting, entitled "Raven Tours West Texas," will be featured in an exhibit shown in museums in five Texas cities this year. The first exhibition will be at the Amon Carter Museum in Fort Worth.

A gala reception for Watercolor Society members and guests of the society will celebrate the opening at 7 p.m. January 21, 2005. A public reception to honor Ms. Jackson will coincide with the museum opening at 10 a.m. Saturday January 22.

At Sea

Willa's advance copy of the press release from the Texas Watercolor Society arrived on December 19 along with a congratulatory letter announcing that her entry had won Best Of Show. Details would follow regarding arrangements for the reception in Fort Worth January 21, 2005. If she didn't show it to Melanie before something appeared in the local paper, her daughter would pout, just as she had as a child. After the predictable upset over Willa's plan to go on a cruise during the holidays and their subsequent truce, they had enjoyed an evening last week putting up the Christmas tree at Melanie's house. Willa hoped to maintain peace with her, at least until after the holidays and her cruise.

So here she was at Melanie's door at six in the evening with two surprises—fresh homemade tamales and the press release. She spent more time these days thinking about keeping Melanie happy than she would like to.

She didn't wait. As soon as she was in the door, Willa said, "I have two surprises." Before Melanie could react, Willa showed her the press release and the letter.

Melanie said, "Mother, I had no idea. I knew you'd been painting a lot the past few years, but . . . Congratulations." She smiled briefly. The frown that lowered her brows moments later made Willa wonder just what she actually thought.

"Thanks. I'm surprised too. Chris was certain I would win. He's pushed me to enter my work in competition. He and Arthur, the gallery owner in Austin."

"You have paintings in a gallery?"

"Chris arranged it years ago, and I agreed rather than

disappoint him," Willa said. She watched Melanie's frown return. She had stopped trying to get Melanie to accept Chris' career as a photographer and artist and his life with his partner Andrew. Rational discussion had no effect. Trying to convince Melanie she was wrong would be no different than the attempts Melanie had made to turn Chris into someone he was not.

"I'd love for you to attend the exhibit opening with me, if you can, " Willa said.

"I doubt if I can. The end of January is very busy at work. I'm sure you'll have plenty of friends and admirers there."

Willa took a deep breath and resisted the urge to tell Melanie if she would attend, she would introduce her to Robert Stanley. But after the scene Melanie created about Mike Ward a few years back, Willa had kept her friendships with men to herself. Melanie might want to pretend to be an aging spinster, living with her cat, singing in the church choir, and hovering over her grandchildren. But Willa enjoyed, actually preferred, the company of men.

Mike had been a mistake, a charming mistake, full of fun, and too quick with a glib lie. One too many times, he evaded a question about his dead wife. Willa used the Internet to search public records. That search turned up two DWIs, an arrest for a domestic disturbance, a bankruptcy, and a divorce. Maybe there were satisfactory explanations for all of those—youth, treatment for alcohol abuse, a deranged wife, investments gone wrong. Regardless, he'd done the one thing that couldn't be explained away, even if she had given him a chance to. He began making plans. She recognized the signs.

Not long after Willa stopped seeing Mike, Melanie asked, "What happened to your old boyfriend from grade school, the engineer? He hasn't been around lately,"

Willa answered truthfully. She told her that she stopped seeing Mike because he was getting too serious and because she wasn't certain she could trust him. Melanie nodded and encouraged her to continue. Willa did; sharing more than the barest facts had been her mistake. When she mentioned, in her recollection of the better parts of her time with Mike, something about sex, Melanie began lecturing her as if she were a willful adolescent. Willa tolerated a few minutes of cross-examination and even enjoyed seeing Melanie's expression when she described a beautiful royal blue gown and peignoir she bought for one of their weekends.

That was when Melanie raised her voice. "How do you know he didn't have HIV or some other sexually transmitted disease? Did you both get tested? Never mind. I'm sure you didn't even think of that."

Her voice low and controlled, Willa said, "You might be very surprised at the things I think about. Unfortunately for you, you'll never know what they are because you treat me like a child you've been assigned to manage, not like an adult."

After that episode, Willa and Melanie had been civil, even cordial, to one another. Their conversations always focused on superficial, safe topics. They chatted on the phone occasionally; Willa usually initiated the calls. They were brief, like quick hands of poker played by strangers—nothing much ever won or lost. Willa made certain that Melanie knew her itinerary when she traveled; Melanie didn't ask for any details.

And Willa never asked about the trips Melanie took to meet her ex-husband Ray in places where they wouldn't be recognized. Melanie probably thought her secret was safe. But Chris had mentioned to Willa a few years ago that his dad told him one evening, over too many drinks, about their odd arrangement and his hope that one day they might remarry. Willa did wonder if Melanie had made Ray show a clean bill of health before she took up with him.

Well, Melanie was nothing if not consistent. "I have one other surprise," Willa said. "I brought supper—fresh homemade tamales. Shall we eat?" Melanie seldom refused Mexican food.

As they ate, Melanie asked a few polite questions about the award. Willa suspected she would want to be able to answer questions from people at work when news appeared in the paper. She even asked when she would be able to see the winning painting. By the time the tamales had all been shucked and consumed, they were discussing plans for Christmas dinner.

When Willa left for the ranch, Melanie was smiling, not pouting. Christmas Eve and Christmas dinner at Melanie's went according to plan, just as anyone who knew Melanie would have expected. Willa had helped with cooking and had thoroughly enjoyed watching the children's antics when they opened their presents. But, she had been eager to leave for this trip. Now, she was in the audience aboard ship and the first art lecture was about to begin.

The lecturer stood before a group of about eighty people. He clicked the remote control to his computer's Power Point projector and the first slide appeared. The title of the lecture series, "Art at Sea" flashed on the screen—everything worked. Willa relaxed; she'd been concerned on his behalf. He'd told her he wasn't comfortable with the cruise line's equipment. The instructions were written in Swedish.

"I'm Robert Stanley, Professor of Art at the University of Texas at Austin. I am pleased to see so many attending the first of seven lectures on History and Trends in Watercolors, our subject for the Art at Sea series on this cruise."

Willa noticed with a bit of surprise that about a third of the chairs were occupied by males, many of them in their thirties or forties. She thought the cruise and the lectures would be filled by Elderhostel travelers and expected mostly females. Dance hosts, another attraction offered by the cruise company probably accounted for some of the women she had seen at departure. Several looked about her age—late sixties and early seventies—probably widows spending the money their husbands were no longer around to enjoy.

The dance after tonight's first dinner at sea should be interesting. She imagined feisty blue-haired, diamond bedecked ladies elbowing one another for position to attract the dance hosts. Melanie could have competed well. Too bad her too-busy daughter had refused to come along. On the other hand, if she had been there, Willa would have had to explain her own dance card's being filled with one name, Robert Stanley. Just as well. She returned her attention to his opening remarks.

"Before I begin with some of the historical aspects of watercolor…" He aimed the remote at the computer. Willa straightened in her chair. She had never seen her own work projected to ten feet by twelve. But there it was. She heard words from the audience—"Beautiful." "So bold." "Can't be watercolor."

"I promised that in this course we would look not only at history but also at trends. I predict this artist's work will set a trend. The Texas Watercolor Society agrees. They chose this painting as Best of Show for 2004, just announced last week. And here's a treat. The artist, Willa Jackson, is with us. Willa, please stand."

She should have known he would have received the press release about the award. But where did he get the slide? Chris must have been the source. Her grandson; her greatest fan. She quickly sat after acknowledging the audience's applause, surprised by the flutter in her stomach. Robert resumed his lecture and she tried to concentrate on its content.

Robert's slides, his deep voice with its Irish lilt, and his store of interesting facts kept the audience's attention for the entire hour. Enthusiastic applause filled the room. Several members of the audience paused to talk with him. An almost equal number approached Willa, offering congratulations.

She and Robert left the room together. "We don't have to be cautious here. No one cares who we spend our time with, as long as the lectures are well received," he said. "Ah, Willa darlin', I'm so glad you decided to go to sea with me."

"You are such an Irishman. Forty years since you left the Emerald Isle and you still have that brogue." She couldn't help laughing. That's why she had come; he made her laugh, and he knew how to let her be.

"Now you must admit, it plays well with most crowds," he said with a wink.

Robert was always fun to be with. Aside from that, she had another reason for agreeing to take this trip. She wanted his advice. And she wanted his full attention when she asked for it. Telephone wouldn't do.

Willa took longer than usual preparing for the fourth night at sea. Having her own cabin gave her the luxury of being alone as she dressed. She thought about how Frank would have enjoyed seeing her in party finery. He had often said that her working with him on the ranch deprived the world of seeing the most beautiful woman in Texas.

The skirt of the black organza dress she'd designed and had made by a woman in Lubbock fell to just above her ankles, a good length for dancing. Her satin camisole bodice was covered by a sheer black organza shirtwaist with long, cuff-buttoned sleeves and a satin portrait collar. The buttons of the bodice and cuffs were covered in the same satin and a narrow satin belt emphasized her still-slim waist. The two wide streaks of white in her black hair, at her temples, made her French twist dramatic rather than severe. A single emerald pendant and matching earrings highlighted her green eyes. She smiled as she polished away a fingerprint from the pendant, remembering Frank's giving the modest pieces to her on their first wedding anniversary—long before they could afford the extravagance.

Robert seemed to have been born to wear a tuxedo. Trim and tall, he looked like every woman's dream of the suave older man who would whisk her away from her kitchen and into a world of carefree glamour, never to wash another dirty skillet. He whistled when she opened her cabin door. "Madam, you are a vision. I'll be the envy of all the men this evening." The slight brogue was back.

"A dashing man like you could turn a girl's head." She stood back and gave him another long look. "Seriously, thank you for encouraging me to come. I'm having a wonderful time."

"There won't be a party like this in Jackson's Pond tonight?"

The ballroom sparkled with New Year's Eve decorations— silver garland draped the walls; tiny icicle-shaped lights twinkled from sconces at each corner; and huge ice sculptures graced every serving table. In three hours, the glittering ball hanging from the ceiling in the center of the room would drop to announce the arrival of 2005.

Just as they entered the ballroom, the musicians, as if on cue, began the opening notes of "I Could Have Danced All Night."

Robert raised his eyebrows at her, as if he might have arranged the entrance, and swept her onto the floor. He was the kind of dance partner she always hoped for and seldom found. As soon as the music stopped, couples who had been watching from tables around the dance floor applauded. "They remember Arthur and Kathryn Murray, I guess," Robert said as he twirled her into a slight curtsy and bowed in her direction. "When we retire we could take this up professionally, if you're willing."

The next song began and one of the dance hosts cut in. Robert nodded and said, "I'll do my job now and dance with the unattached females." He kissed her hand and said, "Save me the midnight dance, my dear."

Robert's cabin, part of the payment for his lectures, was twice the size of Willa's next door. They were having breakfast together, the only time they could talk privately. Robert's "professional Irishman" charm made him popular with all the passengers, not only the lecture attendees. Willa had been busy, also. Several people sought her out to ask questions about her work and wanting to know if she would give painting demonstrations.

"Don't give your art away, Willa. The cruise line pays me rather well to do my lectures. If they want you to do demonstrations and offer lessons, they should pay you also. You have become a commodity, so get used to it."

"I feel like an impostor, like an amateur who had a stroke of good luck, not a real artist who worked hard to merit some attention."

Robert cocked his head and narrowed his eyes as if assessing her. "An impostor, huh? Well, we're all pretending to be something every day, aren't we? You have talent. As long as you believe that and continue demonstrating it in your work, you aren't a fake."

"But I really don't mind answering questions, and I wouldn't mind people watching me paint. And I don't need the money."

"It doesn't matter. In the business of art, part of what establishes reputation is what people pay for your work." She frowned. He went on to explain that she could set up a charitable corporation and give the money away if she didn't have a use for it. "Making your name as an artist is based on your work. But that's not all there is to it. It's tied to people wanting to collect your work; to how much it sells for; to which prizes you win. And maybe just a little bit to creating a legend about you."

"A legend? I won't lie about myself, if that's what you mean." She put her fork down. She looked steadily at him and then her frown changed slowly to a smile. "Maybe I could develop an Irish accent."

He laughed. "Woman, ye're such a devil," he said—all Irish now. "No, you can't have my Irish accent; I came by that legitimately. We'd build your legend on legitimate things about you. Your ranching background, your studying dancing, and your age." He pushed his plate away. He nodded, as if answering a question he'd asked himself. He told her that if she would agree, he would love to manage her, develop her brand. But only if she would be his dancing partner exclusively for two years.

"You should find a younger partner, Robert. I'm seventy-four."

"That's perfect. I'm seventy. Women outlive men, so we'll fade out about the same time, in twenty years or so. Shall we put that agreement on paper?"

"Robert, you are so full of bull. I do need you to be serious, now. I need your advice."

"I am serious, about managing your brand. I would enjoy making your success my project. Promise to think about it." He waited until she nodded. "Okay, now, what advice do you need?"

"First, I need to explain some background information. You'll see later how it's related. Be patient. This has been on my mind for months."

The background information took them through two cups of coffee. Robert listened without comment as she described the Texas Wind Turbines Coalition project that was now in operation near Jackson's Pond. After months of negotiation, the project's lease men finally assembled all the agreements required to site the three hundred towers their wind farm required. Robert smiled as she described Junior Reese, the last hold out. His land, just north of the Jackson place sat in the middle of the project. He bargained and dickered and agreed and backed out. "He was like a virgin," she said, "eager to be taken but holding out for the best proposition."

She and J. D. did a lot of homework to be sure research showed that livestock and wildlife weren't harmed by the presence of the towers. And then she waited for them to approach her. "I wasn't sure they even would, because I had a 'falling out,' shall we say, with their engineering consultant. But sure enough they did."

She told him about her contract with J. D., her partner, who had managed her ranch for the past nine years and who married her granddaughter five years ago. She explained his compensation—a base salary; free use of the tenant house that she had grown up in, the one she and Frank lived in the first three years after they were married; plus an annual bonus of a percentage of the net profit from operations. The percentage increased annually from the original twenty percent to next year when he would receive seventy percent. She owned the land and the big house and met her personal expenses from investment earnings. "You'd be surprised how little I require," she said.

When she and J. D. were satisfied that the turbines would not impede their cattle breeding operation, J. D. agreed that there was no reason not to sign the agreement. She deposited the second lease payment just before she left for this cruise, the sum of $192,000—twenty-four towers, $8000 per tower.

She hesitated after she mentioned the figures and paused before continuing. Discussing financial affairs with others, except for J. D., and then only related to ranch operations, was something she didn't usually do. Remaining independent required competently handling your own money.

Robert sat back from the table. "I had no idea that besides being a fine artist, you are a tough, wealthy business woman and rancher. I'm impressed. What could I possibly offer you any advice about? I only know art and the business of art."

"You also know Chris, knew him as a student. This is partly about him. He's twenty-nine. For the past ten years, he's painted in any free time he has, but has always had a job to support himself. I think he's a good artist. What's your opinion of his potential?"

Without hesitating he said, "His potential lies in his work as an oil painter. He could be great."

"What would it take?"

"More time devoted to his painting, primarily."

"Do you think he has any business sense?"

"I don't know. He's smart and he could learn if he wanted to. What kind of business?"

"Operating a studio gallery. If we were thinking of opening a studio gallery, one that would sell my work and his and selected others, what location would be best? I'm thinking somewhere southwest."

"Anywhere in particular in the southwest?"

"Santa Fe and Taos are the two places that came to my mind."

"I would choose Taos over Santa Fe." He explained the differences he saw in the art market in the two cities and the lower prices of real estate in Taos as important factors. "I'm intrigued by your questions. When will you tell me what you plan?"

"First, one other question. Would you teach Chris about the business of art, if he asked you?"

"For a fee."

"Certainly, that goes without saying. How much?"

His eyes twinkled. Now he was a leprechaun, a tall one. "The price is that you agree to my earlier idea. I create Willa Jackson as a brand. Two years. And you save every dance for me."

She had never been a debutante. But this must be how a debutante feels at her "coming out"—as if her father had paid every man in the room to be certain his daughter never sat out a dance. The orchestra's breaks were the only opportunities she had to catch her breath on their final night at sea. Earlier, during dinner at the Captain's table, the ship's master presented her with a letter from the president of the cruise line proposing that she lecture on three winter cruises next year. A contract to that effect was included. She promised the Captain she would contact the president within two weeks. To Robert she whispered, "I believe I see your fine hand at work already." His attempt at appearing innocent only made him look like a tall leprechaun who had been wounded.

Later that evening they sat in deck chairs, drinking coffee and brandy. Tomorrow morning they would dock in Galveston. "This has been the best time I've had in years. Thank you for inviting me."

"Be assured it was my pleasure," Robert said. The sea was calm and flat. The moon hovered above the horizon painting a silvery path directly toward them. "Have you thought any more about our earlier discussion?"

"About your making me a name in the art world?"

"Yes, the entire package—I teach Chris the business of operating a gallery; I manage your rise to stardom; you dance only with me; we'll have great fun."

Looking across the sea to the far horizon, she felt completely at ease, the same as she felt gazing across wide stretches of High Plains grassland—a serene sense that timeless things are beyond any attempt at human control. A tiny smile crossed her lips as she thought how foolish she was to hope she could control anything.

She took Robert's hand. "I need to think about a lot of things. I don't want to interfere in Chris' life, to try to make him be anything he doesn't want to be. But if there's a way that the money I have can help him be the artist he can be, then I want to make that possible. And about your taking me as a project, I need to think about that, too. I don't want anything to spoil our friendship. You are dear to me."

He didn't respond. The sea and the moon held his view. Then, almost in a whisper, without looking her way, he said, "Willa, nothing could ever spoil our friendship."

They parted at the airport in Houston, he for Austin and she for Lubbock. Two days after she returned to the ranch, she and Robert discussed, in a long phone conversation, the reservations she had about commercializing her art. Somehow any plan to make her a name in even a small part of the art world seemed to detract from the way she felt about making art. She painted more from a need for expression than from a desire to be noticed. He corrected her about commercializing her art. It wouldn't be mass production, he told her—no coffee mugs, no cheap posters of her work, no pressure to remain static in her style or her subjects. He countered her concern about her process as an artist by saying that there are many good artists and a few excellent ones, and that the ones who leave a legacy are those whose work becomes known in the art world. "Your work is beautiful, makes a statement. It should be seen. The key to that today is management, darlin' girl, crass as it sounds," he said. "You have a unique perspective to share. It should be seen—by many, not only by a few."

"I'm not willing to take much time away from painting to spend on publicity," she said.

"That will be my job; to manage your art so that you have time to dedicate to making art."

Two weeks later, she was in his office in Austin signing a letter of agreement that made her laugh. "This part about the dance partner can't be legal, can it?" she asked. Then more seriously she said, "I'm appending a statement that all of this is all contingent on Chris' agreeing to my offer." Robert initialed the document below her handwritten addition. She dismissed the thought that intruded as she placed her copy of the agreement in her purse, the thought that Melanie would disapprove.

Chris had agreed earlier in the week to pick her up after her meeting with Robert. She found him sitting in the hallway as she left Robert's office. They hugged and then she stepped back to get a better look at him. His bloodshot eyes, day's growth of beard, and wrinkled shirt made her frown. "What's wrong? Are you sick?"

He shook his head. "I'm not sick. I'll explain when we get to the house."

She didn't press. One thing that never pays is anticipating the worst. So, they made the short trip to the house in silence except for the "Goddamn!" he exploded with at a driver who suddenly switched lanes from the right, cut in front of him, and then turned left without a signal. "Stupid asshole." Nearly to the house, he turned to her and said, "Sorry, Gran. I'm not usually so crude. A little on edge today."

He unlocked the front door and called out, "Andrew?" The question echoed and died.

"He's gone." Chris sighed and shook his head sadly. He pointed to the sofa.

She sat, not uttering any of the questions she wanted to ask. The house smelled like stale pizza and beer.

"He's been gone two days." Chris fell back against the sofa and sighed. He closed his eyes, then opened them and stared toward the ceiling. "It was about phone calls. From a woman I work with. A feature writer. She and I worked on a project last month. Big piece for her. I did a photo spread to go with it. Took a couple of weeks, some extra hours. I think she thought she might be able to get something going with me. I told her it wasn't going to happen. And I told her why. She laughed and said there was no such thing as a permanent no."

He stopped and stared at his hands, then shook his head and exhaled, a long tired sound. "Then she started calling here and asking for me. I talked to her a couple of times, trying to be polite and professional. She always had some excuse for calling. I started avoiding her at work. She's about our age and a good writer, but…Well, I hadn't said much of anything about any of it to Andrew. Now I know I should have. Then the other night she called while I was out. Talked to Andrew. Fed him some bullshit story about her and me and…" He stopped talking and shook his head. "Stupid."

"Don't answer me if you don't want to, but had you two been having trouble before this?"

"Not between us, exactly. I've been restless. Can't paint because I get called out at all hours for work. He could tell I was getting fed up. And he's been filling in as a nurse manager at the hospital and hates it. Both of us on edge, I guess."

"Will he come back?" Willa asked.

"His clothes are still here." Chris smiled a tired sad smile. "I'm sorry to spill all this on you."

"What's a granny for? Come in the kitchen. I'll make us some coffee. Maybe decaf. You look like you could use some sleep."

"Let's don't talk about me any more. You had something important, you said."

"I do, and it is about you. Probably not the best time, though," she said.

He made a show of standing up extra straight, throwing back his shoulders, then flexing his biceps. "Nope, tell me now. I can handle it."

His tough guy imitation worked on her the way it always had; she laughed and hugged him. "Okay, let's get that coffee and we'll talk, strong man."

They sat at the kitchen bar. She poured two cups of decaf. Then she began by explaining her offer as clearly as she could. For some reason, she felt like a first-time public speaker, worried that the audience might boo or heckle. Maybe this was a bad idea. Chris had his own life, a grown man's life. And now a grown man with trouble at home. She hesitated, searched his face and saw puzzled amazement, and then continued.

She told him that if he agreed to certain conditions, he would receive a portion of his inheritance now, $200,000, to set up a studio gallery in Taos. Further, he would receive additional installments of that inheritance for the next eighteen years, a minimum of $50,000 each year. Continuing funds would be contingent on only one thing, his continuing to work at art—painting and managing the gallery—exclusively, for the first ten years.

During the time that he operated the gallery, his would be the only one representing her art. And he would commit to learning all he could from Robert Stanley about the business of art. She didn't mention the arrangement with Robert to manage her "brand." She still had a little trouble thinking of a brand as anything other than an owner's mark on a steer's left hip.

There, she'd done it. She had never dared dream for herself the freedom she was offering him. Maybe he wouldn't want it. "Don't be concerned that I'll be hurt if you don't accept. I make the offer because I want you to have choices. I don't ever want to make your choices for you." She waited. He closed his eyes again and said nothing. "Do you have any questions? Did I explain clearly?"

"You did. It's perfectly clear to me. It's as if you had been eavesdropping on my dreams. I don't know what to say. I have to ask, though, is it fair to Claire?"

If he hadn't asked, Willa would have been disappointed. She assured him that Claire would receive the equivalent. She reminded him about the wind project and explained it was the source of the money she was offering him.

"Gran, you don't know what it means to me that you would even think of offering me this opportunity. How will I ever thank you?"

"Honey, you have already done enough by being just who you are. Think of this as me sharing my good fortune with you, while I can see you enjoy it."

"Do you think Robert would actually agree to teach me the business side of art?"

"I already asked him. He believes in your talent and your brains." She looked at her grandson and remembered him at twelve, listening to his grandfather's every word, watching her paint, back when his life had been simpler. "Think about this. Take your time. You don't have to decide right away. Your choice can affect the rest of your life."

She insisted on taking a cab to the airport. Chris needed rest. She spent the flight to Lubbock worrying that her offer would complicate his life further, not make it better, as she'd hoped. By the time she got back to the ranch, she had convinced herself that Chris could manage his own life. All she had done was open the way to wider possibilities. He would make his own choice.

Nine days later—she'd marked them on the calendar since she returned to Jackson's Pond—Willa opened a letter that arrived in the morning mail. Chris' address, but not his handwriting. Andrew's signature. Graceful cursive of the sort no longer taught in schools delivered a simple message—he was writing to apologize for being away when she came to Austin. He and Chris agreed they had failed as partners by not discussing problems as they arose. (He used the word arose, a formal, old-fashioned word.) "We are stronger now as a couple than ever before," he wrote. "I hope Chris will agree to your generous offer of freedom. I want you to know I will support whatever he decides." Below his signature was a p.s.—"We repaired the chair and the telephone."

That same afternoon around five-thirty, Chris called. "Gran, Andrew and I are going to Taos this weekend, taking Monday and Tuesday off, too. Collecting information on gallery locations, rental housing, all that. We'll know more when we get back. And I talked to Robert Stanley. He's ready to start teaching me Art Business 101 anytime I'm ready. Gotta go now. Oh, one other thing—we're looking only at houses with a casita in the back." He sounded excited, talking fast.

"Why is that? Wouldn't you want your studio at the gallery?"

"Not for a studio. For you. If we go, we want you with us. In your own place, but with us."

She said, "Your mother…" She hadn't told Melanie anything about her plan to help Chris. Didn't intend to immediately. But moving to Taos would require explanations. "I'll have to think hard about that, Chris. I'm accustomed to having lots of time to myself. And there's your beautiful house in Austin to think about. The two of you put a lot of yourselves into it and you might not be ready to leave it. Don't rush into deciding. I don't want you to regret any choice you make."

"I'll take my time. But this is what I've dreamed about." She could hear the urgency in his words. "And Andrew checked into jobs in Taos. Had a phone interview. He could start tomorrow—relocation bonus, better hours, good pay. Nurses with experience like his are in demand. You'd better start packing."

She couldn't help but laugh. "We'll see. You just go on and do what you need to do to be certain."

Sleep that night was hard to come by; images of mountains and of red chile ristras hanging outside a casita door floated by. Rehearsals of bits of explanation for leaving; Melanie, so upset that her tightly contained French twist sprang free from its clip; a gallery holding walls and panels full of watercolors, her paintings from the years before Frank died, the ones only he had seen; and the pond, shrinking in the distance, all competed for attention. Each time she woke, she smiled into the dark, thankful for those dreams.

Sunday night Chris called again, this time from Taos. And again, in his excitement, he spoke as if he were being chased. They had found a gallery space on Bent Street that fit the budget and would be perfect, a house for lease within walking distance, with a casita that also would be perfect. If she hadn't changed her mind, then could she do whatever was necessary, because in two weeks, after they gave notice at their jobs, he and Andrew would leave for Taos and begin spending money to set up the gallery and house immediately. "And, Gran, you need to come to Taos and look at the casita in a month, no later, and plan to be living here full time by summer. I mean that. Don't disappoint your favorite grandson."

"I wouldn't dream of disappointing you. I'll arrange things at the bank on Monday and let you know the details. We'll set a date for me to visit after you get moved in. You better go now and sit down. The altitude seems to be affecting you. Ask the nurse to check your pulse."

Willa's pleasure and amusement with Chris' obvious joy soon gave way to a question. How to deal with Melanie.

Willa had given Melanie the home territory advantage. No amount of her daughter's dramatic storming around would change her plan, so she didn't mind encountering Melanie in her own home. "There are some things I need to let you know, Melanie. Although only a small part of this affects you directly, it's only right that you should hear it directly from me." She saw Melanie stiffen in her executive model desk chair. Willa leaned back and relaxed as much as possible against the straight back of the chair opposite the desk.

"What now? Another cruise?" Melanie punched some keys on her computer and the screen's glow darkened. She faced Willa again.

"No, but it's something else exciting. I've decided to give Chris and Claire their inheritances early. I've arranged the part that will come to them now and have included the rest in a change to my will. I haven't told Claire yet, but I have talked with Chris. I'm sure she will be as surprised as he was."

"Is there some reason you didn't discuss this with me before you made decisions?"

Willa had expected that. "Since I made up my mind quite a long time ago, it was just a matter of when. And since you have known for years that your grandmother's trust included most of what you would have received from your father and me, had it come to us, what I leave to the children doesn't affect you directly. And not least of all, you have plenty on your mind, with the responsibility of your job. Honestly, I don't know how you do it all."

Melanie gave her a look Willa couldn't read.

"Do you want me to tell you the details or only the overview? I know you probably brought work to do this weekend, and I don't want to take too much time."

"I have time. Tell me what you've planned." Melanie's raised eyebrow alerted Willa. This wasn't going to be easy.

Willa told her that Claire and Chris would receive two gifts, one this year and one next. Chris would receive one hundred thousand dollars each time and Claire would receive half that sum in cash plus the deed to one hundred twenty-five acres of the ranch each of the two years. Subsequently, each would receive a minimum of $50,000 per year for the life of the wind turbine contracts.

Melanie frowned and squinted over the half-glasses she'd begun wearing recently. "Why now? You know, don't you, that this will cause trouble for J. D. and Claire. Men can't stand it. Their wives having independent money."

"What century is this? I know no such thing. I trust Claire to handle her own marriage in her own way. I want to give her this now, when I can see her enjoy it rather than after I die."

"And what do you expect Chris will do with his? I suppose he'll quit work and paint or something like that."

"He intends to do exactly that. He'll open a studio gallery in Taos."

Melanie kept quiet, but Willa could see she was far from finished. She wondered how long it would be before the threats began.

"There are two other things. First, even though you probably hadn't expected it, you will receive annual payments from the turbine leases in the same amount as each of them, beginning next year."

Melanie's expression changed from disapproving to puzzled. "Why would you do that?"

"Why wouldn't I? You're my only child; I want you to benefit from the wind project, too. The final thing I want you to know is that I plan to move from the ranch—

Before Willa could finish, Melanie said, "I'm so glad you finally decided. It will be an adjustment at first, but you'll be so much safer and I will feel better…"

Willa didn't hesitate to interrupt Melanie's interruption. She raised her right index finger and Melanie stopped in mid-sentence. "Wait. I'm not moving into Jackson's Pond or to one of those retirement places in Lubbock. I'm moving to Taos."

She only had to wait a second for Melanie's reaction. Her daughter's range and speed always amazed her—she could go from delight to distress in an instant. Willa predicted icy anger would soon follow.

"No. You absolutely cannot move to Taos. It's too far; it's not safe; you don't know anyone there." Melanie had, as yet, avoided mentioning age. Willa knew she'd get to it soon.

"Chris will be there. It's as safe as any other town. Lots smaller than Lubbock."

"Mother, I warn you. I'll fight you on this."

Willa leaned forward and said very quietly, "I wouldn't make threats if I were you."

"I would hate to do it, but I could have you declared incompetent. You're seventy-four years old, giving away large sums of money and land, and talking about moving to a strange town. Clearly, you're losing your faculties. Forget Taos, Mother or I swear I'll do it."

"Court proceedings are public, can be so messy, and they're expensive. But that's your choice, Melanie. And moving to Taos is mine." Willa smiled and made a show of checking her watch. "I must go. I'm having dinner in Lubbock, staying in touch with some Democratic Party friends."

She stood to leave. Melanie's frown, so unfortunate, Willa thought, spoiled her otherwise tightly composed appearance. Melanie didn't move from her executive chair. Willa let herself out.

FLOYD COUNTY TRIBUNE
Thursday, July 14, 2005
Editorial

Joshua Barnes, age 14, of Jackson's Pond, is a young man with a lot on his mind. His essay, "Effects in Texas of the Continuing Decline in the Ogallala Aquifer." won the South Plains Water Conservation District's essay contest this year. (See essay page 3.)

One of the most alarming points in Joshua's essay is that in many areas of the aquifer, farms now producing cotton and corn will no longer have water for large scale irrigation, as is common on the South Plains.

The situation is similar across many portions of the Ogallala's entire range from South Dakota through the Texas High Plains. In the Texas portion of the Ogallala, only a small part south of Lubbock has not had the severe decline, due to some geological factors.

Although low tillage farming may reduce water demand some, he says, it is likely that crops with lower water requirements will eventually be the only ones that can be produced in the area or perhaps the land will no longer be used for farming. Change in agricultural production can dramatically change the economy and may prompt the demise of many small towns.

Small towns and family farms are important links to the region's history and its present culture. It will be Joshua's generation's task to deal with this important issue. With intelligence such as his essay demonstrates, we expect that he will be equipped to lead.

Continuing Education

Claire listened, at least she heard the words he said, as J. D. talked about the cattle and his hay inventory and how he was going to have to deepen two of the wells because of the declining water table. At the same time, she cleared the table and washed the supper dishes. He offered to bathe the kids, but by the time he did she already had them undressed. She didn't want the two of them, and him, messing up the bathroom.

"Thanks, I'll do it," she said. He'd help like he did everything else, at his own careful pace, as if following instructions printed on the back of his eyelids, one step at a time.

"Well, I think I'll go on to bed if you don't need any help. You feel okay?" J. D. asked. He looked at her the same way she'd seen him watch a calf that seemed a little off, like he might want to pen her up to watch for real sickness.

"I feel fine. I've just got a lot to do. A lot I want to do." She shooed the kids toward the bathroom.

"Don't stay up too late," J. D. said.

That last comment came as no surprise. Always trying to manage her.

Now Amy and Jay Frank were bathed, in bed, and on their way to sleep. Claire couldn't stop. Not now. She started packing; put some of the clothes they couldn't wear in this heat in a suitcase and pushed it back to the back of the closet. Both Amy and Jay Frank were good about sleeping all night.

Back in the kitchen, she busied herself washing the cast iron skillet she'd forgotten to wash, then spun from the now spotless kitchen sink to survey the rest of the room. Okay. Now for the front room. This four-room house had been big enough for the past five years, until the kids. Until lately. She hadn't realized how much they had accumulated until she started organizing to pack for their move.

She couldn't have everything in the kitchen sitting in boxes for the next three days and J. D. would hear her if she started in the bathroom. He wasn't completely asleep yet. She could tell from his breathing.

She slipped off her shoes and stepped out onto the porch. She'd only stay a minute, just to cool off. At least there'd be air conditioning in the big house. The heat today had been the worst so far this summer. J. D. moved into this house when he went to work for Gran— nearly nine years ago. Before him, Gran and Granddad Frank, and before them, Gran's father and mother had lived here. In all those years, no one had any more than a fan. At least, after Amy was born, J. D. put a window unit in the room where the two kids now slept.

Today, when she'd been working, making her rounds of home health patients, every time she was out of the car and in one of the hot little houses so many of them lived in, she tried not to think about the temperature and the dry heat. All afternoon, her clothes had smelled like the cover on a just-used ironing board. Finally, here on the porch, now that it was dark, she felt a little breeze. She thought for a fraction of a second about sitting down and having a glass of iced tea out here. No. Too much to do.

Almost forgot; Wednesday night. Call Chris or he'll worry. Speed dial #1; he answered on the second ring. "Just checking in, big brother. Fine, just fine—no, really. Lots to be done—won't talk more than a minute. Yeah—Moving out.—It'll be lonely with Gran gone, you're right. I'll be fine; we'll be fine.—Wish I could see you, too." She frowned at the dish towel she found in her hand—wiped the glass pane at the top of the storm door with it, nodding as she listened. "How's Taos?—Yeah, I'll bet it is. I guess Gran will be there by Saturday night." Her voice sounded funny and she had to take a couple of deep breaths. "Nothing, it's just I hate talking on the phone. It's not the same.—Oh, yeah everything at work's great. They want to promote me to Nurse Supervisor for the district.—I don't know." She wasn't even telling him about her plan, her dream, yet. "I've got a lot to do before morning. Tell Andrew hi. I love you, too.—Bye."

She could count on Chris, no matter what. He understood her. Seemed like he understood her even when she didn't understand herself.

Maybe she should have talked to him longer, told him how she was feeling and what she wanted to do. But she wouldn't make sense tonight; there was too much to do. Too many thoughts competing for attention.

J. D. occupied their entire bed, arms and legs spread wide, the sheet in a wad near his feet. He slept still, relaxed, like a man tired from work he's proud of. He breathed slowly and steadily, reliably. In the kids' room, Jay Frank huddled in his crib in a curled ball, out from under his blanket. She covered him and pasted a kiss on his forehead with her index finger. He didn't move. Amy muttered, "Jay Frank, stop it," when Claire moved her toward the center of her bed, away from the edge. But she didn't wake. Good, everyone out for the night.

Claire stood in the front room. Where to begin. She bit on her top lip and closed her eyes. She'd felt this way before. Once, it had been so strong she thought she would explode. She'd been sixteen and should have had better sense, but she waited late until Gran went to bed and then she saddled her horse and rode him as fast as he would gallop. And she smiled so widely she thought her face might split. She didn't know where she was going. Or care. Maybe she and the horse would fly.

The horse shied at the reflection of the moon against fence wire. He went from full gallop to dead still in seconds. She hit the ground hard enough to make her wonder if she'd ever draw another breath. At the emergency room, the doctor said she had cracked two ribs and sprained her right wrist severely.

The pain in her ribs and wrist immediately replaced her sense of near-explosion. She slept at Gran's for two days—no food, only juice and water when Gran forced her. Not able to make conversation. Finally, her mother threatened to take her back to the hospital. Or to make her see a psychiatrist. That got her up and eating, but not talking. Except to say she wasn't going to see any doctor. Gran convinced her mother to give Claire some time. For the next three days she moved like a cow blinded by a sandstorm, and then still slowly and cautiously for another three days. *Completely empty* were the only words that came to her mind. She was afraid then to say them out loud.

She stayed at the big house and Gran watched over her the entire time. Chris called every day and when she couldn't talk, told her it was fine; he just wanted to hear her breathe. Neither one of them told her to quit feeling sorry for herself, or to get over whatever was bothering her. They just let her be.

After a few days, she could see the sunshine again and the whole thing seemed like something she had read or seen on television, not something that had happened to her.

After a year, she only recalled the details of the ride or the fall in that distant, television episode way. But a memory of the enormous sensation that each of her senses was hyper-acute that night remained; that she smelled each blade of grass, that she heard the footsteps of coyotes, that the moon's light was hot on her skin, that she saw every barb on the fence as her horse shied, and that the wind rushing past tasted of chocolate and cinnamon. And she remembered the power she felt. As if every dream, every aspiration she ever hoped rushed into her, concentrated into pure energy, lodged at the center of her and threatened to expand, maybe faster than her mind, her body, her soul could accommodate.

And she didn't tell anyone. Not Gran. Not even Chris. Not her dad in any of his concerned daily phone calls from Austin. She knew he would come immediately if she even hinted she needed him. But she didn't want to see that sad look in his eyes, the one that seemed permanent since he and her mother divorced. And she certainly did not tell her mother.

She didn't want anyone to diminish her experience by explaining it away as a psychological problem, or teenage dramatics. And she didn't want to try to tell anyone how she understood what followed that night—that the emptiness afterward hadn't been depression or a concussion or some other easy answer. No, she had been so full of everything wonderful.

And when that fullness, the acuteness, was knocked out of her by the fall, disappeared with the breath she thought was her last, then normal and ordinary felt like *completely empty.*

Her answer satisfied her for three years—until she took the mental health nursing course. The textbook description of bipolar disorder alarmed her. Maybe she did "suffer from a chemical imbalance," as the professor so carefully said in her lecture. Case studies of bizarre manic behavior and crippling depression left Claire suspicious. Maybe her acceptance of that night as an almost-holy one-time event was an elaborate rationalization—denial, the textbook term.

She made an appointment with a psychologist at the college counseling center. The doctor listened carefully, took a thorough history, asked questions that embarrassed Claire to answer, and told her that a complete physical was necessary first, to rule out hyperthyroidism or other possible causes of her mood that night. She was, she said, surprised that Claire had not had any other similar experiences after that one time.

Since she'd already told the psychologist things she never spoke of to anyone, she told her the rest—how she would have welcomed a repeat, just to feel for a minute that ecstatic strength and awareness, even if it meant that the emptiness would follow. She admitted to having energy fluctuations from high to low in the weeks before her menstrual periods. But nothing like that night when she was sixteen. The doctor looked at her like she might see into places Claire couldn't and said, "I think I can understand."

Pronounced free of other disease by the internist, she returned to the psychologist two weeks later. The woman listened, encouraged, prompted, nodded and, for twelve more sessions, led Claire through a brief, scrutinizing study of herself. Claire concluded that she, like every other person, was unique in some ways; that she needed to find at least one other person she could trust to tell her if she ever stepped beyond the limits of acceptable behavior, and that she could continue to learn each day about how to be herself. The psychologist agreed and told her to return if she needed to. The last thing she said lodged firmly in Claire's memory. "None of us learns all the lessons all at once. We revisit the important things again and again. Live long and learn much, Claire."

She immediately told two other people about her work with the psychologist—Gran and Chris. Neither of them commented other than to say that they would tell her if they thought she needed help and would force her to get it if she refused to listen. Later she told one other person. She felt it was the honest thing to do. Eager as she was to marry him, J. D. needed to know that she might not always be easy to live with, or to love. Hearing the story didn't change his mind. They married just after she graduated from South Plains Community College.

Since then, five years now, there were times she had held herself down and some when she had to push herself to get moving. But, those times never lasted longer than a couple of weeks and they seemed to be related to her periods. She learned how to use her energy when it was up and to rest when it ebbed. She could do anything if people would just let her; just stand back.

Now, tonight, the first thing to do was to make a list. All the things she wanted to do and be and get done on any particular day were on her lists; the daily lists she could check off—the lists of things she needed at the grocery store, activities with the kids, meals, housecleaning; the long-term lists of her goals; and the right-this-minute-to-get-her-thinking-straight lists. She needed one of those now—a list of all the things necessary to be ready to move into the Jackson house, Gran's house, on Sunday, four days from now.

A few hurried steps and she was in the kitchen again. Standing at the counter, she wrote fourteen items in less than two minutes. Yes, that made things clearer. She stood very still for a second and then returned to the front room.

Three hours later, she closed and taped the last box after noting the time on the clock as she placed it in the box—one twenty-two. Everything in the living room plus part of the glassware and dishes from the kitchen waited—boxed, taped, and labeled both by description and its intended location at the big house.

She blinked to clear the gritty sensation under her contacts, then closed her eyes. A little girl and an older woman—Claire and her Gran—danced to the music of Tchaikovsky. The ballroom at the big house was both their studio and the theatre where Claire performed for her mother and father and Chris. Becoming a ballerina had been on one of her lists a long time ago. Later, she replaced professional dancing with a different goal—marrying J. D. The fatigue she expected tonight, hoped for, dangled just out of reach, just beyond those dancers.

Her list of preparations for the move offered nothing more she could accomplish tonight. She drew a red line through *Pack Living Room*. Tomorrow promised plenty of activity—eight patients to visit.

She listed their names and procedures to be performed—a dressing change, an IV drug administration, observed oral medications administration on a patient with multi-drug resistant tuberculosis, INR blood draw on a woman taking Coumadin, follow up assessment on a man recently out of the hospital after an MVA. After each procedure she noted what she called "value added"—her label for the difference she would make, the things that she would attempt to accomplish that would make her visit different from that of other nurses. *Check nutritional status for the tuberculosis patient, teach the husband of the Coumadin patient about signs to observe for bleeding, teach care of the IV port to the daughter of the post surgical patient*—the list continued.

Those extra things weren't required by the Sunflower Home Health Company; she required them of herself. She was a professional nurse, with a Bachelor's degree from Tech's nursing school to prove it. J. D. had been skeptical that she could complete that second degree, work full-time, and deal with toddler Amy, all at the same time. Her mother weighed in on the subject too, advising her to wait. Said after all she was already an R.N. Claire didn't wait. She wanted to be more, know more. She graduated three months before Jay Frank was born.

She flipped the page in her notebook to the Goals section and looked, for probably the hundredth time, at the most recent item—Master's degree, Nurse Practitioner. Tomorrow or the next day, she'd begin working on that by talking with J. D. Later, when, or if, it actually happened, Chris and Gran would be happy for her. Her dad, too. She could imagine what her mother would say. Something like, "You have responsibilities to your children. You should wait. I don't understand why you are so driven." If anyone knew about being driven, her mother should. Melanie Jackson Banks, the Acting Superintendent of Schools for Floyd County Consolidated, never slacked up, at work or in attempting to run her daughter's life. She'd given up on Chris.

Supplies. She'd get the supplies ready for tomorrow's patients and then she'd rest, maybe actually get some sleep. Without any sound, she slipped out the front door and walked toward her car. A breeze stirred the dry air. A short walk would help her think, clear her head. She should probably worry about stepping on a snake on a night like this. She didn't.

Exercise always helped; it was just so hard to tear herself away from working at whatever she was intent on, but she had learned. Without the clock she wasn't sure, but an hour probably passed while she took the walk and then sorted out the things from the car trunk that her patients would need tomorrow.

She slipped back into the house, as quietly as she slipped out. She turned off the kitchen light; changed into her short gown, brushed her teeth and rinsed her face without turning on the bathroom light; and looked in again on Amy and Jay Frank. Outside the kids' room, her eyes searched the dark, as if a neon list might materialize, blinking, to direct her to do one more thing tonight. From their bedroom, J. D. said softly, "Claire, I need you to come here."

She hurried to his side of the bed. "What's wrong, honey?"

He scooted over and pulled her down beside him. "Nothing now. I just needed you to be here. And you need to try to rest, even if it is hard for you to." She willed herself to relax against him; he was right. He held her, gently, loosely, the way he did a child or a skittish animal, sharing his calm.

She woke when the sun rose near six a.m. By then, she had slept three hours. J. D. had left coffee for her and gone to the barn to gather tools for his day's work. Sunflower's dress code specified that employees should look professional while on duty and that the name tag should be clearly visible. No uniforms required. Some of the nurses, the fat ones in particular, wore scrub suits that made them look like sacks of flour tied in the middle. Not Claire. She believed that her appearance could make a difference in how her patients felt when they saw her. For her, work clothes meant tailored slacks and blouses or sweaters with a color-coordinated jacket. On days like today, when she was feeling full of energy and optimism, she reached for the brightest colors in the closet.

She showered, dressed, drank coffee, and ate yogurt and toast, all before she woke the kids. Their breakfast cereal waited on the kitchen table while Amy chattered to herself in the mirror as she dressed. Jay Frank came to slowly, so he was the perfect audience for Amy's non-stop talk. He didn't say a word.

Even though she often zipped from one of her own tasks to another, Claire tried never to hurry, or slow down, the children. Each of them had a different speed, different from each other's and different from hers. She wanted to let them move at their own pace, to give them what she wanted for herself. That meant she was often completely ready to go long before they were dressed for the day. That presented no problem except on Tuesdays and Thursdays when she took them into Jackson's Pond to Parents' Day Out at the Methodist Church. It would have been simpler to leave them here at the house and have a sitter every day, but they needed to learn to play with other children. J. D., or if he was too busy, Gran, would pick them up just before noon and bring them back to the ranch. A schedule posted on the refrigerator kept everyone organized and the children seen to. Today was Thursday.

She helped Jay Frank into his high-chair seat and poured milk on cereal for him and Amy. Then she said, "I'll be on the porch, big boy. Call me when you're ready to get down and get dressed."

J. D. came out of the barn and stepped up on the porch. "Hi there. How're you feeling this morning?" He kissed her on the forehead and then stepped back to look her over. "You look good. Like a bright, fresh flower. I don't know how you do it on so little sleep."

"I feel good. We'll be packed and ready to move on Sunday morning. I got a lot done last night." She stood next to him and put an arm around his waist. Looking from the porch across the early morning shadows on the grass pasture, to the low grey clouds in the west, she hoped for the rain they needed.

She led Amy in singing nursery rhyme songs on the drive into town. Jay Frank repeated words he recognized and smiled all the way. Eight o'clock start time for the kids' day left her with an hour before she would visit a patient. She hated to waste the time, so she headed for the café where she could have coffee and read the Lubbock newspaper.

The two blocks of storefronts on Main Street with their few remaining businesses stood ready for another slow day, made slower by the July heat. She ordered a cup of coffee and a glass of orange juice in the City Café. The only other customers sat together at a table near the front window. The Harper twins. Sixty-two years old, dressed alike, wearing shorts, with their dyed red hair in pony tails. Both showed the result of their years in Dallas. One, she had trouble recalling which was Linda and which was Louise, waved at her. "Come sit with us, Claire, and tell us what we need to do about our wrinkles." Maybe she could have told them thirty years ago not to drink and smoke so much and never to enter a tanning booth. It was too late now.

"Be right there." She finished the last bit of juice and took the paper and her purse. She would stop briefly and then make a quick getaway. Forget reading the newspaper. She'd have run straight out the door if her intention wouldn't have been obvious. What did those two women do all day?

She finished her first three patient visits before noon. The library offered a cool place to work on her charts. She had to discourage Mamie Mundt from conversation and she felt bad about doing it. Mamie volunteered two days each week to keep the library open. Otherwise, the city would have to close it down entirely due to lack of funds. If she chatted with Mamie, her charts would go unfinished. She bent her head toward her work and did not make further eye contact with Mamie. She scribbled a reminder in her notebook. *Kids to library-visit Mamie.*

She left the library and drove to the last street on the north side of town where she parked and ate her apple and cheese and reviewed the procedure for IV port care she was going to teach Mr. Colson's daughter.

Forcing herself to focus on the remaining five patients and on adding value to each visit became more difficult as the afternoon wore on. So many things needed to be done before the move on Sunday and she wanted to talk to J. D. about her plan. Better to do it soon. And if she let herself, she'd start dreaming about opening a clinic in Jackson's Pond.

She sat in her car to complete the final chart notes. Before she put the records away, she made herself review each one for completeness. On her high energy days, that's how she thought of them, she might move too quickly, might omit important information. She had learned to make herself take this extra step, even if she had to put it on a list to be sure she did it.

Late Friday afternoon, at home after work, she walked through the house's four rooms, slowly. The edge of the urgency had receded, no longer able to reach her. As of early this morning, everything she could do for the move had been done. "Kids, let's go see Gran," she said. They beat her to the car.

At the big house, she found Gran sitting on her bedroom floor surrounded by boxes and pieces of newspaper. Except for this bedroom, every room Claire walked through held labeled boxes similar to the ones at their house. "I hate to see you doing that. It will be so hard knowing you're not here."

"I'll be here. You'll see me around every corner, every day."

"I know I'll see you upstairs in the ballroom. Who'll teach Amy to dance?" Before she finished her sentence, she began crying. "I'm sorry. I should be happy for you. You're going to do something you've dreamed of—live in a beautiful place and paint every day. But, I will miss you so much." She wiped her eyes and tried to smile.

"I'll miss you, all of you. But you can come visit and I'll

come here anytime you need me." Willa placed a small painting wrapped in newsprint into a box. "Come here and let your Gran hold onto you." The two of them sat together on the floor, arms around one another. "Are you feeling okay?" Willa asked.

"I'm fine. Don't worry about me. J. D. does enough of that." She hugged her grandmother tight and then stood. "I promise not to cry again. I'm going to check on the kids."

The three of them returned and both of the children ran to Willa and hugged her. Kisses all around. Claire said, "We'd better go. I finished packing, except for the last of the kitchen things and the beds. Now that it's all done, I think I can rest. Oh, I want to tell you one thing. I'm thinking about going back to school."

"When?"

"Fall, I hope. What do you think?"

"As long as you take care of yourself and your family, I think that you should do what you dream of. Is there anything I can do to help?"

"No, just keep being the way you are, always. I'm going to go before I cry again."

Amy danced around her as they went to the car. She pirouetted and said, "Hurry Mommy! Mommy, why are you walking slow?"

"I'm thinking, Amy." And she was feeling herself assemble, the edges of the expanded, scattered pieces joining. She ruffled Amy's black curls. "Thinking that when we get home we'll have a snack and then a little nap."

She finished washing the last plate from supper. She rinsed it and handed it to her husband. "I've been thinking about something," she said. She might as well start this discussion now; it could take a while to settle.

"Just one thing?"

She smiled. He knew her too well. She bumped him with her hip and winked. "One thing more than the rest."

"I suppose you're about to tell me." He flicked the dishtowel he'd been using to dry dishes toward her, aiming at her butt.

She grabbed his damp weapon and deftly twirled it into a tight length. "Oh, no you don't, mister. You know you can't win this game. I'm the dishtowel popping champ." She flicked the towel. Snap! She'd aimed wide, but he jumped back.

Both hands above his head, he laughed and said, "Okay, I give up."

"Say it."

"You're the champ." She watched his hands as he spread his arms wide apart. "But you cheat."

"I cheat? When did—"

He grabbed her, pinning her arms to her sides. "Get out of this, champ."

She kissed him, hard, pressing her body against his. He relaxed his grip. They kissed again, gently. "You cheat," she said.

"Yes, ma'am. I'm the champeen cheater." He leaned back and cocked his head to the right. "You look mighty good with that tomato soup on your cheek." He smiled, watching her scrub at her cheek. "Are you going to tell me the one thing you've been thinking about now or after?"

"After what?"

"After I conduct a thorough examination to be sure you don't have tomato soup anywhere else." He fiddled with the top button on her blouse. "Like maybe in here."

She swatted at his hand. "I'll tell you now. That tomato soup thing could take a while."

He sat at the kitchen table. She sat across from him. She wanted to be able to see his eyes. "I've been thinking about this for quite a while. I want to go back to school, get a master's degree, be a nurse practitioner." She always told him things straight out, to the point. She knew some women who bragged about tricking their husbands into agreeing or shaming them into buying things for them. Not her. She didn't want J. D. to agree with her out of obligation or guilt or pity.

"Do you need it for your job?"

"No. It's for me. I want to know more and do more for people than change dressings."

"Are there any jobs for nurse practitioners around here? Or would you end up educating yourself out of a job?"

"There's one practitioner in Calverton. I think I could get a clinic started here in town. One reason businesses won't locate here—no health care. I'm not saying I could save the town, but maybe I could make a difference. I could be good at it, with the education. I know I would."

"There's no question in my mind about that. But—"

She amazed herself by waiting, not saying anything. She could, if she had to. If he didn't agree now, she still had choices. She could wait until next year; she could apply for admission without his agreement; she could—

"This can't be about money," he said.

"No. We have plenty. We'd be fine if I never worked at all." She thought about how to explain. "I need to work; I need to always be doing something useful and interesting." That was the truth. The rest of it, what she couldn't explain, was that part she hadn't quite learned; why she had that need.

He nodded—maybe he did understand; she thought he probably felt the same about his work.

She told him the details; classes were held in Lubbock one full day a week, a two-year program, how she would manage the studying, and she could apply for one of the incentive scholarships for rural students—they had already reserved the money from Gran for the kids' education. She told him all the things she had worked out in her mind and on her lists. His watching her as she talked made her stumble a couple of times. "Well, what do you think?" she asked. He hadn't really balked yet. She expected he would. Easing into things was his style; hers was jumping in headfirst.

"I worry about how much it might take out of you. Maybe I never said it out loud, but I want all of you; I've felt that way since you were sixteen years old." He looked away, looked a little embarrassed. "Sometimes I'm even a little jealous of the kids. I worry about you when you get to moving so fast, doing so much. It would kill me if anything ever happened to you."

She didn't know how to answer that. There was so much of her, plenty for everyone, she was sure. She reached across and took his hand. "That's the best, sweetest thing you ever said to me. I love you. "

It would have been so much easier if he had tried to tell her flat out she couldn't go, or that he didn't want her to go to school because the kids needed her at home, or because he didn't like the idea of her getting a graduate degree because he didn't have one, or because commuting to Lubbock would be too expensive. All those arguments she could have countered and overcome. And she could have stayed angry with him for not supporting her or for being weak-egoed and old fashioned. But he hadn't.

They sat looking at each other for a long minute. She said, "We don't have to decide this now. Let's both think about it for a while." She stood, still holding his hand. "About that tomato soup. Would you take a look?"

WICHITA FALLS TIMES
Friday June 2, 2006
Archer County Ranchers Honored
    Archer County's McDuffie Ranch was designated today in Austin as a Texas Land Heritage Program member. James McDuffie received the Family Land Heritage certificate from Governor Parsons.

    "This program honors families who continue to demonstrate the value of our rural heritage even though many rural areas are in decline," the Governor said.

    The program, operated by the Texas Department of Agriculture, recognizes families who have continuously conducted agricultural operations on their land for at least 100 years.

Marking Time

S tanding near the kitchen trash can where she deposited the junk mail, Melanie read the article Ray sent with his letter. The item was about a ranch in Archer County receiving recognition as a Family Land Heritage ranch. She didn't know anyone named McDuffie. She reread it. The Jackson Ranch could qualify for the program and its recognition certificate. No one in *this* county had one. She was almost certain. The Jacksons could be the first. They *would* be the first.

She looked at the picture attached to the article. That was why he'd sent it, the photograph. The note scrawled along the edge said, "Governor's bad hair day," with an arrow pointing to the accompanying picture of his boss at the Land Heritage ceremony. The governor's trademark Kennedy-like hair was standing up at approximately a sixty-five degree angle. It revealed an unattractively high forehead; his face looked like an egg, decorated with two tiny slits for eyes and a toothy, pasted-on politician's grin. Apparently the wind had been blowing in Austin, or some reporter, probably not a Republican, knew a lot about Photoshop.

More and more often, Ray made derogatory remarks about the man he had worked sixteen years for and about his job—Executive Assistant. A fine title, he said, but the job consisted exclusively of cleaning up messes other people made. The governor and Ray had been fraternity brothers at Tech.

Before she and Ray divorced, they argued frequently about his job with Parsons who was, at the time, a State Representative. She distrusted Rich Parsons; disliked Ray's constant travel; and suspected him of seeing other women. But his job hadn't been the only reason for the divorce. Truth was she couldn't really remember all of the reasons. After all this time, they really didn't seem to matter much.

There hadn't been a phone message or one of his long silences on the answering machine when she got home. He'd call, regardless of whether he was tied up with work. She could count on it. That fact still amazed her. After all these years.

She fed Elsa and stroked the cat's black fur, only once, because Elsa flicked her tail, narrowed her eyes, and flattened her ears against her sleek head. Melanie's one companion apparently wasn't in the mood for people. "I feel the same way sometimes, Elsa." The cat stalked away, leaving her half-empty food dish at Melanie's feet.

She took a glass of wine and headed toward her bedroom, but changed course and went to the computer in her home office. Texas Land Heritage Program. The Agriculture Department's website appeared. She skimmed through the information to the Frequently Asked Questions—one hundred years continuous agricultural production—ownership continuously in the family— certificate—ceremony in Austin—can purchase signage for the property—listed in registry. The Jackson Ranch *would* qualify.

Junior Reese and that Warren bunch would choke. Deadline for application—September 15. She reached for her calendar, but it was in her briefcase. She'd left her briefcase in the car, trying to wean herself from working every waking moment.

She hesitated. *You made a promise to yourself.* As she thought it, she heard the tone that would have gone with it, the one she had come to detest—disciplinarian, administrator. She inhaled deeply through her nose. The sound, the only one in the room, bounced inside her head. She printed the FAQ sheet and shut down the computer. If she didn't, she would stay at it.

A large Heritage sign would require a larger gate. And she would see that the largest available version of the sign was placed at the ranch. All these years and there had never been anything other than a rusting, dented mailbox on a cedar fence post to indicate that the Jacksons owned the property.

Her son-in-law, J. D., had made many improvements around the place since he went to work for her mother. He added an equipment barn and replaced the old cedar fence posts with miles of sturdy metal t-posts, all painted green with silver tops. He restrung or replaced all the sagging or rusty barbed wire. She liked that, liked the posts that stood firm and erect like slender soldiers wearing flat-topped helmets, and that the fence wire declared a tightly maintained boundary. The big house, where J. D. and Claire and their two children lived since her mother moved to Taos, wore a fresh coat of paint and a new roof.

Of course, J. D. hadn't spent all that money for ranch improvements without Willa's collaboration. Her mother's insistence on going her own way no matter what anyone in Jackson's Pond thought often irritated Melanie. But she had to admire how she had managed the ranch. After she made J. D. her partner in the operation, she had not ceded her role as the other half of that partnership. Now, at seventy-six, Willa still ran her own show, doing what she wanted, whenever she wanted. Her move to Taos was clear evidence of that.

The Land Heritage application required documentation of family ownership and operation of the ranch for at least one hundred years. Willa would be the best source of that information. But her interest in markers and plaques was, as far as Melanie knew, non-existent. Melanie willed herself to stop thinking about the marker, about adding another thing to her to-do list. She folded the FAQ sheet into neat quarters, laid it on the corner of the desk, and left the office.

Usually, if she had choir practice, or a visit with her grandchildren, or a school-related evening meeting, Melanie didn't consider waiting at home for a telephone call. Since April, though, she surprised herself by guarding the hours from eight until ten p.m. If at all possible, she was home, near the phone, preferring to talk there rather than on a cell phone. Missing Ray's call and hearing only the long silence on the answering machine between the "begin your recording" beep and the end of the allotted message time gave her a vacant feeling that kept her from sleeping. He told her she could call him any time; but so far she always waited; never called. She stared at the kitchen clock— 7:48. There was time for a shower.

Last night, just as they were about to hang up, she mentioned something about how sorry she was she'd ever taken her job. It was the first time she had ever said anything negative to Ray about her work. She avoided mentioning work to him at all. He said she probably needed to talk about it, that it would help. He was probably right. Who else would she tell? Not a counselor. She was finished with counselors. Not the other women at work; they were her employees. Not Claire; her daughter had all she could say grace over right now, going to graduate school and keeping up with J. D. and her two kids. Not anyone in Jackson's Pond; she didn't have close women friends. She didn't know anyone she had enough in common with; she was too busy; she disliked gossip. Those were the reasons she used to explain to herself why the women she knew were acquaintances, not close friends. And for some reason, even when her mother asked about her work, Melanie never hinted that she now detested the job she worked so hard to get. She glanced at her watch. She straightened the phone cord. She watched the cat stretch.

When she had been about thirteen, her grandmother Jackson engineered opportunities for the two of them to have what she had called "confidential chats." More often than not, the chats had been lectures on topics Delia considered vital for Melanie, warnings mostly, and matters of proper female deportment. Melanie could almost hear the tone in which Delia once said, "Your mother should cultivate some women friends. It's unhealthy, her being such a loner." As a teenager, she couldn't have named the faint disdain in Delia's voice or understand the discomfort she felt hearing it. Now, here she was, just like Willa, a woman her grandmother would have pitied for her lack of female intimates. Delia Jackson wouldn't have been a person the adult Melanie could have confided in either.

She went down the hall toward her bathroom. The sensation of being watched as she passed the extra bedroom made her shoulders tighten. She stood perfectly still, listening—nothing. The door stood partially open. She tensed, then pushed it wide open with her bare right foot. In the glow of the nightlight she saw only the usual occupants—the twenty-five dolls her grandmother had collected for her—their self-satisfied, pristine porcelain faces prim as always. But tonight the collective gaze of their fifty staring eyes felt intrusively human. Melanie backed out and shut the door, tired of being watched.

In her bedroom, she shed her clothes and walked naked to place them in the hamper in her closet. She stared at the neat row of blouses and dark suits she wore for work and then looked above them to the hat box. She pulled it down and took out the wig. *You are so foolish. A grown woman playing dress up.* She thought it, but that didn't stop her. Four steps and she was in the bathroom carrying the wig and the clothes she chose for tonight, not one of her dark suits or the contrasting tailored blouses.

Back in March, she found a UPS box on the front porch when she returned home after work. She checked to see who it was from—no sender' name, only Ray's street address in Austin. She looked toward the houses to each side of hers. No one in either yard. The box was large, but fairly light. She had hurried into the house with it and slit the packing tape. She frowned at the contents, a black, curly, long-haired wig on a mannequin head and a pair of red-framed sunglasses with very large, dark lenses. *What in the world?* Elsa ran under the kitchen table when Melanie set the wigged head on the countertop.

Near the bottom of the box, under a mountain of Styrofoam packing bubbles, lay a single sheet of paper. The message was assembled, like a ransom note in a bad movie, out of letters cut from magazines. "No fooling. Wear this to meet arriving flight at Lubbock International Airport Friday, April 1, 4 p.m. If anyone speaks to you, respond in Spanish accent, chica. Pack hiking clothes. Code word—Bienvenidos, Senor."

Ray's April Fool's Day surprise was a weekend trip to one of the lesser-traveled parts of New Mexico. He had reserved a room at the Night's Rest Motel in Logan, New Mexico. The motel featured hand painted horses' heads on the top panels of the doors, a different horse for each of the ten guest rooms. It sat just down the street from the town's bar, an establishment named Whiskey—Road to Ruin. There they drank beer and danced to juke box country music and played pool, alternately competing with a man who claimed to be a CPA from Clovis and a kid who probably used a fake ID to buy his beer.

By the time they left, both Texas fugitives were mildly drunk, intoxicated by beer and the remoteness of the place and nostalgia for all the funky little bars in small towns they'd stopped in during their college days. They walked arm in arm back down the state highway that served as Logan's main street to arrive at room #1, where a palomino rolled its eyes suggestively from the top panel of the door.

The next day they drove north past Roy to Mills Canyon. They hiked around the ruins of Melvin Mills' grand venture, Orchard Ranch. In the late 1800s, in a canyon carved by the Canadian River, Mills developed a large system of fruit orchards and vegetable fields in the canyon floor's rich soil. Melanie felt better that day than she had in years. Tired and hot and relaxed and free.

She tried to imagine Mills' small empire spread all green and lush before her. She could almost smell the peaches. Mills had built a tram railway to carry cars full of Orchard Ranch's produce to the canyon rim some eight hundred feet above. He succeeded and became a New Mexico tycoon. Ray read to her from a brochure, "In October, 1904, prolonged, heavy rain caused the Canadian to rise as much as seventy feet. The entire canyon bottom, the orchards, fields, and irrigation system were wiped out and the entire area was covered with silt. Crops could no longer be cultivated there. After many years of unsuccessful attempts to resurrect the project, Mr. Mills died a pauper at age eighty."

Ray shook his head and stared out at the ruins of the tramway and demolished bits of concrete irrigation flumes. "That just goes to show you, doesn't it?

"What?"

"We're not in charge of anything, really. And we're kidding ourselves if we ever think we are."

Melanie didn't answer.

They stayed in the canyon until near dark, hiking and poking around the ruins. They ate supper in Roy and afterward walked the few streets in town. A police car passed them, slowly. The officer nodded, a solemn acknowledgment of their foreign presence on his street, and raised two fingers from the steering wheel in a small salute. Ray nodded and raised an index finger in response. They ambled on to the car.

Melanie turned in her seat to watch Roy, New Mexico, disappear behind them. She told herself it was silly to want to cry. Ray drove slowly back toward Logan. The silence between them was calm, easy. Outside Mosquero, just before the highway descended sharply back onto the plains, he pulled to the side of the road and turned off the headlights and ignition. Shadowy hills, dotted with juniper and yucca, rolled away in front of them in a scene that suggested they had traveled to another planet or another time—no sounds, no other vehicles, no electric lights. The silence and the darkness surrounded them as gently as a velvet cushion in a jewel box. "Let's get out, honey. There's something you need to see."

He stood beside her so closely that their shoulders touched. He pointed east. "Keep looking right out there." As if cued, the moon peeked above the horizon and quickly rose to show its full diameter. "I ordered that just for you."

The pale, smiling orb rose, its size doubled by the tears in her eyes. And she felt it tug at all the tides within her.

The shower made her alert, more eager for the phone to ring. She dressed in red leggings and an oversized white shirt, an outfit she would never wear outside the house, and the wig.

Since that New Mexico trip, she'd put the wig on several times. A different person looked back from her bedroom mirror. The curly black hair transformed her face. She could see Claire and even found a resemblance to her mother. She'd never thought before that she fit into the line between Claire and Willa, the two of them with their lean figures, black hair, and green eyes. Her own blue eyes and blond hair, always carefully contained, made her seem more like Delia Jackson's direct descendant. The woman in the wig was carefree, appealing. She shook her head to fluff the curls and smiled back at her reflection.

She picked up the phone when it rang, but waited until she heard Ray say, "Melanie, are you there?" before she answered.

"Si, hola, Raymondo. Como esta?" Her accent could have been authentic.

He laughed. "I'll bet you're wearing that wig again. I wish I could see you. Have you worn it to work yet?"

"Not yet, but I've given it some thought."

"Speaking of work, let's talk about it."

She had promised. "This may not come out too clearly. You're the first to hear it, the only one who will." Before their divorce, she would never have trusted him enough to tell him.

"Doesn't have to be clear. I'll just listen, maybe ask a question. No advice, I swear."

"You've gotten to be a very good listener."

"I can hear you stalling."

He knew her. "You're right." She sat on the loveseat. It helped that the mirror across the room showed her a woman who wouldn't care a bit about being superintendent of schools. After a long pause and a drink of wine, she began. "Okay. When the board asked me to take the superintendent position as Acting, two years ago, I thought I wanted the permanent job. I was a fool to accept it as Acting. They didn't even begin to search for a permanent appointee until three months ago. Then, when they announced the search, the board president said something like, 'of course, we would welcome your application also.' Obviously an afterthought." She wondered if Ray could hear in her voice the sensation that she felt just now, like a hand clutching at her throat. She swallowed; she would tell him all of it. "I think that means they'll offer me the position only if they don't find someone with a doctorate. A man with a doctorate."

"Does the position description require a doctorate?"

"Or equivalent experience. But that bunch of small-minded—well, they'd prefer a man and they'd like to be able to brag about his degree. A lot of good that did with that last one."

"Small-minded, you said."

"What I mean is bigoted." She ticked off several examples of how they had outright resisted her efforts to recruit Hispanic or Black teachers or staff. And she cited figures; the student population was forty-nine percent non-white and the faculty ninety-two percent white. Her voice rose and she didn't try to stop it. She'd started now, so she continued, giving several examples of almost daily interference by board members in operations in every area from personnel, to athletics, to curriculum. She said, "If they offered the job to me now, I'd refuse." Then she stopped talking, felt herself swallow again.

"You've told me what you *think*. I haven't heard you say how you *feel* about all this," he said.

"You're really good at this. I should be paying."

"For you, ma'am, it's free of charge."

Neither of them spoke for a minute or two. She imagined him holding the phone and smoking a cigarette, watching the smoke rise toward the ceiling.

"I *feel* weary. Too weary to fight all that I know is wrong." She hesitated, searching for words that were accurate. "I'm angry at myself for being used. And I don't have the energy to go back to graduate school for a doctorate."

"Energy. You? Is there something I don't know about?"

"No, I haven't even had a migraine in two months. Maybe that's one advantage of being officially menopausal." She pulled off the wig and stuffed it between the cushions of the loveseat. "Let's not talk about me anymore."

"I wish you had let me in on some of this before." A long pause told her he wasn't sure about what he wanted to say next. "You're tired. We'll talk again tomorrow night." She thought he was going to hang up. Then he said, very quietly, "Remember this. No matter what job you have, or whether you even have a job, I love you. I always have."

"Thanks for listening."

After they hung up, she sat still with the phone in her lap.

Then she took a deep breath and went to the kitchen. She finished her wine with the dinner she heated in the microwave. Without bothering to start a to-do list for tomorrow, she went to bed.

The phone fell to the floor when she fumbled for it. Sound asleep, Melanie had added its ringing to her dream, something about a kindergarten full of happy, active five year-olds. She tried to say, "Hello," but it came out muffled. She laughed.

She laughed again. "Yes, Mother, it's me. I was dreaming."

"It must have been a good dream. It's great to hear you laugh. I'm sorry I woke you; you're usually working this time of the evening."

"Turning a new leaf. No work at home." She knew she sounded addled, but couldn't seem to completely wake up, or maybe she didn't want to.

"Really? You must tell me about that leaf. I'll be at the ranch tomorrow night by supper time. I just talked to Claire. She said she'd make chicken fried steak and to tell you she's setting a place for you, if you're available."

Melanie was fully awake now, finally, and a little surprised. "Is there a problem at the ranch?"

"No, no problem. Going to Dallas. Some of my paintings were selected for a juried show. I'm going to the opening reception Saturday night."

"Okay, I'll see you tomorrow night." Then she remembered. "Oh, there's something I need to talk to you about."

Melanie hoped to return to her dream. The last thing she remembered was that every one of the five year-olds looked like Chris had at that age—angelic, perfect.

After supper the following evening, Claire and J. D. shooed Willa and Melanie out to relax on the front porch while they cleared the kitchen and put the children to bed. Willa chose the glider and Melanie sat in her granddad's big rocker. "Melanie, you said last night you wanted to talk about something."

Melanie mentioned the Texas Land Heritage Program. She was prepared to have to persuade Willa and had her key points in mind: tribute to her father and grandparents, she'd do all the paperwork for the application, Willa would only have to supply a few documents, Junior Reese would choke. She was about to launch into her sales pitch, but stopped when her mother stood and walked to the front door. Willa said, "Wait a second, I'll be right back."

None of the usual late June afternoon clouds had formed before sundown. Now the clear dark sky was decorated only by the constellations whose forms Melanie could never quite discern and the single blinking light of an aircraft passing from the southwest toward the east. An occasional gentle breeze ruffled her hair, left loose from its usual tidy restraint. She lifted it to cool her neck.

The front screen door clapped closed. Willa said, "Here's all the information you'll need about ownership and operations. I got it together several years ago when the Land Heritage program was first announced. I never got around to applying after the year the ranch was eligible. It's been in a file cabinet in there in the office."

"You certainly made that simple. Thanks. We should be the first in the county."

Willa nodded and looked at her daughter. She said, "Your hair looks so pretty that way, Melanie. It reminds me of the way you wore it in college, layered and curled."

Melanie nodded. A thousand years ago. "Thanks, maybe I should get it cut that way again sometime."

Willa slid the glider gently and hummed quietly, a tune Melanie couldn't recognize.

There were a thousand things they might talk about, but now that her purpose had been so easily accomplished, Melanie couldn't find any words. She gazed toward the blinking beacon of the rapidly disappearing plane.

As she left the ranch and turned onto the county road, Melanie felt in her purse and found her PDA. Operating it with her right hand, she extracted the stylus. Functioning by rote, and still one-handed, she opened the scheduler to today's list, ticked off the final item, and scrolled to tomorrow's. Less than fifteen minutes later, she was back in Jackson's Pond, in her house behind locked doors. No message on the answering machine.

She opened the lock on the upper kitchen cabinet. Her bottle of Pinot Grigio was half empty. She took two cigarettes from her pack; she never allowed herself more. *"No work tonight. No lists. You're already slipping. You're hopeless."*

The phone rang, preventing her from lecturing herself further. Elsa sauntered by, flicking her tail. *Even the cat knows I'm hopeless.* She waited for Ray's voice.

"Melanie, are you there?"

"Hi, Ray."

"Don't have much time to talk tonight. I'm supposed to be at a big do at the Mansion right now. The governor expects me to stand beside him and remind him of people's names and to point out anyone who owes him a favor. I just wanted to check in and to ask you something."

She waited.

He cleared his throat. "I have to be in Lubbock tomorrow." And then he asked if she would she let him stay at her house, not would she meet him at a hotel or see him in some out of the way restaurant, but at the house they had bought not long after they married in 1975. "It's been a long time since April," he said.

She didn't answer. She couldn't because she was concentrating on her chest, the fast, ascending-elevator sensation, that sudden awareness of gravity and the exhilaration of upward thrust.

"Melanie?"

"Uh huh." Her voice belonged to a small girl.

"Does that mean yes?"

"Yes."

"Don't worry about the neighbors. I'll take care of that. I'll leave a message on the machine tomorrow about when to expect me. Got to go."

She said, "Goodnight," to the dial tone.

She lit a cigarette and sipped the wine and paced the

kitchen. The cat followed. She stopped the aimless walking. The cat retreated to shelter under the table. Melanie crushed out the cigarette, finished the rest of the wine in two quick drinks, and headed down the hall. Two hours later, all the Madame Alexander dolls in their frilly frocks, still peering straight ahead with their blank porcelain stares, were carefully stowed in boxes on the top shelf of the closet, at the back.

Ray's message on the answering machine when she came in from work the next day asked her to park so there would be space in the garage for a second vehicle and to open the garage door after the neighbors' lights were out. He'd be there between eleven and midnight. At eleven twenty-five, she watched as a vehicle with its lights off pulled into the driveway. The only light she had on in the house was in her bedroom at the back of the house, their bedroom.

She heard the garage door close. He hadn't been in the house for sixteen years, not since the day she'd told him to leave and never come back. Waiting for him tonight, she told herself they were different people then. Arguments about his work, her jealousy, about living in Jackson's Pond, her rushing to finish her Master's degree, about Chris, about the rumors of other women in other towns—all those things had seemed important to those people, the ones they were then. People she didn't know anymore.

Like a pair of teenagers at their first dance, they made a few missteps. They got as far as the kitchen before they began circling, palms sweaty. "Did anyone see you?"—"The house looks good."—"Where do you want to put your bag?"—"How are the grandkids?"— "Is that a new perfume?"

Melanie laughed, a high-pitched strained sound. "Listen to us. Don't say another word for a minute." She made them both a drink. Then she led him by the hand into the family room.

"I can use this," he said. He raised his glass to her. "I'll admit, I'm a little nervous."

"Me too."

"I've got some news," he said. "The kind that makes me wonder if I've lost a mule or found a bridle."

"Tell me."

"Two rental houses I bought when I first moved to Austin sit on a piece of property that's going to be developed as an office park. I got a call yesterday morning and a written offer this morning for $300,000." He sat back and shook his head.

"That doesn't sound like a lost mule to me."

"Right. After I pay off the mortgage, there would be enough left to fund the rest of my retirement plan. I can stop saying, 'Yes, Governor,' anytime I want."

"What would you do? You've got some good years left in you."

"I hope so. I don't know what I'd do. I never let myself think seriously about it." He leaned forward and swirled the ice in his drink. "What would you do?"

"I'm not you."

"No, I mean if you quit your job. Is there anything you've dreamed of doing?"

She peered into her glass for an answer. "I used to think I knew."

He settled back on the couch. "Big questions to ponder at midnight. Maybe we should talk about this tomorrow."

Close to him in bed, she felt him twitching during the night, as if he were running. She managed to lie still, but her search for a dream to replace the one that had made her acting superintendent of schools kept her awake. The five-years-olds eventually arrived, laughing and tugging at her skirt, and led her away to sleep.

The aroma of bacon sizzling and coffee brewing brought Ray to the kitchen. "I thought this might get you out of bed. The waffles are ready," she said.

He poured a cup of coffee and kissed the back of her neck. "I could marry a woman who cooks like this."

"You did. 1975."

"Melanie, let's get married, again."

She dropped the waffle; didn't pick it up from the floor, stared at it as if it were art.

"I mean it. We love each other. We've been sneaking around like criminals for nine years, just to see each other. That's long enough." He picked up the waffle and pretended to dust it off. She pointed to the trash. He aimed carefully and tossed it in from across the room. She rolled her eyes.

Smoke rose from the bacon. She concentrated on moving the pan to the back burner. She held her breath while she extracted the strips and arranged them on their plates. She placed them on the table, took a deep breath and said, "I don't want to spoil things. We have fun; we don't argue, and you're right, we love each other. But ..."

"But what?"

"If we lived together, that all might change. I don't want us to be unhappy together again." She pointed at the plates. "Eat."

"We're smarter now." He ignored his plate.

"I'm not sure I am. You don't know what I'm like when you're not with me."

That got a laugh from him. "I'm willing to take my chances."

She felt him watching her push a waffle around in the pond of syrup on her plate. When she looked up, he winked at her and smiled the smile that she always had trouble resisting. "Okay, let's eat before your waffle turns to mush," he said.

That afternoon, they watched DVDs of old black and white movies. Between movies they ate popcorn and had a long disjointed conversation that reminded her of watching people playing pool—questions and answers colliding, caroming, occasionally landing in a pocket, the play moving quickly, and the advantage changing rapidly. Lots of balls on the table to begin with—Where would he want to live? Austin? No, he'd had enough of Austin. Somewhere quiet, maybe a place where they could have some animals and chickens. Where would she want to live? A different house, not this one. Did she want to work? Not for pay; maybe volunteer. Never to be in charge again. What would people think? Who cares?—And then they were down to the only real question, the last ball on the table. It was her play.

By Sunday, she believed he was serious. That morning there was none of his usual joking, no waltzing her around the kitchen to interrupt her cooking. No attempts to get Elsa to play. It was time for the hard parts. "I believe you now. You're serious about getting re-married. But I can't imagine your being happy out here, not after all these years and not in a town that doesn't even have a grocery store. And I can't see myself moving very far away from Claire and the children, at least not until they're older. I need them."

He didn't argue. Instead, he said, "That's important information." He grinned and cocked his head to the side. "I never thought I'd be competing with my own grandkids."

She took a long time clearing away the evidence of yesterday's matinee, picking up stray popcorn kernels and arranging DVDs in their boxes, not saying anything.

He said, "I know we can't decide this today. Will you promise me you'll think seriously about how we can make it work?"

"I will."

"Good. Come with me while I pack. Got to leave before two."

She walked behind him to the bedroom. She straightened the pillows on the loveseat. Next, she placed her hairbrush, her comb, and her jewelry box in a perfect line on the dresser.

Without looking up from his packing, Ray said, "You're straightening."

She took a deep breath and held it. When she finally exhaled, the words followed in a rush. "Do you see Chris? Do you talk? Is he healthy?"

"Yes, to all three." He sat down and beckoned her to sit beside him. She slumped forward, staring at a clump of cat hair on the carpet. "Do you hate our son?"

"*No*, I think of him almost every day. He was such a sweet child. And then when he got older I didn't know him anymore. I didn't know what to do with him. I made so many mistakes. Oh

Ray, I know I made him hate me."

"He doesn't. He's a good man, an excellent artist. And he and Andrew are a committed couple—eleven years." He touched her shoulder. She leaned against him, huddled under his right arm.

"Chris misses you," Ray said.

Tears ran down her cheeks and onto his shirt. "There are so many things I regret. Not just Chris, lots of things. I don't know what to do about any of them. Too much time may have passed. Why would you want to marry me?"

Ray kissed her on the forehead. "You're my girl, have been since the day we met. We belong together. We can work out the tough parts."

After Ray left, thirty minutes on the exercise machine didn't help. And an hour of house cleaning only aggravated the weariness that made every step an effort. A nap was what she wanted, just a short one.

It was five on Monday morning when she woke. Three cups of coffee and a shower finally made her alert enough to dress and consider a Monday at work.

The engine that usually propelled her forward seemed to be entirely out of fuel. Finding something for breakfast taxed her. The car keys hid behind the toaster. The PDA's "battery low" message blinked. Her briefcase inserted itself under the passenger seat in the car. Elsa twitched her tail at her favorite food and turned over the dish. Melanie surrendered. Her assistant sounded surprised when Melanie called and told her to cancel all her appointments and file a sick day report for her. She sat for a while, wondering why she hadn't told Ray that she had didn't really have to work anymore, with the "early legacy" money from her mother that she still had trouble accepting as hers. And then she went back to bed.

She woke for the second time that day at three-thirty p.m., finally feeling rested. A lawn chair seduced her to the backyard where she stayed, doing nothing at all, until the sun went down.

That night, the phone rang. "Melanie, are you there?" It was Ray, with loud talking and music in the background.

"I'm here. I can hardly hear you."

"Noisy room. Another fund-raiser. San Antonio. I rejected the $300,000 offer. They countered with 325 and I agreed. You're talking to a soon-to-be-free man. And honey, I meant everything I said this weekend. Everything."

"I'm thinking about it. Seriously. I need time."

"Take all the time you need, darlin'. I'll call you tomorrow night. I love …." The background noise muffled his voice and then the connection was broken.

Early the next morning, she quickly found her now fully charged PDA and opened the organizer. She stared it intently with the stylus poised above the keys. First, a tentative stroke, then several others completed the short list.

To Do List--Tuesday June 13

#1. Call for haircut appointment

#2.

FLOYD COUNTY TRIBUNE
Thursday, October 1, 2009
County's Oldest Cemetery Closes

Lack of space has forced closure of Memorial Cemetery in Jackson's Pond to further burials.

The Jackson's Pond City Council voted Monday night to no longer permit additional burials, according to the minutes of the Council's meeting.

Mayor Garland Clements said, "This was the only choice. There is no more space and the city doesn't have the money to buy more land to expand. Besides, since the funeral home closed two years ago, services are seldom held here in town. The last burial, two months ago, was in the last remaining space in the Andrews plot. That filled the cemetery."

Local rancher, Junior Reese said, "The Cemetery Association will continue to maintain the grounds through volunteer clean up days. We've always done this, although the city owns the land. There are only a few of us, but we'll always decorate the graves with flags on Veterans Day and Memorial Day. We won't forget."

With Honor

Until today it wouldn't have mattered that finding just the right card took several hours. What else did she have to do? Lie here in this bed? Watch the bag of formula drip slowly into the tube inserted in her intestines? Follow the progress of the crawler that crept across the screen below the serious looking faces on CNN? Wait for someone to come to help her move? Count the minutes until her next pain medication would be due, begin asking for it, begging, really? Stare at the bony, bruised hands lying on the sheet, hands which bore no resemblance to the ones that had been hers?

But, today Ann Mason Pruitt snapped at the woman who couldn't even find the boxes of cards in the closet, the woman her daughter referred to as "your caregiver." Care giver. Nothing was given. Her care cost forty dollars an hour twelve hours a day; a woman registered by the state to sign R.N. after charting any care she gave. Her entries, if truthful, would surely be brief. Searching for cards seemed beneath her, or beyond her. Finally, Ann could tolerate her milling in the closet no longer. "Help me up. I'll get them myself." She came very close to calling the woman Sairey Gamp. It probably wouldn't have mattered. The nurse didn't seem the sort to read Dickens.

Back in bed, after the struggle across the room, she panted and wished for the other ones, the night ones. Cheaper, less expensive, they took turns, one on Monday, Wednesday, and Friday and the other on the opposite nights, sleeping on a cot near her bed. Ann spent those nights listening to their soft snores—they sounded exactly alike—and watching the ceiling. Onto that blank expanse, she projected her waking dreams and recently, her plan.

Before they bedded down, those women did their best to entertain her, telling bits of soap opera plots and mentioning their grown children's troubles. MWF—Ann never recalled their names—spoke in a soft alto drawl. She was the one who would have been able to find the cards. One night she had asked Ann if she minded if she just looked at some of the pretty things in the room and at her clothes. Maybe she was planning a robbery. Ann doubted it. She still trusted her ability to estimate people. MWF, a strong, round woman, from somewhere in the South, with her kind eyes and soft voice, knew about misery. She wouldn't steal; she provided care. Ann would have given her all the clothes and the pretty things in the room, might still.

An hour later, after she summoned a bit of strength, Ann requested, afraid to demand, help getting to her chair. She didn't want the bed inviting her to sleep while she chose the right card. Where had her daughter bought all these cheery, childish cards? The card must convey the importance of the message she would write inside. The woman she remembered as her friend would take it all in, not only the words, but also their medium. She was an artist.

She eliminated one after the other of them as possibilities. As she rejected cards, she planned what to write. "I wouldn't ask you to make the trip if it weren't important." No, important was insufficient; extremely important, urgent, crucial, a grave matter. That last one made her laugh. She decided on "Ill for some time now—situation worsening—something only you can do for me."

She proceeded methodically through the two boxes of cards. Each one, she took in her left fingertips, the only digits that had a tiny bit of remaining sensation. All the cards were examined and those that had a message on the inside were eliminated. Then she placed all the ones with glitter pasted on or with any hint of religion in a separate stack. She'd save those for tonight.

The fifteen cards that remained, she sorted into two stacks, one of those with art of some sort on the front and the other, the plain ones. One from each of those two stacks remained after she spent another forty-five minutes considering the effect of finding each particular card in the mail after not seeing its sender for nearly fifty years.

She eventually chose one made of heavy, ecru, linen-textured stock with a thin navy border. Getting from her recliner back to bed made her wish that wheedling worked on the nurse. So far, the woman had never varied from the prescribed schedule for the pain medication. In that contest of wills, the nurse always won. It wasn't that Ann couldn't tolerate the pain; it wasn't unbearable, but why should she have to accept it at all? She didn't bother to mention her next dose as the nurse helped her back to bed. As soon as she found a position to lie in, after checking the time, Ann closed her eyes. She heard the nurse leave the room and seconds later, heard cabinet doors opening and closing in the kitchen.

What could she be looking for? She didn't cook. Ann heard the microwave. The nurse returned and situated herself in a chair next to Ann's bed, the best position for viewing the television. Ann watched as the woman located the remote control and selected a channel, never once consulting her patient. The nurse arranged a tray on her lap and chewed with her mouth open while Ann sipped flavored water and watched the formula dribble its way into her intestines.

Ann gave a few minutes' consideration to retaliating. But she didn't have time to waste on petty revenge fantasies, no matter how lacking in empathy the high-priced nurse. Action must be taken to assure that her son didn't bury her where she would never rest. She closed her eyes and ignored the talk show. Willa Jackson would understand.

She flinched when the nurse touched her shoulder. "I've brought your pain medication. Do you want it now or would you prefer to wait?"

Ann saw that the nurse's tray was gone and the television was off. The afternoon could have slipped entirely away and joined all the others. There were things she must do. She said, "Yes, thank you, I'd like to have it now. After it has time to take effect, I want to take a walk and then sit in my chair." Now there was a reason to try to maintain some strength. The exercise would sap her energy, but might help keep her ready. The card had to be written today. It was the first step in her plan.

After the few steps that constituted a walk, propped again in her chair, Ann began the task of writing the message for the card. Achieving legibility taxed her patience. The last round of chemotherapy left all of her fingertips, except two on her left hand, numb. Nausea, vomiting and hair loss produced terror the first time the oncologist began treatment. Somehow she had lived over those insults. The hair grew back and she quit vomiting. Sensation lost from her fingers was gone for good.

The first note she wrote as a draft on plain paper. The caregiver had managed to find a lined pad and a pen in the kitchen, the room she seemed to favor over Ann's. She didn't blame her. She'd prefer any room to a sickroom. The actual note went more smoothly than she expected. She inserted the newspaper article inside the card and sealed the envelope. She addressed the card to Willa Jackson, Jackson's Pond, Texas 79306 and wrote PLEASE FORWARD across the left side of the envelope.

That night, the first thing she said when MWF started her shift was, "There's something very important I need you to do for me." She explained that the envelope must be mailed first thing the next morning. She knew that days might go by before she would receive the phone call she hoped would come in reply. Her plan called for other action while she waited. "And you mustn't tell anyone." The sweet-faced woman didn't ask why. Ann said, "Would you like to have these cards?" She pointed to the stack of glittery ones. "I doubt I'll ever get around to using all of them and I thought you might like them." Her caregiver beamed.

That night Ann did not search the ceiling.

Seventeen days passed after she prepared the card. Two nights after she handed the card to MWF, Ann had asked if she had remembered to mail it. The gentle, caring woman assured Ann she'd gone directly to the mailbox the next morning.

Since then, Ann had put the time to good use. Every morning she leaned on the nurse's arm to walk from the bed to the door. Each afternoon, she opened the door and pushed her walker a few steps down the hall, farther each day, accompanied dutifully by the nurse. Today she counted thirty-one steps before she'd felt the now-familiar evaporation of her strength. She allowed the nurse to lower her into the chair, the one Ann had her move each day one step nearer to the room that was her objective. After a few minutes' rest, she slowly returned the way she had come, her eyes focused on the bedroom door. By the end of the week, she intended to make it to the den.

Sixteen years ago when the General had selected this house, the Realtor insisted on calling that room the family room. There was no family. Her husband made a show for the Realtor of asking Ann's opinion about the house, but she knew from all the other times they had moved that he would decide. And she knew that this was the house. He had a pattern.

Each of the twelve times they changed location after those early years of living in base housing, they looked at exactly four houses. He always chose the fourth one, never bothering to return to any of the previous three. After all, he'd rejected them for some reason. No turning back. She imagined that four was the magic number because by then he would have exhausted the time he scheduled for the chore, not because the house was any better or different from the other three. The general's lady never publicly disagreed.

This was the final house decision that he made. The year of his retirement, with his medals and framed citations and his three stars and the bitterness about not having a fourth, they moved here to Colorado Springs. "I like being near the Academy," he'd said. Six months later, at the age of sixty-five, the lieutenant general died from a ruptured aortic aneurysm while playing a round of golf. The burial was at Arlington National Cemetery. Full military honors.

Cynthia, their daughter, arrived from Los Alamos National Labs, where she worked as an astrophysicist on a project she wasn't allowed to talk about. There had been some question about whether she would be allowed to leave her job long enough to attend the funeral; a small jet stood by to return her to New Mexico. She shed not a single tear at the funeral nor at the interment. She and her brother, both unsmiling and stiff-backed, their faces blank, talked briefly to one another before he and his family, a small group in tight formation, left the gravesite. Ann wasn't surprised; the two of them had never been close when they were children. But the long embrace Cynthia held her mother in before she strode away after the ceremonies had been a surprise.

Their son, Lieutenant Colonel Carleton Pruitt, Jr., and his wife saw Ann to the plane back to Colorado the day after the funeral. Her son already had taken care of the paperwork to assure Ann's pension income, and he sounded reassuring and decisive when he said, "You will be buried here too, Mother. It's your right. You have served, too. For now, you should plan to stay in Colorado Springs where you know people and have the support of the military community." His wife nodded and patted Ann's hand and watched her husband for cues. Their sons Matthew and Mark both said solemn goodbyes and departed toward Concourse B for their return flight to college. Everyone had a schedule to keep.

The relief Ann felt when she was finally alone in the departure lounge embarrassed her a little. Later, when the plane reached its cruising altitude, the sense of freedom that spread through her left her smiling and elated. She was no longer the general's lady. She was Ann Mason Pruitt.

Until she called to inform her children of the cancer diagnosis four years ago, during those ten lovely years alone, the occasions on which her son contacted her were the days on which families were supposed to see or hear from one another— Christmas, Thanksgiving, birthdays. The pattern hadn't varied in all the years since he'd gone from college into the Air Force. He might as well have been hatched from an egg laid by one of the giant birds he flew. The Air Force was his birth family.

Cynthia continued to surprise her, though. Since the funeral, Ann received a call from her each Thursday night at precisely eight p.m. She made Ann a part of her vacation each year and they spent every Christmas together. She sat in the hospital waiting room during that first surgery, took time off and came to drive Ann to her appointments with the oncologist and the rest of the medical parade. Maybe she did what she did out of a sense of duty; it certainly wasn't because she anticipated a large inheritance. Ann didn't suspect her, she simply didn't understand. She did wonder, though, how long it would be before Cynthia decided it was time to begin making decisions for her.

The house always had seemed too large to Ann; now it seemed enormous. The thirty-one steps on her return trip seemed like mile twenty-six in a marathon. She focused on the bedroom door. Even with the oxygen, each breath resisted her effort. She imagined the general standing there in his dress uniform saying, "Never give up. Strive on." She muttered, "Easy for you to say."

"I'm sorry, I didn't hear what you said," the nurse said in a voice fit for the hard of hearing.

"Nothing, I'm—" The phone rang. It insisted—five times before she landed safely in the bed and the nurse helped her into a somewhat comfortable position.

"She's a bit tired just now. Would you ..." The nurse's voice sounded irritated.

"No, I'll take it." She pushed herself up on her pillows to a sitting position. She drew an easier breath and said, "This is Ann Mason Pruitt."

She could feel strength return as she listened. "Willa, I'm so glad you called. I know I'm imposing to ask after all these years. But can you come? I need to talk with you—not on the phone." She leaned back against the pillows and waited with her eyes closed.

"You're here already? In Colorado Springs? Yes, in the morning. Is nine too early?" She sat up straight and ignored the pain in her bones, the heavy ache that was her constant, unwelcome companion.

That night, MWF's soft snores provided the soundtrack for memories of Ann's college years at the University of Texas.

Excelling in the math and science classes she loved. Worrying about her application to medical school. She and Willa sharing a room. In their senior year, Willa listening, the only person she could tell about her problem. Her solemn, proud parents watching her receive her degree, Summa Cum Laude. Hurriedly arranging her own wedding to Air Force Lieutenant Carleton Pruitt, a Northerner from Connecticut, two days later. Willa as her only attendant and witness.

She could only hope that Willa had forgiven her the pride that had kept her from contacting her all these years. Ann thought of it now as false pride, her misplaced attempt to allow her friend to think that she managed to forget her dreams of medical school and to be satisfied being a career military wife. If she had written Willa or seen her she would not have been able to sustain the lie.

Ann woke early the next morning, did the best that could be done with her hair and face, and willed the feeding to hurry into her intestines before Willa arrived. The nurse raised her eyebrows when Ann said she would wait for her pain medication until later, that she wanted to be alert for her visitor. And then Ann sat alone, hovered over by the pole the formula hung from and propped up, surrounded by a pile of pillows, waiting.

When the doorbell rang, she smoothed the sheets, closed her eyes, and took a deep, cautious breath. She opened her eyes and saw her friend standing in the bedroom doorway, a hazy nimbus of morning light around her. "Willa, come in. I'm so glad to see you," she said. Willa hugged Ann carefully, as if she were afraid her friend might shatter.

Willa took the card from her purse. Ann held up a hand to stop her. She couldn't tell from Willa's face if she was angry or concerned. "I know, that's the main reason you came. We'll get to it. But first, let's enjoy a visit, please." She wished that she'd lost her sense of smell instead of touch, so that just for a few minutes, she could not detect the odor of the colostomy bag she had to wear. Willa was sure to notice. How could she not be repelled? How could she not want to escape?

They zigzagged through unconnected stories stored all the years since they'd seen one another. Willa remembered Ann staying up all night cramming for a chemistry exam and falling asleep in the Student Union before she could get back to the dorm after the test. Ann recalled Willa's first college ballet recital and her mistaken arabesque left when the rest of the corps turned right. "Thank goodness the soloist was in the spotlight at the time," Willa said. "You were the only one who noticed, I'm sure. Except for the teacher." They both laughed and Ann relaxed a little.

When tears fell at stories of the sadnesses in their lives, and they reached to touch one another's hands, she knew that Willa was still the friend she could rely on. She said, "I thought you might be angry because I never wrote. Just that birth announcement about Carleton, Jr. my mother wouldn't let me send until two months after the fact."

Willa shook her head. She said, "You had your parents and a new husband and baby to deal with. You could have just as easily wondered why I didn't try to find you. We're here now. That's what matters. Tell me some more about your life."

Ann had never gone back to Jackson's Pond after she married. But all the years in the military, wherever the Air Force sent them, and since, she subscribed to the Jackson's Pond paper. She knew about changes in the town and she knew of Willa's success as an artist. Since the *Gazette* folded, she took the county paper.

Ann veered past life in the military with one brief story about her orientation at Lackland—"Duties and Demeanor for Officers' Wives." She described in more detail the ten years between her husband's death and her first cancer surgery—my ten years of freedom, she called it. She'd taken classes, traveled, and volunteered for liberal causes her husband would have forbidden. "He loved who he thought I was," she said. "He didn't know me."

"And you?" Willa asked.

"I loved him in my way." She started to say something more, but instead, smiled at her friend.

"You must be wondering," Ann said, "about all this. Cancer, first in my lungs, now almost everywhere." She paused for breath and made the mistake of inhaling deeply. The smell of the deodorizer in the colostomy bag produced a wave of nausea. How could Willa sit so close so calmly?

"I'll spare you the grisliest details of my treatment. It will do to tell you I've had four surgeries, three rounds of chemotherapy, targeted radiation, and countless scans, scopes, and other indignities. And now..." Ann waved a hand toward her hospital bed and the room's array of medical equipment. She stared a moment at the hand that had gestured as if she didn't recognize it. She hid it beneath the sheet.

"My son frequently refers to my 'battle against cancer.' Cynthia uses the words 'cancer survivor' as if they should be a mark of distinction," Ann said. She smiled wryly and shook her head. "I take no pride in living on while being reduced bit by bit to skeletal remnants. I can't say this to my children, and I'm sorry to sound ungrateful, but I don't see the point of surviving." She leaned back and closed her eyes. She had spent her strength far sooner than she intended.

Willa didn't say anything for a long time. Then she said only, "I think I can understand."

Ann returned her steady gaze and said, "I believe you do."

Willa was exactly as Ann remembered her, at least in all the important ways. Her green eyes never left you when you talked; she laughed easily and often; she never interrupted a silence. Even though she had aged—who hadn't by seventy-nine—beauty remained. And the expressive hands Ann remembered were still as graceful as strong-winged birds.

"Did you ever wonder why we weren't close friends in high school?" Ann asked.

"Not really," Willa said. "I never had close girlfriends. Most girls seemed silly. Until your parents arranged for us to be roommates at UT, I never knew what it was to have someone to talk with the way we did."

"Oh, Willa, you are the only real friend I ever had. Isn't that a sad thing to say? It's true. It's no one's fault but mine—always studying, set on medical school, no time for foolishness. And since..." She took a breath, almost a gasp; she'd been ambushed by a pain bolting through her upper abdomen, left to right. The next breath, she held, then exhaled slowly. Gone now. It had been a scout, a lone pain, a probe into enemy territory. Guerilla warfare.

As if she had heard Ann's sharp breath over the sound of the tiny kitchen television, the nurse appeared at the bedroom doorway. Without entering, she squinted at Ann and asked if she wanted her pain medicine.

Before Ann could answer, Willa said, "Ann, take the medicine. I'll go to the hotel and rest a bit and come back after lunch. Don't worry. I have all the time we need."

When Willa returned two hours later, Ann pointed at the formula bag. "My lunch. Takes ninety minutes exactly. Leisurely dining. How was yours?"

"A burger. It was fine. Ann, while I was eating, I remembered one time you did participate in silliness in high school. The Senior Play. You were quite funny. Do you recall?"

"I do remember. I learned one important thing in that play. How to make an entrance." She laughed at the memory.

"Out of a cake?"

"That for one, but generally how to make every eye turn to you. Hesitate on the threshold, stand erect, survey the entire room as if owning it pleases you. A skill I often used later in life. Stopped conversation at many an officers' cocktail party. Entrances and exits."

There had been so many. Entering each of the new duty stations, charming the officers and the wives in order to help advance her husband's career. Never upstage a higher ranking wife; never exit a cocktail party or a volunteer activity until every obligation, every social duty was completed. And then, when finally, you are the general's lady, stay on stage and try to recall who you were before, when you had a name of your own.

"Yes, and you did exits better than anyone," Willa said. "You slammed the door and never looked back. Remember, the set had to be reinforced. The entire thing threatened to collapse at every rehearsal. You were quite the actress."

"I used that later, too, the acting. There are some people who believe to this day that I enjoyed being the general's lady." She paused. Her smile disappeared. "I've retired from acting except on special occasions."

"Seem futile?" Willa asked.

"At this point. I know you understand." Ann tried to slow her breathing. Panting would wear her out. "Tell me about your family and the town and the ranch and the pond."

Willa's response included a brief mention of Jackson's Pond as now less a town than a wide spot in the road. She talked more about the present than the past, except for saying how much she had missed her husband after he died, still missed him every day.

Otherwise, she told Ann facts, not dwelling on problems or heartaches or triumphs. Ann knew she was sparing her, concentrating on the old, sick friend whose card had brought her here.

Willa told her about her daughter Melanie and her career in school administration, about her granddaughter, Claire, and how making Claire's husband a partner in the ranch freed her to paint and to move to Taos. And she described the gallery that she and her grandson Chris owned there. She stopped talking. Ann opened her eyes and smiled. Willa said, "You need to rest again. I'll come back tomorrow."

"Wait, I need to ask you one other thing. Are you religious?"

Willa frowned a tiny bit and sat silent. Ann could tell she was thinking before answering. "I don't attend church. I believe that God is all around us, in nature, in other people."

"Do you believe God makes decisions about individuals, takes a hand in the particulars?"

"Probably not."

"Me neither." Ann closed her eyes again.

Willa said, "I'll be back in the morning. I need to make some phone calls—confirm some appointments in Denver day after tomorrow."

"Business?"

Willa nodded. "A gallery contact and an appointment with a doctor."

"Don't let doctors get their hooks in you. They won't let you die in peace." Ann waved to Willa as she left. "See you in the morning."

The next day, after more hours of reminiscing, gaps and silences began to outnumber sentences between the two of them. Ann knew she either had to begin talking about trivial things or to deal with the reason she had asked Willa to come. "Do you have the card I sent, and that clipping?" she asked.

Willa nodded and took the card from her purse. "It said you needed my help."

"I do. Will you promise to do something for me, Willa?" She leaned forward in her chair, then retreated when pain clutched her back.

"If I can."

"It's about my burial—disposing of my remains. My son expects me to be buried next to his father at Arlington National Cemetery. The honor of the burial and the little pageant that goes with it are just the sort of things he'd love to talk about with his officer friends." She stopped for a breath; she hated the panting. It made her pitiful to watch, she was certain. "I can't stand the thought of being buried there. I'll have no peace surrounded again by the military. Until I saw that clipping, I intended to be buried at Jackson's Pond cemetery, near my parents. Now I know that can't be."

"What do you want me to do?"

"Two things. First, I want you to receive my ashes. Did you know they call them cremains now?" She made a disgusted face at the sound of the word. "I'd like to have them scattered at the pond on your ranch. I remember it as a happy, peaceful place." Ann watched Willa's face for a clue.

Willa sat up very straight in her chair. She shook her head, just once. "I don't want to interfere with your family. I did that years ago in Austin and your parents never spoke to me again. They seemed to believe I had something to do with your being pregnant."

Ann laughed. "They would have preferred to believe that than think their perfect daughter was a participant." She reached for Willa's hand. "I can have my attorney develop a directive. Then I will tell Cynthia and Carleton when the time is right. They will have to accept my wishes, even if they don't agree." After a minute, she said, "Carleton definitely won't."

"And about the pond," Willa said. "It's not as you remember it. It's drying up. Before long it will be gone."

"I'll be gone before then," Ann said. "The pond is perfect for what I want."

"You said there were two things."

"Yes, I want you to speak at the memorial service I am planning. You are the only person alive who knows who I am. Please let those who come know that I was more than a general's lady."

Willa looked steadily at Ann, not speaking. Then she asked, "Is there anything you're not telling me?"

"Nothing you don't already know." Ann waited. In the silence, she focused on the pain she now felt grinding and shocking along her lower spine, like a dentist's drill against a sensitive tooth. "Please tell me what you're thinking."

"Your children don't even know me."

"But I do." She clenched her jaw, determined she wouldn't cry. "This is important to me, Willa."

Willa returned the card to her purse and spent a while studying the floor near her feet. She rose and stood near Ann's chair. "I need to think about this. I hope you understand." She stopped talking long enough to find a tissue in her purse. It was more than a minute before she spoke again. "Can I give you an answer in a week? Can you wait?" She looked directly at Ann. "Will you?"

Ann nodded. "I will." She reached up and pulled Willa to her in a tight hug. "Goodbye, my friend."

She heard the front door close. It took more effort than she could afford to waste, but she managed to make the nurse hear her call. When the woman appeared at the doorway, Ann said, "Please help me to bed and please bring my pain medication." She needed rest; there were still other steps she must complete. The general would have been impressed.

At nine the next morning, the phone rang. Ann turned from staring at the formula bag's interminable dripping to watch the nurse as she answered. The woman said, "I'll see if she's able to talk." She put her hand over the mouthpiece and said, "It's Mrs. Jackson. Do you feel like talking?"

Ann reached for the phone. When she moved, nausea threatened; she took a deep breath to conquer it. She answered, hating that her voice came out as little more than a whisper. She understood her friend's reluctance, and refused to think about what this quick response might mean. Willa said, "I will do what you ask. Have your attorney send me a copy of your directive and the plans for your memorial. I will do my best to honor you properly when the time comes. Please promise me that you will explain to your children." There was a silence, then Willa added, "Soon."

Ann promised. Before they hung up, she thanked Willa, knowing the words were insufficient, and said she would be in touch again. She immediately had the nurse call Carleton's number, not really expecting to reach him directly. He was a general now, after all. The message she left with his aide was brief—she needed to speak to him in person, in Colorado Springs, next week, Thursday at the latest. The same aide called an hour later to tell her the general's estimated time of arrival next Thursday.

Her next call arranged for her attorney to come to the house tomorrow afternoon.

A few minutes later, after her formula finished its slow journey, she began the trek toward the den, down the endless hall again, assisted by Nurse Gamp. Ann would need all the strength she could muster before the skirmish with Carleton. With each slow, painful step, she imagined herself nearer to her final objective.

THE TAOS OBSERVER
September 1, 2013
National Honor for Taos Artist
by Feature Editor, Jan Fox

The spotlight of national attention focused on Taos artist Willa Jackson and her art this week. Honored by the National Watercolor Society with its Best of Show Award, 2013, Jackson said, "I never really intended to make my art for sale or exhibition until my grandson convinced me to place a few of my pieces in a gallery.

"Soon, there were a few patrons who began collecting 'Willas.' That's what they call them."

As we talked, the eighty-two-year-old painter packed her easel and materials for a day of capturing northern New Mexico scenes. Dressed in jeans, a blue chambray shirt, western boots, turquoise jewelry, and a black cowboy hat, she looked like the Texas rancher she was before devoting her time to painting.

Jackson came to live in Taos in 2005. Asked if she had painted during her years in Texas, she said, "Yes, and I've always favored watercolors. For a long time, my favorite subject was a pond on the ranch. I painted it in every season from the time it was a young pond until it finally was overgrown by native grass and mesquites."

It was a series of three of those studies of the pond that captured the attention of the National Watercolor Society judges. As a result of the Best of Show designation, the paintings will be shown as part of a traveling exhibit in 10 major American cities, beginning in January, 2014, in New York City.

Jackson turned her artistic sights to northern New Mexico when she arrived in Taos. "I enjoy creating studies of the same view, or general location, over time, across seasons and the differing light those seasons create. I've found so many spectacular scenes near Taos. I recently finished what may be the final painting in a series of views from near the Rio Grande Gorge. I'm often uncertain when I begin how many a series must include for me to feel it is complete."

Marvin and Susan Maxwell, of Taos, collect Jackson's work. Susan Maxwell said, "Willa is not a Taos native, but she is a Taos Treasure. She's become a vital part of the community. She's active in the local Democratic Party, and the Chamber of Commerce, and on the Holy Cross Hospital Board, just to name a few of the things she's involved in. But, there is one other thing you need to know. She lies about her age. She can't be a day over 65."

"She's ageless and her work is timeless," said Patricia Carmichael, a Taos artist and owner of Fine Prints gallery. "Her style is unique, bold, yet there's something very tender in her treatment of natural beauty. I carry her prints in my gallery, by special arrangement with The Pond. I can't keep them, they're so popular."

Jackson's paintings are available exclusively through The Pond, the studio/gallery co-owned by Jackson and her grandson, Chris Banks.

A Complete Series

News of Willa's Best of Show Award arrived during the family reunion that Andrew and Chris arranged as an early gift for her eighty-third birthday. Several local collectors of "Willas," gallery owners, and other friends hosted a hastily arranged reception in her honor at Pat Carmichael's print gallery.

Melanie, ever efficient, had arranged for the six from Jackson's Pond to stay at a hotel, saying she didn't want to crowd anyone. After the reception, she asked Willa to drive her there to rest a bit before dinner. As they walked to her Jeep, Willa stumbled. She grasped Melanie's arm to keep from falling. "These bifocals will do me in yet," she said and laughed as if it were a joke. She saw concern in Melanie's face.

Seconds after they drove away, Melanie asked, "Mother, are you sure you're feeling well?"

"This minute? I feel great. The reception was so nice. And having all of you here together for my birthday was the best present I could have." She drove slowly away from town, east toward the ski area. "Why do you ask?"

"I thought you seemed unsteady during the reception and then just now... At your age some health problems wouldn't be surprising. I worry. You might not tell Chris. I know how you hate to trouble anyone."

"You forget we have a nurse on the premises. Andrew watches over us both." Willa slowed her Jeep and pointed toward the mountains. "Look, Melanie, isn't the light beautiful this time of year, particularly in the late evening? It's the same near dawn."

"Yes, it is. I'm ashamed to say I hadn't noticed. Now that I'm here, I can see why you like Taos. It's not at all like home." She flipped down the visor and quickly applied lipstick, touched her hair, and frowned at her reflection in the mirror. "Do you miss Jackson's Pond at all? Eight years." She pointed to a parking space near the entrance to the hotel's parking lot.

"Occasionally the ranch and the way the pond was years ago, but not the town." Willa passed the space Melanie pointed out and circled toward the front of the lot. "Don't my visits count?"

"They're never long enough. I'd feel better if you'd come back to stay. At least for the winter; surely eight winters here are enough. You could live with me and Ray." Melanie cleared her throat. "Or we could find a nice senior residential facility for you in Lubbock."

"That would make you feel better?" Willa slowed almost to a stop.

"Things can happen. You might fall or get sick. Besides, I want to take care of you. It's something I should do." Melanie glanced around the parking lot and then seemed to search her lap. "Mother, I love you."

Willa couldn't recall a time since Melanie was a child that she had said those words. Willa's chest hurt and her eyes filled. What had she missed? She touched Melanie's hand. Melanie didn't move; she focused on her lap.

Willa spoke softly. "I love you too. That's why I want you to live your own life. That's what you should do. You and Ray and your children. I don't need to be taken care of, not yet. But I appreciate your offer." She stopped talking, concentrated on parking.

She turned off the ignition and looked at her daughter. If she painted portraits rather than landscapes, she would try to capture the difference she saw in Melanie—softer, more open, not the stern school administrator who had hurried through so many years pursuing a career, and at this moment, a little sad. After a silent few seconds, Willa asked, "What time will you be coming over this evening? I'll get out the dominoes and the popcorn popper and light a fire in the kiva."

"About two hours," Melanie said. She got out, then hesitated before closing the car's door. "Thanks for the ride." She looked around the lot as if she'd lost something there. "At least promise me you'll think about coming back."

Willa smiled and nodded. "We'll see you in a little while. Enjoy your rest." As she drove away, she shook her head and sighed. Her daughter had changed a lot in the past few years, but she still carried her agenda wherever she went.

As much as she had enjoyed the weekend with her family and Robert, who, to her was now family, she didn't hurry to rejoin the others at her casita. She drove back toward the main road to town and then continued and turned south on Lower Los Colonias. She stopped on the roadside and gazed west, toward the final rays of the setting sun.

Andrew had been the instigator of this Labor Day weekend reunion that brought all of her family together for the first time in twenty years. Her incidental remark, back in July, about how she would like to see all of them together, here in Taos, inspired him. She couldn't imagine how he negotiated dates that worked, wondered what manipulations he had used to accomplish their arrival two days ago.

Since Melanie and Ray's surprise remarriage—no one knew about the ceremony at the magistrate's office in Clovis until after the fact—they lived in Jackson's Pond in their completely remodeled house. She operated a small private kindergarten and he managed Claire's clinic. With the clinic expansion to operate the additional site in Calverton they seldom left town for more than two days. Willa knew Claire hadn't taken a vacation from the time she opened the clinic until last year when they added a third nurse practitioner. Her two kids were in school; J. D. always had work to do at the ranch and there was the annual bull sale to get ready for.

Chris and Melanie were probably the most difficult to sell on the idea of an extended family gathering. Willa chose not to ask Andrew about their reactions. Although this weekend she saw nothing but harmony between mother and son, the change from their earlier estrangement might still be tenuous.

She knew Melanie had made the first overture. After her wedding she called Chris and asked if he would meet her, alone, in Albuquerque for dinner. A single meal ended up as a weekend together for the two of them, their first since he'd left home for UT. When he returned to Taos, Chris had only said he was glad he went. He'd never returned to Jackson's Pond, but since that weekend he and Melanie talked often; sometimes he was the one who called. Melanie knew about Andrew, but for some reason—Willa didn't know why—until now they had never met face-to-face, had only spoken on the phone.

A splice in a barbed wire fence came to her mind. A splice like that could be stronger than the original wire. She hoped this new connection between mother and son would hold.

The sun setting beyond the high desert plain that stretched west from the rim of the Rio Grande Gorge gave her a peaceful feeling; some things seemed eternal. She leaned back against the Jeep's seat and absorbed the drama of the sun's descent.

Tomorrow, everyone would leave and she could return to her painting. As happy as she had been when they arrived, she relished knowing she would be able to think of this time, with these people she loved, as a memory. For her, spending time with her memories was not living in the past as much as a small way of slowing the onrush of the future. The sun dropped below the horizon. Time to go. She wanted their last evening together in Taos to be as memorable for her family as it would be for her.

Robert, Chris, and Andrew were already busy when she arrived home. Robert was tending the small fire he had started in the kiva and Andrew and Chris had found the corn popper and had begun popping enough corn for all of Taos. "Nothing better than the smell of corn popping or the sight of men working," Willa said. "Anything I can do?"

The two younger men shooed her from the kitchen. Robert took her hand and led her to the couch. "Willa darlin', it's time for the two of us older folk to sit before the fire and reminisce." She leaned against him lightly, appreciating the support of his arm. The day had tired her.

"Well, County Cork, I see you've charmed my daughter as you do most females," she said. He raised his bushy white eyebrows and then winked. She pictured Melanie's face when Chris had introduced Robert Stanley as the man responsible for Willa's "brand" and her recognition in the art world. Willa had overheard her asking Robert later how long he and her mother had known one another. It was a tribute to his Irish blarney that Melanie seemed quite taken with him. More than once during the weekend, Willa found them talking seriously about the business side of art.

The Jackson's Pond contingent arrived soon and the house filled with chatter and music and the sound of dominoes clicking. The popcorn disappeared rapidly, along with beer, wine, and for the kids, soft drinks. Later, another round of eating began when Ray and Andrew teamed up to make nachos.

Willa saw J. D. studying her small collection of handmade walking sticks. They hung from leather thongs on pegs arranged in a frame on the living room's east wall. They were made of different woods, some polished, others stained, some straight, others showing the twists and gnarls of their growth in stubborn soil, some inlaid with local gemstones. "Do you like those?" she asked. She touched the turquoise on the top of one made of polished aspen.

"They're beautiful. Would you tell us about them?" he asked. "Amy, Jay Frank, come here. Let your gran tell you about her collection."

She took them down from the frame, handed him five and brought four with her. She settled in her armchair and gathered the sticks all together, surprised at their interest in her small collection. As she began to answer, Robert took a place on the ottoman near her chair. He cocked his left ear toward her, as if he didn't want to miss a word. Chris, Claire and the two children joined J. D. on the couch. Ray, Melanie, and Andrew stopped washing and drying dishes and stood together in the kitchen archway to hear. Seeing them all together made Willa mistrust her voice. She looked at them, memorizing the scene.

She then began by answering J. D.'s original question and went on to tell something about the person who had crafted each stick. To her the maker was as important as the piece itself; the maker was reflected in the work, she believed, as she was in her painting. Each stick had spoken to her in some way—the color, the shape, the wood, a whimsical design, or some other feature drawing her eye, she told them. Two had been gifts from the artisans who crafted them.

As she went through the stories she passed eight of the sticks around the group, a little surprised that even her great-grandchildren seemed interested. She managed to skip the ninth one, the not-quite-straight mesquite stick. Neither Chris nor Andrew mentioned her silence about that one stick, but she saw Chris nod at Andrew's questioning look. She had told the two of them its story for the first time just before the rest of the family had arrived.

She hadn't known she was searching for the raw material for a walking stick. She saw the fallen mesquite at the pond the evening before she left to move to Taos. That particular tree had been a focal point in one of her early watercolors of Jackson's Pond, she was almost certain. It had been one of the first that had moved toward the shrinking pond. The fact that no green was left in the small branch she broke off told her that several months had gone by since it had died.

She hated that mesquites had crept up onto the Caprock, but watched their growth and recorded it in her paintings of the pond. It was a natural consequence of the pond's life cycle coming to an end. She would not interfere by trying to eradicate the mesquites, although there were chemicals she could have used to do the job. For her, the delicate-appearing but extremely hardy trees were part of a landscape crafted by a master architect. She watched them and preserved their stages in her art and marveled at the grand plan in which they played a tiny role.

And now this one had died without her noticing. She sat on her pickup's tailgate and stared at the tree and bit her lower lip. She called herself a silly old gal for wanting to cry about the death of a tree that nobody loved. And then she did cry, glad that only the mesquite and the small muddy remnant of the pond could witness it. She didn't have a choice; if she didn't cry, she wouldn't be able to catch another breath.

She spoke to Frank, to her memory of him. She explained that she had to leave here or else she would end up boxed in and haltered and that she couldn't tolerate that no matter how well-intentioned Melanie or anyone else who wanted her to stay put. The pond was all but gone, dried up just like the town. She didn't plan to stay here and turn to dust or wither and fall over like that mesquite; she had things left in her to do. He knew what she meant, she was sure.

The mesquite's trunk was less than three inches in diameter, but its dense wood and remaining branches made it more of a load than Willa could lift. By the time dark arrived an hour and a half later, she'd used the Boy Scout hatchet she kept in her pickup to remove the branches, the dried roots, and part of the trunk. Wrangling the five-foot section of the mesquite into the truck's bed, she laughed, thinking what her daughter would say about her safety and sanity if she could see her. "You'd be wrong, Melanie. I'm not feeble yet."

The next morning, no one asked—maybe no one noticed—why she was hauling the wood up to Taos. She waved goodbye—Melanie, Claire and J. D. and their two children all had assembled for the send off—and drove out of Floyd County as fast as the law allowed. In three hours she was in New Mexico and by evening, all the way to Taos before anyone asked.

When she arrived, Chris and Andrew unloaded the things packed in the pickup bed. Chris lifted the mesquite and said, "Gran, I told you not to worry, we have everything you'll need out back in your casita. You didn't have to bring firewood." She told him it wasn't firewood. "It must be important if you had to haul it from Texas. What is it?" he asked.

She answered, as if she actually knew what she said was true, uttering the thought that came to her first. "It will be a walking stick." Both Chris and Andrew nodded as if they understood. Chris stroked his chin and looked at the sky. Neither asked any more questions.

That night after she unpacked the few possessions she'd brought to her new home, she opened a small deerskin pouch and poured out its contents—five perfect arrowheads. Frank had given her the pouch and the arrowheads more than sixty years earlier.

They had stopped for the horses to drink at Jackson's Pond. The day had been warm for December and, uncommonly for the High Plains of Texas, there was almost no wind. All afternoon, they had ridden along the east and south fence lines tightening slack barbed wire and replacing missing staples to fasten the wire to the weathered cedar fence posts.

Sitting on the pond's bank next to Frank, she told about her first semester at the university—stories about her classmates and her professors and about the differences between Austin and Jackson's Pond. She'd come home for the holidays as soon as classes were out, eager to see her father and Frank.

Frank had begun his third year at Texas Tech in Lubbock. He talked a little about his classes and the ones he would take next semester. And he talked about the work he was doing on the Jackson place. Each weekend, he returned home to work alongside Willa's father and the other tenant and the occasional day-work cowboys. He would assume management of the ranching and farming operation as soon as he completed his degree. Frank told her his father offered him the opportunity because his dad preferred business that involved trading and talking about cattle rather than working them, and Fort Worth suited him better than Jackson's Pond did these days. Frank's eagerness to be in charge sparked him to spend every free minute on the place.

Willa knew his parents didn't force him to do it. And she suspected his mother had other hopes for her son. He told her that his mother had said to him at breakfast one Sunday morning, "How will you ever get to know any suitable girls if you don't have some dates? You spend nearly every weekend at home. We didn't send you to college to make you a ranch hand or a bachelor." He'd said he hadn't answered. Instead, he'd excused himself from the table and gone to the barn to grease the tractor.

They both stopped talking as the sun began to set. As they watched, it fell behind a narrow line of clouds just above the horizon. The clouds' color changed from pale gray to dark blue. In seconds, the scene changed again as the sun outlined the entire line of clouds in deep pink. The wind picked up, rippling the surface of the pond.

Frank took her hand. "I have something I want to give you, and I'll warn you I want something in return."

She said, "If you think I can give you that new bull you have your eye on, you've got the wrong girl. But I did get you a present, too. A nice notebook from UT. Your friends at Tech will love it. There's a picture of Bevo on the front. I think he's a steer, not a bull." She winked and poked him in the ribs.

"No, I'm serious." He nodded as if encouraging himself to continue. "This time I'm serious." He handed her the pouch. "I made that for you from the hide of that deer I shot last fall." He had tanned and worked the skin soft and beaded one side with a circular pattern in red, purple, and white with a buttercup yellow border outlined in black.

"This is beautiful. I'd love it even if you hadn't made it. But knowing you did makes it perfect." She reached to hug him.

"Open it." Five perfect arrowheads slid out into her lap. "I've collected these here on the place since I was fifteen. That's how long I've known I was going to give them to you someday." He took a long time telling her about how he imagined the Comanches who camped in the area, how they hunted with these, maybe had given them as gifts sometimes. All the time he was talking, he watched the ripples on the pond in the fading twilight.

Willa studied the pointed flints, tracing the edges with a finger. She said, "You must have spent a long time searching for these. Every one of them is perfect."

"That's why I saved them for you. You're perfect, too."

Still looking toward the arrowheads in her lap, she took his hand and held it in both of hers, not speaking for a long time. "Thank you—for saying that and for the best gift I've ever had."

She looked at their hands linked together. "That notebook seems kind of pitiful compared to this. I'm embarrassed."

"Don't be." He lifted her right hand and kissed it, gently. "I told you there's something I want you to give me in return."

"What is it?"

"A promise. Will you promise to marry me when you graduate?"

She had found a man to make her walking stick not long after she settled in Taos. He understood immediately when she explained the importance of the materials she brought. He had complimented her on her choice of the piece of wood and said that she understood the soul of the tree or she could not have chosen so well. He had added a raven feather to the beautiful thing he created from her treasure. "For wisdom," he'd said.

When she finished telling Chris and Andrew, she said, "That's the story of this walking stick and that was the kind of man your grandad was, Chris. I wanted you to know that about him, along with all the rest you remember."

About three weeks after the reunion, on Tuesday afternoon, Willa opened the casita door only wide enough to peek out. Andrew had his hand raised to knock a second time. She enlarged the space just enough to show her face. "You again? I already told Chris I plan to spend tomorrow evening alone," she said. Andrew's pitiful look would have been believable if she hadn't known him. "You're a mighty sad case, mister. Like every other hobo that's passed this way. You can come in if you promise not to steal anything."

When she opened the door completely, the long rays of afternoon sunlight painted a gilt path across the tile floor. She replaced the walking stick she'd been holding when she opened the door among the rest of the collection.

Her tone less serious, Willa said, "One of the benefits of getting to be an old woman is that if you display them prudently, some of your less desirable traits can be accepted as charming eccentricities. Don't you agree?" She turned slowly and took Andrew's arm and led him to the couch.

"What—you're planning to put tin foil over the windows, bar the doors and become a recluse, to dedicate full time to studying conspiracy theories? No ma'am. I've been a psych nurse too long. You're busted. We know you have a secret date taking you out on your birthday. Chris sent me to find out who it is."

She couldn't help laughing.

"I'm his secret weapon. Year of practice make my technique irresistible. Everyone must tell me their secrets." He narrowed his eyes, spoke in a hypnotist's drone. "Look deep into my eyes. You are getting very, very sleepy."

She laughed again. "Nice try, kiddo. You've met your match." They often bantered this way. His quick wit and gentle manner were two of the many reasons she was glad that he and Chris had been a couple all these years. He had become her friend. "Joking aside," she said, "I do enjoy spending time alone."

"Actually, I think I understand wanting time alone on your birthday. Time to take stock as your new year begins. What are you thinking about on this birthday eve?"

"I was thinking it's been a really good year for me. And you have been an important part of making it so," she said.

Andrew didn't speak immediately. He took an audible breath and said, "Thank you, Willa. That means a lot to me. I feel more related to you than to any of my kin."

She grasped his left hand, felt the platinum wedding band Chris had placed there, felt strength and gentle warmth.

He squeezed her hand and said, "Now, will you party with us tomorrow night? You wouldn't want to disappoint me would you?"

"Another good try, Mister Psychology. Guilt never works on me. Time for you to go."

He stood. She took his arm and walked with him to the door. "You must have other old women to badger today. I don't want to keep you from them. Please report to Chris that I am a poor subject, unhypnotizable, a hopeless, eccentric recluse, but very charming." She opened the door and gave him a gentle shove. "Do come back again if you're in the neighborhood."

He drooped his head and let his shoulders sag. "I'm a

complete failure. Beaten down by an eccentric eighty-three year old woman. The shame of it."

"You'll get over it. You're young. Success will find you," she called after him as he made a show of shambling across the courtyard to his and Chris' house.

He responded without turning around. "You'll be sorry. You'll miss a good party."

After she closed the door, Willa stood before the display of walking sticks, straightening one, rubbing a smudge off another. She took down her favorite, the mesquite one inlaid with arrowheads. She steadied herself with it as she cleared a tiny cobweb from the top of the frame.

The next afternoon, she was lying in the living room floor, doing stretching exercises when she heard a tap on the door. She didn't have time to speak before Chris walked in. He nearly always stopped by after closing the gallery. He asked, "You okay?"

Willa nodded and looked up at him with a smile. She sat up and said, "Hi, sweetie. I expect to be up and out early tomorrow morning. Don't wait for me for breakfast. I'm going to the gorge again. The series may need one more to be complete."

"I thought you'd seemed preoccupied with something for the past few days," he said. He sat on the sofa as if he'd been invited to watch a performance.

"It's been on my mind since I finished that twelfth one the first of this month," she said.

Chris watched as she extended her left leg to the side and folded herself gently to touch her left toes with both hands, a movement she made seem effortless. "I remember upstairs at the big house at the ranch watching you practice ballet when I was a little boy. You stretched and did barre exercises before you danced. Is that how you've stayed so flexible all these years?"

She switched her position and stretched to the right. "That, and attitude," she said.

"Attitude?"

"Flexible mind and flexible body, the secret to a good life."

"Did I ever tell you that when I watched you dance, I thought you could fly?" he asked.

"There were times I thought I could. At least it felt close to flying." She moved into a lotus-like position, knees flexed and ankles crossed. Extending her arms above her head, she clasped her hands and inhaled deeply, catching a scent of piñon from the fireplace. She closed her eyes and sat silent for a long while.

Chris made no sound. Then she moved her arms, wing-like, in a single gentle flutter toward her breast. Willa held Odette's pose briefly, then opened her eyes and smiled at her grandson. "Back to the series, what do you think about it?"

"I think it's complete when you say it is. Only the artist knows. What makes you think, or feel, that it's incomplete?"

"Nothing more than a feeling that I might not be quite finished. Maybe it's the light at dawn this time of year. Fall light here is perfect—long shadows, warm tones. It reminds me a little of the colors developing along the edge of the Caprock just before sunrise. I wonder if I could capture it."

She changed position, extending her legs in front of her, stretching forward to clasp her ankles. "I need to see before I decide. I'll go prepared, just in case. I won't need to paint the scene, just to mix and try colors to find what I remember. A wash beneath the entire piece could be the answer." She concentrated on another stretch in the same position.

Chris said, "I could take you out to the gorge so you won't have to be the only person in the parking lot in the dark."

"I've been out there at dawn alone before. Remember last May? I was there early every day for two weeks. No need, but thank you."

"Gran, you are the hardest person in the world to do anything for. No birthday dinner, no early morning chauffeur service. How can I ever repay all you've done for me, if you won't let me help?"

"Honey, you know I appreciate your offering. You save up all that help, I'll need it soon enough."

He glanced at his watch. "Okay, this is me saving it up. But, if you change your mind, call me. I've got to run back to the gallery now. Supposed to meet a couple from Santa Fe in fifteen minutes." He turned back after he opened the door. "Guess what they're interested in."

"That piece of yours that was in the show at the State Museum last month?"

"No. They want to see our Willas. You're making us both rich."

"I've felt rich most of my life, with or without money."

"Love you, Gran."

She waved to him as he left, but stayed on the floor until she heard Chris open his back door across the courtyard. Then she slowly got to her feet and with the aid of her mesquite stick made her way to the bedroom closet. With no one to see her, she used the stick to prod the portable watercolor kit to the edge of the shelf.

Recently she often couldn't trust her legs, or maybe it was her balance. Keeping her feet flat on the floor helped avoid falling. Twice in the past two weeks she'd found herself on the floor with no throw rug or bumpy surface to blame. And there was that near miss that Melanie witnessed. Precautions were necessary. If she implemented them carefully, no one would know—no one would demand she use a walker or offer her a wheelchair. At least not for a while, yet. She looked at the kit, just beyond her reach near the shelf edge.

She should get the stool. She sighed and crumpled to sit on the bed, hugging her mesquite stick to her chest. A tear dropped onto the arrowheads. Another fell, reflecting as it rolled down the length of the raven feather.

She knew what Frank would tell her if he were there. He'd say, "You can quit any time you want to. You don't have to finish everything you start." Or. "You've done more than your share." He said it when they had worked gathering cattle and fixing fence six days in a row after a snowstorm. And when she plowed all day so he could sleep after staying up all night with a first-calf heifer. He told her the same thing when she took care of his mother after her strokes. "We'll hire nurses. You've done enough," he'd said. She kept going because he never quit. Even when he got sick, he didn't really quit.

She closed her eyes and saw her husband as if he were there with her. She remembered his courage and patience and felt bad for even thinking about quitting anything. *But, the truth is, I'm just plain tired—tired of being careful not to fall, of feeling like I have to force myself to get up and get moving. I'm tired and we both know it's only going to get worse. Before long I won't be able to help myself. And the worst part is that I'm tired of people. I'd rather spend my time talking to you.*

She stood abruptly and waited until she felt steady before pulling the low, single-step stool from under the bed. *Stop feeling sorry for yourself. There are things to be done.* One careful step, stop, balance, repeat, reach—she'd worked out a slow, careful choreography. Success! She held the portable watercolor kit in one hand as she reversed her combination of steps.

She laid out insulated underwear, a sweater, her barn coat, and gloves along with her usual painting clothes. Next, she busied herself checking the kit's supplies—six sheets of 9 x 12 hot press 400 weight paper; two plastic cups for water; five brushes—two flat, three round; watercolors; collapsible easel. She took the final item, a one quart water bottle, to the bathroom to fill. She saw her worried looking reflection in the mirror and thought Melanie would have her in a nursing home and on dementia drugs if she saw her mumbling and easing around to keep from falling. She'd have her declared incompetent before the sun set. Tied down for sure, taking care of her properly.

The next morning, before dawn, Willa parked in the lot on the east side of the Rio Grande Gorge Bridge. She smiled back at the face in the full moon hanging low in the west, directly in front of her. It lit the way as she crossed the bridge on the pedestrian walkway.

The morning came close to perfection, warm for late September and without a whisper of wind. For that, she was thankful. The bridge had seemed to vibrate with the wind last May when she painted the gorge. At least once, the vibration had set off a rush of nausea strong enough to make her stop and clutch the railing. She had never been able to force herself to drive across. She worried that if nausea or vertigo began she would injure someone.

She matched each step of her left foot with her walking stick, making consistent progress with nary a wobble. At times like this, she thought maybe the neurologist in Albuquerque had been wrong. But she knew better, had known for nearly four years. Her deteriorating cerebellum would be her undoing, sooner rather than later. Degenerative, idiopathic, he had told her. A second opinion in Denver had confirmed. Walker, then wheelchair, then completely uncoordinated, and bed until she died, as helpless as her mother-in-law had been.

Fifteen minutes later, just as the moon went down, she stepped to the west rim of the Rio Grande Gorge. She scanned the nearby campground. Only one RV occupied a space. No sign of life. She wouldn't be disturbed. She sat on a large rock, telling herself she was waiting for a bit more light, knowing she needed to rest to assure that she would remain steady enough for what she intended to do.

After a couple of minutes, she rose and walked past the short fenced area at the end of the bridge. She eased herself onto the ledge just below the fence. She had painted from this perfectly horizontal ledge several times before. It held her and her easel with a bit of room to spare. She quickly unfolded the legs of her easel, opened her paints, and poured water in each of the two cups. The steps of preparation were automatic after years of painting outdoors.

She looked east, past the gorge, watching the outlines of Taos Mountain and then Wheeler Peak emerge as the dark paled and shadows emerged. The bare peaks above the timberline reflected an almost lavender light. She could have watched the mountains for hours. The view would continue to change minute to minute throughout the day. She scanned the scene, searching for the answer she thought she would have this morning. Just before the sun's corona appeared over the farthest ridge, the color she recalled from Jackson's Pond flooded over everything in view. She drew a long breath, inhaling piñon scent and color together. Then, as quickly as the outflow of a single breath, both were gone.

If people had been watching, they might have thought she'd forgotten something. They would have been wrong. She left the ledge and walked back to the bridge's midpoint, using the same cautious movements as before, but more quickly. She stopped in the observation area and turned slowly in a circle, her arms positioned as if she might pirouette.

A raven sailed near, passing under the bridge. Its wings made a single sound, a whoosh, as it lifted to catch an updraft. The Rio Grande far beneath seemed full of life, busy. She imagined the rapid water chattering noisily as it passed under her, cheerily greeting the rocks and ledges in its path—live water six hundred feet below. The glow behind the mountains warmed. A young ballerina danced with the raven across grass-covered plains edged by high mountains, all bathed in that perfect shade she had come here to see. Willa's answer had found her.

A tap of her stick matched each step as she returned to her ledge, her face placid, her bearing regal. She leaned her stick against the easel and selected her favorite brush. She stood perfectly still in the glow. Then she took a step forward and began to paint.

CPSIA information can be obtained at www.ICGtesting.com
Printed in the USA
BVOW07s2326261014

105BV00004BA/292/P

9 781626 770034